"I've tried to answ
your questions

Jake said, "because that's what you said you wanted to hear. But you haven't said much about you, Susan. Really, you're still a bit of a mystery lady. Is there anything you want me to know?"

Tongue-tied, Susan sat thinking about all the things she'd kept hidden from him. Now was the time to tell the truth, surely. But when she did that, what would be his reaction?

Jake, so handsome that the sight of him made her heart ache, was looking at her with the eyes of a man in love. How could she risk losing something so wonderful when there was so little time to savor the experience?

"Jake," she said softly, "would you like to sleep in my room tonight?"

ABOUT THE AUTHOR

"With each Byrnside book, I've come to like
Jake Caine and Susan Bonner better and
better," author Jane Silverwood tells us.
"These are characters who truly deserve to find
each other and fall in love. So I've been
eagerly anticipating telling their story. And
now, at last, here it is." *Bright Secrets*, which
concludes the Byrnside Inheritance trilogy, is
the author's sixth Superromance novel.

Books by Jane Silverwood

HARLEQUIN SUPERROMANCE

282–THE TENDER TRAP
314–BEYOND MERE WORDS
375–HANDLE WITH CARE
434–HIGH STAKES
438–DARK WATERS

HARLEQUIN TEMPTATION

46–VOYAGE OF THE HEART
93–SNOW MELT
117–A PERMANENT ARRANGEMENT

Bright Secrets

JANE SILVERWOOD

Harlequin Books

TORONTO • NEW YORK • LONDON
AMSTERDAM • PARIS • SYDNEY • HAMBURG
STOCKHOLM • ATHENS • TOKYO • MILAN

This book is dedicated
to my mother

Published March 1991

ISBN 0-373-70442-9

BRIGHT SECRETS

PROLOGUE

"I'M SORRY, OWEN. I wish I were bringing better news. But so far we've come up empty-handed on this. Lynn Rice is still a mystery woman," said Jake Caine.

The tall, dark-haired lawyer stood in front of a massive oak desk in Owen Byrnside's paneled library. Opposite him, a highly disgruntled expression on his hawklike features, Owen Byrnside sat ensconced in a wheelchair. A thick plaid blanket was tucked over the ailing multimillionaire's lap and around his knees.

Catty-corner to the two men, Susan Bonner, Jake Caine's assistant, sat on the edge of a leather wing chair with her legs primly crossed at the ankle. Like Jake, she wore a tailored gray business suit. Pearl earrings peeked out discreetly from the smooth blond wings of her ear-length hair, and a pair of horn-rimmed glasses perched on the bridge of her slim nose.

It was to her that Owen turned. "What do you have to say about all this, young lady?"

From behind her glasses, Susan's golden-brown eyes looked out warily. "I'm just Mr. Caine's assistant. I have nothing to add to what he's just told you."

"But, if I heard Jake right, you're the one who's been coordinating the investigation. And you've got all the files on the girls who might turn out to be my granddaughter right there, don't you?" He jabbed a bony finger at Susan's briefcase.

"Yes, sir."

"Then tell me what you know about the last of my three missing orphans. I'd like to hear it from someone with a pretty face, for a change." He shot Jake an irritable look which the younger man met neutrally.

Susan cleared her throat. Over the past year she'd heard a great deal about Taleman Hall, Owen Byrnside's castlelike New England estate, yet this was her first visit. It seemed strange to her that despite all the work she'd done on Owen Byrnside's desperate search for his missing granddaughter, this was the first time she'd actually met the elderly founder of Byrnside Enterprises.

Susan opened a folder and glanced through the contents, though actually she knew all the material pertaining to the Byrnside quest well enough to need no cue cards. A year ago an anonymous letter had set the quest off. It had informed Owen that before his only son's fatal car accident, Christopher Byrnside had fathered a child with a rock singer named Gloria Dean. Twenty-seven years ago on April 1st, that child, along with two other female infants, had been abandoned at the Broadstreet Foundling Home. One month later the home burned to the ground, all the records were destroyed.

If that child still lived and could be found, she would be Owen Byrnside's heir. Already two of the three candidates had been located and brought to Taleman Hall to meet their possible grandfather. But whether or not either was the actual heiress to his international communications and publication network was still in question.

Owen Byrnside intended to determine which was his true granddaughter with a sophisticated laboratory procedure called DNA fingerprinting, but only when all three orphans could be gathered together on his estate. Unfortunately, the third and final young woman was proving elusive.

"So far all our efforts to trace Lynn Rice have failed," Susan began. "We do have quite a few facts about her, and even her photograph." Susan withdrew a somewhat washed-out identification picture of a young woman in a police uniform. She had long, pale brown hair and a stern expression.

"As you can see," Susan continued after she'd laid the picture on the small table in front of Owen Byrnside, "Lynn's face is badly scarred. We know that this is the result of that fire at the foundling home where she was abandoned. Because Lynn's face was damaged, she was unadoptable and grew up in a series of foster homes."

The expression on both men's faces had become grimmer. "Poor kid," Jake murmured. "What a rough start she had in life."

Owen remained silent. The bleak light in his pale eyes said it all.

"Rough," Susan agreed briskly. "But it appears she survived okay. After graduating from high school she joined the Boston police department where she did well enough to be considered for promotion to detective. Eighteen months ago, however, she requested and received a leave of absence. At the end of that leave she sent in her letter of resignation. She hasn't been heard from since."

Owen picked up the photo and stared at the sadly scarred young woman depicted in it. Then he dropped it and balled his gnarled hands into fists. "That a granddaughter of mine should have to go through such hell...!"

"Owen," Jake warned, "there's only a one-in-three chance that Lynn Rice could be yours by blood. You've already met Kate and Maggie and think the world of both of them. I've got a detective working to track Lynn Rice down now. But even if she doesn't surface, there's still every likelihood that you've already met your true grand-daughter.''

Owen shook his head. "Maybe, but I can't rest, or die—'' he touched his ailing heart ''—until I've laid eyes on all three of my lost girls.'' He gazed starkly up at his lawyer. "Find Lynn Rice for me, Jake. Do it soon.''

CHAPTER ONE

"WELL, WHAT DID YOU THINK?"

"About what?"

Jake Caine shot Susan Bonner's neat profile an impatient look. "About Taleman Hall, about Owen Byrnside, about this whole fantastic situation."

"The situation's not new to me," Susan pointed out, keeping her gaze pinned to the car's side window and the wintry New England countryside unfurling on the other side of it. "And as far as Owen Byrnside and Taleman Hall go, they're both very impressive, of course."

"I wouldn't have known you were impressed by the way you handled yourself back there."

He was doing it again, Susan thought, probing, pressing, trying his damnedest to get a rise out of her. She half turned in her seat. "What do you mean? Did I behave inappropriately with Owen Byrnside?"

With minute movements of his sinewy wrist, Jake Caine maneuvered his Mercedes around a sharp bend flanked by tall birches. When the road had straightened out again, he flicked another glance at Susan. "Oh, not at all. As always, you were calm and cool under fire. In fact, you never behave inappropriately, do you?"

"I try not to," Susan said calmly. She knew what this was all about, of course. Last week when he'd gotten into town after one of his many lengthy business trips, Jake had asked her to have dinner with him again, and again she'd refused. Since most other women fell at his feet, his male pride was hurt, and he was irked.

"Honestly, Miss Bonner, I don't think you have to try at all. I think you were born behaving appropriately."

At that, all Susan's anger drained away, leaving her merely amused. The flash in her long-lashed golden eyes was replaced by the glint of laughter and her finely cut mouth lifted at the corners. If only he knew!

"Yes," she replied, "I was born wearing ruffled diapers and clutching a copy of Emily Post. Not unlike some people I know who came into this world with a full set of silver spoons," she added pointedly.

Jake, whose privileged background reeked of substantial old brick houses, substantial old pedigrees and stacks of old money kept under judicious control, knew Susan was referring to him. He raised his dark brows as she smoothly changed the subject.

"I just saw a sign for Lowerton. Isn't that near where Christopher Byrnside had his accident?"

Jake nodded. "We passed the spot only a couple of minutes ago, as a matter of fact."

"You mean those hairpin turns back there?" When he said yes, she asked, "Could we turn around and take a closer look, do you think?"

Jake shot her a surprised glance and then put his foot on the brake. It was half a minute's work to swing the big car in a circle on the narrow country lane, and soon they were purring along in the direction from which they'd just come.

"Any particular reason for wanting to inspect the scene of the tragedy?"

Susan kept a careful control on her voice. "Just morbid curiosity. Do you mind?"

"Not at all. I'm in no rush to get back to the office."
Jake pulled off the road by a clump of bushes. "We'll have
to walk back. There's really no place to park any closer."

"That's fine with me. I could use a little exercise."

When he opened the door for her, she stepped out on the
rutted gravel and pulled up the collar of her belted tweed
coat. It was long, just brushing her trim, booted ankles—
a good thing, since a cutting January wind whistled
through the leafless trees.

As Jake took Susan's elbow, she glanced up at him.
Though the icy wind riffled his usually neatly combed
brown hair, he appeared unaffected by the freezing temperature. His navy cashmere overcoat hung open. He was
the sort of man who never buttoned his coat, Susan
thought. It was as if no winter winds, no matter how severe, would dare discommode such a fine and perfect New
England specimen as Jacob McClellan Caine.

As they walked along the side of the road, Susan said,
"Tell me about Christopher Byrnside's accident. I know
he was supposed to have been drunk and high on drugs
when it happened. But was there anything else unusual
about the circumstances?"

"To be honest, I haven't looked into the matter. It happened almost thirty years ago, after all."

"Yes, but it might be worth studying the police report.
You never know, there's always a chance it could have
some bearing on what's going on now."

"You mean the attacks on Byrnside's second orphan,
Maggie? I doubt there's any connection, but you're right.
It's worth doing a little research." He shot Susan a half
amused, half curious look. "I think you missed your calling. You should have been a private eye."

"Oh?" Susan kept her gaze on the uncertain footing.
"What makes you say that?"

"We've been working together long enough for me to have formed an opinion of you, you know. You're meticulous, have a sharp eye for detail, a cool intelligence and the patience and tenacity of a bulldog. If I were an evildoer I'd hate to have you on *my* trail."

"Well, I'll take that as a compliment, though I can't really say it sounded terribly flattering."

"Then you must not know when a man is trying to compliment you. Which is strange. I'd think an attractive woman like you would have the opposite sex all figured out by now."

Instead of responding to that leading remark, Susan pointed a gloved finger at the sharp bend in the road just ahead. "Is that it up there?"

"That's the spot. I only know, actually, because on one of my early trips up here Owen's chauffeur pointed it out to me."

"Oh, was he working for Mr. Byrnside at the time of the accident?"

"Yes. Owen may appear gruff, but he seems to inspire deep loyalty in his employees. I know of several of his staff who've been with him for decades, including Loretta Greene."

Recalling Owen Byrnside's haughty personal secretary, whom she'd met for the first time that afternoon, Susan made a small face. She and Loretta Greene had taken an instant, though discreetly unspoken, dislike to each other. It had been as potent as a chemical reaction, like two cats with rising fur facing each other on the boundary of a disputed territory. Sometimes you could react to strangers that way, Susan knew, but it wasn't usually so severe.

Susan and Jake had reached the spot where the road swept sharply to the left. On the right it dropped off into a deep, bracken-filled ditch. Jake stopped and pointed.

"Christopher didn't make this turn. He was driving a lightweight sports car, probably much too fast. It swung wide, rolled over into that ditch and exploded."

Susan stood beside him, staring at the site of the decades-old tragedy and imagining how it must have been, the squeal of the brakes, the smell of burning rubber, the sound of grinding gears and rending metal and then, perhaps a moment or two before the explosion, Christopher Byrnside's scream of terror.

"Are you cold?"

"W-what?"

"Susan, you're shivering. Your teeth are chattering."

"Are they?"

"My God, yes. You're pale as death. Why didn't you tell me the cold was getting to you so badly?" Jake put his arm around her shoulders. "C'mon, let's get back to the car."

The interior of the Mercedes was still warm. Nevertheless, Susan huddled in its deep leather seat, her hands buried in her pockets and her face averted to the side window. Behind her haunted eyes she still saw a horrifying image of a young man who had everything to live for screaming in terror while his car burst into flames around him.

As he drove, Jake Caine shot the pale, silent young woman beside him worried glances. "You're awfully quiet."

"Sorry." She shook herself a bit, changed her position and tried to relax.

"It's been a long morning. I know a nice old inn near here. How about stopping there for lunch?"

Susan shot Jake a wary glance. "All right."

A distinct look of satisfaction settled around his chiseled mouth. "We'll be at the Red Tub Lodge in five minutes."

The Red Tub was a sprawling, half-timbered old structure nestled in a stand of tall pines and cedars. There were only two other cars in its gravel parking lot.

"Good. Looks like we're going to have the place to ourselves," Jake said as he helped Susan out of the passenger seat.

Inside the hostess placed them at a table near a huge open hearth where a small fire crackled. "This is charming," Susan commented. She glanced up at the copper pots, warming pans and bunches of dried herbs dangling from the beamed ceiling. A stuffed owl with a quizzical expression perched on a small shelf and antique photos, mismatched bits of china and pierced tin pie plates decorated the rough-plastered walls. "Why do they call it the Red Tub?"

"Because a century or so ago guests bathed in a red tin tub that was brought to their rooms on request. I believe since then the plumbing's been modernized."

"I certainly hope so."

Jake grinned. "Oh, I don't know. In the right company bathing in an overcrowded red tin tub might be fun."

"I can't imagine how."

"Can't you? No, I suppose you can't." Shrugging, Jake draped his and Susan's coats on a wooden rack. "I discovered this place the first time Owen summoned me up here to discuss finding his orphans," he commented.

While his long, lean back was turned, Susan allowed her gaze to rove over the rangy lines of his tall figure. Actually, she could imagine quite well how it might be fun to be naked in a tub with him. Nevertheless, the instant he turned, she restored her attention to the menu.

"I've been stopping here ever since," Jake continued as he folded himself into the chair opposite her.

"Mr. Byrnside never invites you to stay for lunch or dinner at Taleman Hall?"

"No. He's very restricted in his own diet, and I get the distinct impression from Miss Greene that an unscheduled guest at meals would not be welcome."

Susan looked up from the list of sandwiches. "I know she's been with him for a long time, but I couldn't help noticing he's awfully gruff with her."

"Don't let that fool you. When Owen's wife died half a dozen years ago he went into a period of utter despondency. Miss Greene took over. She runs Taleman Hall."

"He doesn't seem despondent now," Susan pointed out.

"No. This search for his granddaughter has really been a turnaround for Owen. Finding these girls, helping them just as if they were his real granddaughters has given him a new lease on life. Maybe he didn't look like the picture of health to you, but believe me he's in much better shape now than he was when all this began. That's why locating Lynn Rice is so important. Finding all three has become his reason for living."

"His, maybe," Susan countered, "but someone else has other ideas for the orphans."

Jake frowned. "You mean the attacks on Maggie Murphy? But those have stopped."

"Only because whoever's behind them is lying low. Jake, it's obvious that someone out there is not anxious to have Owen Byrnside's granddaughter found. If that person could set a contract killer loose on Maggie Murphy, he's bound to try again, and not just on Maggie but on the other two orphans as well—provided one of them isn't the actual culprit."

"I have a detective working on it."

"He's working, but so far he hasn't come up with anything concrete."

Jake shrugged. "Maggie and Kate don't know it, but I've got a guard keeping an eye on each of them. When we find Lynn Rice, we'll protect her, too. But we can't do that until we know where she is. Meanwhile," he added with his most charming smile as the waitress approached their table, "I recommend the barley soup. The smoked turkey salad is excellent, too."

After they'd ordered and Jake had persuaded Susan to try a glass of mulled wine, he sat sipping from a tankard of ale and regarding her thoughtfully. "A few minutes ago you asked if Owen ever invited me to stay for lunch at Taleman Hall. Truth to tell, even if I were invited, I'd probably refuse. After a session there I'd much rather relax over a meal in a place like this."

"I can see why," Susan agreed with an appreciative glance at the glowing fire next to them.

"Until now, that's always meant eating alone," Jake added smoothly. "It's a pleasure to have someone like you sitting opposite me."

"Someone like me?" Susan studied her employer. She hadn't seen much of Jake Caine this past year. He traveled so frequently. Still, keeping the man at arm's length on the rare occasions when he *was* around hadn't been easy—not when he was so attractive.

Oh, he wasn't the handsomest man she'd ever met. Yet he was certainly one of the most appealing. She couldn't help but admire his tall, rangy physique, his easy grace and the quick, decisive way he did everything. Except when a real smile lit his expression, there was no softness in his aristocratic face. It was all strong lines and lean angles, and behind his wire-rimmed glasses his gray-green eyes had a cool, assessing intelligence that drew her. For Susan that was Jake's greatest attraction.

But Jacob Caine wasn't for her, Susan reminded herself. Not in this tricky situation, not when the stakes were so high. Besides, he might enjoy flirting with the various pretty women he squired around, but anyone who knew him had to be aware that he wasn't about to get serious with a mere hireling.

"You must know that I enjoy working with you," Jake said. "I've been out of the office a lot, but you've kept things running smoothly. In fact, you're the best executive assistant I've ever had. You're intelligent, efficient, and self-motivated."

"Why, thank you," Susan responded. "Does this mean you're going to give me another raise?"

"Not for a month or so," Jake responded with a grin. His gaze played over her. "You're a consummate professional, Susan. But you're also a very private person, aren't you?"

"How do you mean?"

"I mean that we've worked together for almost a year now, even traveled together, yet really I know very little about you."

"As you just pointed out, you've been away so much that we really haven't seen a lot of each other. Even so, you've learned all you need to about me. You've seen my work and read my résumé. That's all most people who work together know about each other."

"Yes," Jake admitted. "Though actually when you were first hired by my partners I only glanced at your papers. It was a busy time and I trusted their judgment— rightly so, obviously." He rotated his mug between his open palms. "However, it might interest you that a couple of weeks back I dug your résumé out of the files and studied it with more care."

"Oh? Why did you do that?" Beneath the table Susan's hands clenched.

"Just curiosity. I confess, I'm very curious about you. There's something unusual about you, an aura—I don't know how to explain it. Anyhow, your résumé was most impressive—especially your education. You went to some good schools."

"I think so."

"I was interested to see that you were an undergraduate at Radcliffe the same year as my niece, Molly Ashmore."

He looked at Susan inquiringly, but she schooled her expression to blandness. She'd learned over the past year that you keep your mouth shut and your feet on the floor until you've been given all the information you were going to get.

"Do you remember her, by any chance?"

"No. It's a big school," Susan responded guardedly, "and we wouldn't have run in the same social circles. I was there on scholarship. Your niece, I'm sure, was a legacy."

Jake stiffened slightly. "It's true that the women in my family have attended Radcliffe for several generations. But that doesn't mean Molly couldn't have gotten in on her own. She's a very bright girl."

"I don't doubt it. In fact I'm sure she is. I'm sure everyone in your family is put together with superior quality material, just as you are." As soon as the words were out, Susan wished she could take them back. They were too sardonic, too revealing—and where Jake Caine was concerned, she didn't want to be revealing.

But it was too late. A fresh alertness had come into his eyes. "That didn't sound very friendly. Do you dislike me, Susan?"

"No, of course not."

"I wondered," he went on, ignoring her denial. "You've turned down all my dinner invitations and all my other overtures, too. I've made it pretty clear that I'd like to get to know you socially, but you've made it even clearer that you're not interested. Is there something about me that turns you off—my family background, my choice of socks, the way I knot my tie?"

The waitress came and set their meals down in front of them. Ignoring his club sandwich, Jake waited for Susan's answer.

"There's nothing like that. I just don't believe in dating the boss, that's all. I prefer to keep a professional relationship professional."

"I see." He picked up his fork. "Well, I guess I can't fault you for professionalism, now can I?"

"I hope not." Susan picked up her own fork. The food smelled delicious, but she had totally lost her appetite. It wouldn't do to show that to Jake Caine, however. She dug into her salad with a will and changed the subject to a problem that needed solving at the office.

THREE HOURS LATER Jake pulled into the small garage of his Beacon Hill town house. When he'd let himself in through the private entrance and climbed the staircase to the first floor he stood gazing around his living room. Slowly he removed his overcoat and then his suit jacket and dropped them on a chair. The cleaning lady had left the place spotless. Nevertheless, as he inhaled the fragrance of lemon wax, there was a discouraged expression on his handsome face, and his eyes were tired.

Jake's town house had been furnished by his wife in discreet good taste and at a great deal of expense. Though Janet had been dead for over four years now, Jake had made very few changes. The walls were painted and pa-

pered with the soft dove gray she had selected and the upholstered furniture was exactly as she'd placed it. Only the
pile of newspapers stacked by the fireplace, the legal briefs
heaped on an end table next to a wing chair and the
vaguely deserted air of the place testified that a man who
spent most of his time at the office or traveling lived here
without a woman.

Sighing, Jake loosened his tie and strolled into the
kitchen where he took a soda from the refrigerator. After
uncapping it, he switched on the answering machine next
to the telephone.

"Hi Jake, this is Alison Steel," a voice chirped. "Remember me? We met at the Turnbulls. Anyhow, I just
happen to have two tickets to *Salome* and I remember you
said you liked opera. Call me at 555-4960 if you're interested."

Jake cocked his head. Yes, he did remember Alison
Steel. Pretty little thing in a ruffled cocktail dress—ran an
art gallery or some such. He'd been interested enough in
her to think he might call sometime. So far he hadn't gotten around to it. It was flattering that she'd decided to take
the initiative—and after being held at arm's length by the
enigmatic Susan Bonner all afternoon, a man could use all
the ego-boosting he could get. Jake made a mental note of
Alison's phone number.

The next message was from the detective Jake had hired
to track down the orphans for Owen Byrnside. "It's possible that our chase may take us back to Europe. I've got
a new lead."

Jake's ears pricked up.

"Nothing I can get my teeth into yet," the investigator
continued, "but when and if it begins to shape up I'll be
back to you with bells on."

Jake grimaced. So far there'd been too many leads that fizzled to nothing. What he wouldn't give to have this Byrnside thing sewn up!

"Of course you're not home. Are you ever?"

Jake recognized his sister Freddie's cultured Bostonian tones issuing from the tape.

"Please call the minute you step in the door," she exhorted. "There are legal questions regarding the Art League Ball and the library fund I must discuss with you. Oh, and I'm planning a dinner Monday night for Molly and this fiancé she's finally lassoed. Now don't put on your forgetful act. You do have a family, Jake. And you do have obligations."

As if I hadn't figured out by now that I have a family, Jake thought wryly. He'd have to be deaf, dumb and blind not to know about his obligations. The Caines had been a New England fixture since Jeremiah Caine had stepped off the *Mayflower*. A portrait of Jeremiah's dour-faced great-grandson still hung in the mansion where Jake had cut his milk teeth along with his other siblings, all of whom still lived in the area.

Jake heard out the other taped messages on his answering machine and then took what was left of his soda back to the living room. He dropped into his favorite chair, stuck his feet up on a stool and considered how he was going to spend the rest of the evening. There were a number of options. He could call Alison Steel or several other equally attractive ladies he knew, dine out and take in a play or concert.

He could go to his health club, gulp down something nutritious at the juice bar, tackle the weights and then pick up a game of squash or racquetball.

Or he could sit home alone and brood. The ring of the telephone shattered the silence.

"Oh, I just knew it. You're home, and you certainly must have got my message on that answering machine of yours, so you've no excuse. Why haven't you called?"

As he listened to his older sister Frederica, Jake rolled his eyes. "Freddie, I just got in and it's been a long day. Give me a chance."

"Oh, pooh. I suppose that means you don't want to talk about the library fund."

"Perceptive of you. Not tonight, no."

"What about dinner Monday? You know Molly adores you. She'll be heartbroken if you're not there to meet her fiancé."

"I adore her, too, and I'll put it in my calendar."

There was a tiny pause and Freddie cleared her throat. "Would you like to come over for dinner tonight? We'd love to have you."

"Yes, I'm sure Howard is panting for my cheery presence in his dining room."

"Now that isn't fair. You know he likes you, Jake."

"I like him too, but tonight I think I'll leave him to his roast beef and potatoes in peace."

"You're every bit as stuffy and unimaginative about food as he is, and you shouldn't be alone tonight, Jake. Do you have any plans?"

"Nothing concrete as of yet, but I haven't had much chance to think about it."

"You've had a year to think about it," Freddie, who'd never been one to mince words, declared starkly.

Wearily, Jake passed a hand over his brow. "Whatever I do tonight, Freddie, I promise it won't be a repeat of last January 9th."

"My God, I hope not!" A year ago on this date he'd disgraced himself. Freddie had stopped by with one of her charity ball friends and found him passed out on the living room floor, a bottle in one hand and a fire still smoldering in the fireplace mere inches from his outstretched fingers. She had, of course, been horrified—perhaps as much by his appalling dishabille as by the fact that he could easily have set himself ablaze.

"Tonight will be uneventful," he stated flatly.

"Do you mean that, Jake? Do you really promise me?"

"Yes, I do."

"I don't worry about you the rest of the year. It's just on these hideous anniversaries. I know you can't help but think about Janet. It's no wonder you get depressed."

"Freddie, I don't want to talk about Janet. Just take my word for it, I'll be all right. Now goodbye, and don't worry." And with that, Jake gently replaced the receiver.

He stood with his hands on his lean hips. Then he went back to the kitchen, flicked on the small TV on the counter and tuned it to a local news station. Listening with one ear to the murder and mayhem which poured from it, he pulled a gourmet entrée out of the freezer and prepared it for the magic zap of the miracle microwave.

He'd given up any idea of going out—though that was probably what he should be doing. Freddie, as always, was dead right. He should have made plans. He should have packed these hours so tight that they'd pass in a blur of activity—the way most of his days did. But he hadn't, and it was too late now.

Still, Jake told himself, it had been four years and he was a big boy. It wasn't as if he couldn't find plenty of work to keep him occupied right here in his study. Somehow he'd get through this night without embarrassing himself the way he had last time. He was a Caine, after all. And for a Caine, dignity was all.

With a wry smile, Jake plucked his packaged gourmet feast out of the microwave, set it on top of a plate and then poured himself a large glass of chocolate milk. After his solitary dinner he headed for his study and set to work. Legal briefs and the letters kept him busy until past ten o'clock. After that he was tired, or at least he told himself he was tired. Deliberately keeping his mind blank, refusing to think of anything but putting one foot in front of the other, he went upstairs and walked through the ritual of bathing, brushing his teeth and switching off the bedside lamp. Then, still stoically blank-minded, he closed his eyes and willed himself to sleep.

But disciplined as Jake was by nature as well as nurture, he couldn't turn himself off completely. Just before he slipped into unconsciousness he saw them again—the horrible pictures that had haunted him for the past four years. He saw a Caribbean night sky acrackle with lightning, black storm-tossed water and his wife's hand reaching desperately for his just before she disappeared beneath that water and drowned.

CHAPTER TWO

THE INSTANT SUSAN emerged from the corner grocery an icy wind lashed at her hair and swirled her long coat around her ankles. A heavy purse and stuffed briefcase weighted Susan's slender shoulder and she juggled an overflowing grocery bag in each arm. It was late and so overcast that the street lamps already burned. She hurried along and, from habit, kept an eye out. Her apartment building was not in the safest of neighborhoods.

Ten minutes later Susan climbed the steps of her brownstone and heaved a sigh of relief as she stepped into the warm shelter of its small white-tiled lobby. After checking her mailbox, she tapped on the door to the right.

"It's me, Mrs. Crumper," she said when the door opened a crack. "I've brought you some milk and tea and those fig cookies you like."

The door creaked open and a tiny, withered old lady with a nimbus of thin white curls peered out. At the sight of Susan, her faded blue eyes lit up. "Oh, look at you, struggling all this way with those heavy groceries after a hard day's work. Come in, come in, come in!"

Smiling, Susan shook her head. "I'm leaving to spend the weekend on Hull, so I really must get upstairs and pack if I'm to make the ferry on time. But I wanted to make sure you had everything you needed."

"Oh, you are the sweetest girl. Your mother must be so proud of you." The old lady's hand fluttered. "Oh, but I keep forgetting, you never knew your mother, did you?"

"No," Susan admitted. "I'm an orphan."

"An orphan." Mrs. Crumper *tsk-tsked*. "And that's why you go to Hull on the weekends, to visit this woman named Maudie that you told me of?"

"Yes," Susan said. "Maudie Walters was my foster mother. She got me past my wild and crazy teen years. And that was no easy task, believe me."

"Well, she did a wonderful, wonderful job," Mrs. Crumper declared.

SUSAN ALWAYS ENJOYED coming to Hull, a peninsula that hung off Massachusetts like a plump appendix. Most of the people who lived there year-round were fishermen, and Susan loved its isolated feel, its old-fashioned houses and its leisurely pace of life. Only forty minutes by ship across the Atlantic from Boston Harbor, it felt like another world. Or so Susan thought as she paid off the taxi driver and walked up the lane that led to Maud Walters's ramshackle Victorian manse.

It sprawled at the end of a partly paved street within hearing distance of the ocean's open-throated winter roar. Other houses on the street were boarded up for the season, but the lights in Maudie's diamond-paned windows glowed cheerily.

"My sweet baby!" Maudie cried when she threw open the front door. Instantly her sturdy freckled arms circled Susan's shoulders and drew her into the warmth of the living room. "The weather's so stormy, I was worried you wouldn't get here."

"It was a rough crossing," Susan admitted. "I made the ferry just in time, and then, with those storm warnings flying, they weren't sure they were going to sail at all. But they did, and here I am." Susan hugged Maudie back and then set her overnight bag down and began unbuttoning her coat. She sniffed. "Is that dinner I smell?"

"The girls are in the kitchen working on a Mulligan stew in your honor."

"Oh?" Susan pictured the three teenage girls Maudie currently mothered, and grinned.

But Maudie didn't return her smile. There was a quizzical expression in her hazel eyes, which had stayed pinned to Susan's face. "Lord, after all these months I still can't get over the way you look. You're not my poor scarred little duckie anymore. Those Swiss doctors turned you into a swan."

Susan shook her head. "Seeing isn't necessarily believing, Maudie. I'll tell you a secret. I can't get used to the plastic surgery either. Every time I walk past a mirror I get an anxiety attack. 'Who is that snooty-looking blonde?' I wonder. It can't be me, can it? Sometimes I feel like an alien who's been planted in the wrong body."

"You'll get over that," Maudie said wisely.

"I don't know. It's been a year now."

"You've had it rough, but you're a survivor." A reminiscent look came into Maudie's eye. "I'll never forget the day I brought you home. You were like a starved kitten who'd been abused by a pack of bullies. You kept your face down, trying to hide that burn mark on your cheek and hissed and spat whenever anyone tried to get too close to you. Talk about streetwise—you called me some names that made my hair curl, you did."

"I know I was awful to you. Don't remind me."

"You were pretty bad. But it didn't last long. A hot meal in your stomach, a clean bed and a little love—that's all it took for you to get over it. That's my point. When this

Byrnside business is taken care of, you'll settle down and make friends with the new, good-lookin' you. And then— oh, my, won't you have some fun! I'll bet the men are already coming on to you strong.''

Susan looked uncomfortable. "It's just my brand-new face they're attracted to—not really me."

"So what else is new? That's how it is with men and women, at least at first. You have to like the package before you get around to appreciating what's inside."

"Maybe, but I'm not ready to deal with that yet."

"Which means they're snapping at your heels." Maudie winked. "How about I get you a nice hot cup of coffee and then you can fill me in on all the details?"

Susan agreed. The two women walked through the huge living room with its worn rug and threadbare but comfortable furniture and past the swinging door into a big high-ceilinged kitchen.

Three giggling girls huddled in front of a chipped enamel stove. They were the latest set of runaways and hard cases that Maudie had rescued from the streets and taken into her home and her motherly heart. The teen named Sherry was arrow-thin in her black spandex pants and magenta top, and so heavily made up that her face resembled an artist's palette. Next to her, in skintight jeans, was Patsy, a sallow adolescent with stringy brown hair and a sulky expression. The other, Tamara, was black, chunky in her sweat pants and loose T-shirt and wore her hair in tight cornrows. All three carried large wooden spoons and gazed into a bubbling iron pot.

When Maudie and Susan came in, the trio swung around. "Hey Suze, right on!" Sherry exclaimed. "So you made it!"

"Yes, but just barely. You guys should be flattered that I'd brave the high seas on a rotten night like this just to spend the weekend eating your cooking. Double bubble, toil and trouble, what have you got in that pot?'' Dubiously, Susan peered between their shoulders.

"It's our secret recipe. Wait until you taste it!" Sherry exclaimed. Her spiky bleached hair shimmered under the fluorescent light.

"Hey, just smelling it may be enough." Susan inhaled and pressed a palm to her solar plexus. "I feel full already."

"No fair," Tamara declared. "You can't get away with just sniffing. After all the work we've put in, you've got to eat it. It's okay—no dead rats or anything, just all the leftovers in the refrigerator that weren't moving or colored fuzzy green."

"Sounds irresistible," Maudie commented dryly.

"Hey, superbo threads," Patsy said, coming away from the stove to run a covetous finger down the arm of Susan's gray cashmere sweater. "This must have cost some major bucks. Got yourself a sugar daddy?"

"Got myself a good-paying job," Susan corrected.

"Well, goody for you, straight shooter. Can I borrow your sweater?"

"Are you kidding?" Sherry interjected, rolling her eyes, which were circled with glittery shadow. "Patsy, with your figure you'd never fit into something of Susan's. Anyway, this stew is ready for action. Are we going to sit down and float it past our taste buds or what?"

"If you've got the nerve for a little floating action, then so do I," Susan teased. "But that concoction's not oozing into my mouth until I've seen it slide into each of yours."

"That goes for me, too," Maudie seconded. "No dangerous living for this old lady. Now, who gets to set the table?"

For the next hour smart remarks and high-pitched giggles bounced off the kitchen's slightly cobwebby ceiling.

"Hey, you know what?" Susan said as she forked up the last bite on her plate. "This stew wasn't half bad. In fact, it was pretty good. Maybe you three should consider opening a restaurant."

Sherry and Tamara made faces at each other. "Yeah," Tamara quipped, "we could call it Bad Girls. Catchy, huh?"

"Maybe, but I don't like it," Maudie shot back. "I think Better Girls is more what I'm aiming for. Speaking of which . . ." She surveyed the dirty dishes littering the table and shot a meaningful look at the sink piled high with dripping cookware. "Who's going to clean up after this gourmet feast?"

The teens looked at one another, but no one said a word.

"Since they did the cooking, how about we do the cleanup?" Susan suggested.

"Yeah! Right on!" Sherry, Patsy and Tamara sang out.

Maudie rolled her eyes. "Foiled by the brat pack once again. Okay, but only if you three skedaddle out of here and produce rooms that are ready for inspection by nine o'clock tonight."

"That's not the best proposition I've ever heard," Sherry whined. "But for tonight I guess it'll have to do."

It took some further encouragement, but a few minutes later the teenagers were out of the kitchen and Susan and Maudie had cleared the table and planted themselves elbow to elbow at the sink.

"The girls seem to be getting along pretty well together," Susan commented as she scraped and stacked. "I have to admit I was a little worried about how Patsy would fit in. When she first came here a month ago she seemed so—"

"Hostile? Tough? Foul-mouthed?" Grimacing, Maudie squirted some liquid soap into the hot water she'd run. "Yeah. Well, she's settled down some, but that girl worries me. She's only fourteen, you know. She ran away from an abusive stepfather when she was barely thirteen and wound up out on the streets. All of these girls have seen too much of the rough side of life. But Patsy's been more ground down by it than the others. And then there's Bucky."

"Bucky?"

"Her so-called boyfriend. He's found out she's here and he's been hanging around. The guy's got to be at least thirty-five, and he looks like Charles Manson's less popular twin. He gives me the creeps."

Susan frowned. She knew exactly the sort of sleazeball this Bucky character probably was. Such men were like vultures, preying on the frightened young runaways who arrived in the big cities. They were expert at spotting and exploiting a kid who was alone, helpless and vulnerable. Susan knew about the Buckys of the world from personal experience. For she'd once been a runaway herself.

Susan started to chuckle.

"What are you laughing about?" Maudie demanded. "I don't remember saying anything funny."

Mouth still twitching, Susan scrubbed at the bottom of a burned pot. "Oh, I was just remembering a conversation I had with my boss this afternoon."

"The classy lawyer I see pictures of in the society pages?"

"That's the one. Anyhow, he took me to lunch this afternoon and ..."

"Oh, ho," Maudie interrupted. "The plot thickens. I thought you were so determined not to get social with this guy."

"I'm not getting social," Susan denied. "This was strictly business. We were driving back from Owen Byrnside's place in Jake's car so there was no way I could avoid eating lunch with him. Anyhow, he told me he'd been re-reading my résumé and was impressed by all the good schools I went to. If he only knew where I really got my education!"

"You learned a lot in Police Academy."

"Yes, but that's a far cry from the fancy college he imagines I attended." Susan laughed again, but Maudie's expression sobered.

"You know," she said, "I've been thinking. Maybe it's time you gave up this charade and came clean with Mr. Byrnside. Think of all the money he's spending trying to find you."

Susan shook her head. "Not until I'm good and ready. Not until I know what's really going on with this Byrnside business. All Owen Byrnside's risking is money, and he has plenty of that. For me it's my one and only life. Have you forgotten what happened in Switzerland? While my face was still in bandages, someone tried to kill me, Maudie, and nearly succeeded. If I hadn't been able to unwrap a new face and run away, if I hadn't dyed my hair and got myself a new identity, I might be dead by now."

The older woman sighed. "I haven't forgotten, and it worries me. I wouldn't have lied to Mr. Caine's detective about not knowing where you were if this whole thing didn't worry me." She put a hand on Susan's arm. "I love you like a mother, remember? If anything happened to you, well I just don't know if I could go on. I can call you Susan in front of other people," she whispered so that no one else in the house could hear. "But to me you'll always be my little Lynnie. Be careful, Lynnie."

"FUN WEEKEND?" Jake Caine sat at his desk, surrounded by stacks of paper. He had his suit jacket off, and the sleeves of his tattersall shirt were rolled to his elbow, showing muscular forearms sprinkled with fine dark hairs.

"Nothing special, but it was okay." Susan stood in his doorway. The ferry back from Hull hadn't been on time that morning, and she'd hurried into the office half an hour late. Jake, as always, had been at his desk to register the fact, and she wondered if she was going to get a lecture on punctuality.

But apparently Jake wasn't in the mood to lecture. "I hope you haven't made any lunch plans."

"No."

"Good. Then I have a favor to ask. You must have heard me speak of Winston Deeping."

Susan relaxed slightly. "The CEO at Byrnside Recording? Of course. I handled the paperwork on the Flying Rats litigation, if you'll remember." She managed to keep a straight face—just barely. The Flying Rats were a British rock group who lived up to their title. After their recent American tour they'd been sued for unpaid bills and breakage by hotels, restaurants and bars all up and down the East Coast. When they'd winged their way back across the Atlantic, they'd left a nest of trouble behind them. And since Foster, Brighton and Caine represented Byrnside Enterprises, Jake's firm had been charged with cleaning up the mess.

Jake responded dryly. "Yes, I remember it well. And so does Owen. He didn't like their music and he doesn't like them. Winston Deeping's flown in from London for a conference with Owen. Owen's raising a ruckus over some new directions Winston wants to take with the British branch of the company. I don't know all the details, but I do know that Deeping's here to try and argue the old man over to his point of view."

Susan pictured Owen Byrnside's flinty jaw and shook her head. "Good luck to Mr. Deeping," she murmured ironically. "He'll need it."

"Exactly," Jake agreed. "Owen may be past eighty and in ill health, but Winston Deeping is still no match for him. On the other hand, to give Winston his due, he's shrewd, determined to have his way, and a smooth negotiator. Before he tackles his boss, he wants to pick my brains, find out if there's anything I can give away that might help his argument. At least, I assume that's what this lunch meeting he's ordered up is all about."

Jake paused, seesawing a pencil back and forth. While Susan waited for what he would say next, she watched the dexterous movement of his long fingers. He had beautiful hands, she thought, strong and masculine yet sensitive.

Her gaze focused on the gold ring he still wore. She knew, of course, that Jake was a widower. It was common knowledge that his wife had been a beautiful former debutante who'd drowned while they'd been in the Caribbean on a second honeymoon. Two years after her death Jake had started dating other women, and in fact now had a bit of a reputation as a man-about-town and a heartbreaker. But he wouldn't still be wearing his wedding ring if he were completely recovered from his wife's death, Susan thought.

Abruptly Jake dropped the pencil. "I want you to come along to this lunch of Deeping's."

"But I was supposed to..."

"I know, I know. Never mind the Burton brief. It can wait. Instead I'd like you to spend the morning digging out all the files we have that involve Byrnside Recording and familiarizing yourself with them. I'll be in a meeting with the partners until eleven. When I get out you can brief me."

Jake stood and shrugged on his suit jacket. He glanced at her from under his thick, straight brows. "You may enjoy lunch with Winston Deeping. It's at the Upperview Shooting Club, for one thing. Upperview is an interesting place if you've never been there before. And for another, Winston's got quite a reputation for charming the ladies."

After the Flying Rats episode, Susan doubted that any amount of charm would recommend their sponsor to her. But she was curious to meet him, and to get a look at this hoity-toity shooting club.

"Isn't Upperview a members-only club and very exclusive?" Susan asked early that afternoon as she and Jake cruised through the outskirts of Boston in Jake's Mercedes.

"It is. You have to have old money and they prefer that their members own a pedigree that dates back to the *Mayflower*."

"Then how is Winston Deeping entertaining us there? He's a Londoner."

"Yes, but Winston lived in the States for many years and has a lot of contacts in this country. As a matter of fact, he began his rise in the Byrnside hierarchy here on the East Coast when he was a talent scout for the American branch of Byrnside Recording. He's a charmer who's always been able to gain access to the most exclusive circles. What's more, two years ago he married a British aristocrat— Tabissa Walthram. Her fancy pedigree alone would give him entrée to the Shooting Club. They dote on anything English."

The Upperview Shooting Club was a sprawling private complex situated in a picturesque valley a half hour's drive from the city. It featured a stone clubhouse that boasted a

rustic restaurant complex with beamed ceilings, obsequious waiters, tables covered with crisp white cloths,
sterling silver cutlery and monogrammed china.

While Susan sat at one of these tables picking at her
shrimp salad platter and taking notes, Jake and Winston
Deeping talked over the situation at Byrnside Recording.
Though Deeping's rock artists had embarrassed the company repeatedly, he contended that they were potentially
big money-makers and therefore worth all the trouble they
caused.

From time to time Deeping glanced Susan's way, a
predatory glint in his shrewd, assessing eyes. He was an
impeccably groomed man of about fifty, and though he
was below average height and slightly built, he fairly oozed
upper-class self-assurance.

"Well, old man, what would you give for my chances of
persuading Byrnside to see things my way?" he asked Jake
as he lit a gold-tipped cigarette while the waiter removed
his plate.

Jake shook his dark head. "I don't know, Winston.
You're the expert on the music business."

"I'm thrilled to know that you, at least, recognize that
incontrovertible fact. Now if only Owen would do the
same."

"He's given you a pretty free hand until recently. But
I'm afraid the Garbage Boys and the Flying Rats have left
a bad taste in his mouth—no pun intended. You may be in
for a rough time with him."

Winston downed the last of his martini and grimaced.
"When it comes to contemporary music the man's a di-
nosaur. Pleased as I am that his health has improved lately,
I do wish that instead of poking into my business he'd
concentrate his renewed energy elsewhere." He shot Jake
a narrow look. "For instance, on this bizarre search for a

missing granddaughter that you were telling me of the last time you were in London. How's that coming along?"

Jake's brow creased. "Well enough, but if you'll remember I also told you in strict confidence and only because I needed your help."

Winston glanced at Susan. "Oh dear, have I let the cat out of the bag?"

"No, Miss Bonner knows about the search, and in fact has been helping with it. But let me repeat, please don't mention it to anyone else."

"No, of course, old man, mum's the word. I know how to keep a secret. But really, aren't you going to tell me anything more?"

"Not at the moment. You'll find out soon enough."

Winston looked amused rather than offended. "My, my, now you really have piqued the old curiosity. But I won't breathe another word on the subject. Now, do let me get that," he added as the waiter brought the check and Jake pulled out his credit card. "You're here at my invitation. Besides," he added, casting another approving glance at Susan, "any lawyer smart enough to hire such an attractive and obviously capable executive assistant deserves a meal on the house now and then."

As the dapper Britisher signed the check, Susan began to pack her briefcase. But Deeping laid a hand over hers. "No, no, my dear. Jake and I haven't finished our discussion yet. But I quite agree that a bit of fresh air and exercise might be in order. Jake, since we're at a shooting club, what do you say to a spot of target practice? Tabissa and I are going on a shooting party at Lord Beechmeyer's estate when I get back to England. My name will be mud if I don't bag a decent quota of his birds, so I daren't let the old trigger finger get rusty."

"Fresh air sounds like a good idea, but no target practice for me," Jake said easily. "I'll just watch, if you don't mind."

Deeping scraped back his chair and got to his feet. "Very well. Miss Bonner, you won't object to accompanying us outside, will you?"

"Not at all."

The day was sunny and unusually warm for January with temperatures into the forties. After they had all put on their coats and Winston Deeping had retrieved a shotgun in a leather case from the trunk of his rental car, they strolled to a flat, grassy area where targets had been set up on wooden posts. Men—and some women—dressed in smart sports clothes stood shooting, obviously trying to put holes close to the centers of the bull's-eyes.

"This standing around popping off at bits of paper is all right," Deeping remarked offhandedly, "but not my or Tabby's style, really."

"Oh?" Jake shot him a questioning look.

"Not to sound bloodthirsty, but we like our targets moving," Deeping said with a wink.

As they walked along over the dry grass Susan glanced from Deeping to Jake, noting Jake's tall, wide-shouldered build and easy stride and Deeping's prowling gait. Suddenly she got a sense of the two men as animals. Jake, for all his control and sophistication, made her think of a timber wolf. He was a man who dominated the world around him, but who also played by the rules. Deeping, on the other hand, was a jungle cat, cunning and—she suspected in a sudden insight—capable of ruthless and erratic cruelty.

They came to a trapshooting station where Deeping had already made himself known. After giving some instructions to the operator he removed the well-oiled rifle from its case. "I often travel with this gun," he said, patting the stock familiarly. "It's like an old friend."

For the next quarter of an hour the three stood in the January sunshine. While Jake and Deeping continued the business discussion they'd begun at lunch Susan took more notes. All the while, Deeping snapped off shots at the clay pigeons that flew out at regular intervals. Most exploded in the air. A few, however, got past him. Once when this happened he scowled and muttered, "Dear, dear, Tabby wouldn't approve. She's a crack shot, you know."

At long last he turned to Jake and offered his rifle. "Care to try?"

"No, thanks. Tennis is my game. I hardly know one end of a gun from the other."

Deeping's smile was patronizing. "This is a dangerous world we live in, Caine. Someday you may wish to know how to handle a firearm."

"I'll take my chances."

"Oh, well, to each his own." Deeping turned to Susan. "How about you, Miss Bonner? Care to live dangerously?"

"I don't know."

"Don't be shy. Take a lesson from my wife, Tabissa. She's beautiful, intelligent, glamorous—if I do say so myself—and a very feminine and aristocratic lady through and through. But on a horse, with a fencing foil or holding a gun in her hand, she can beat every man she knows hollow." Deeping chuckled and patted Susan on the shoulder. "Now, of course I wouldn't expect anything like that from a pretty young thing like you. But it never hurts to try."

Against her better judgment, Susan—who'd never been able to turn down a dare—nodded. "It does look like fun." She handed her pen and pad to a bemused Jake and stepped forward.

Deeping beamed. "Have you ever handled a shotgun before?"

"Yes, though it's been a while, and I've never shot at clay pigeons."

"Ah, then before I load it up for you, you'll want a little refresher course." Unctuously, the man explained the workings of the shotgun. "Now, after you've sighted, follow the pigeon with one smooth movement and squeeze. There's quite a knack to it. It takes a steady hand and eye, so don't be disappointed if you don't hit anything."

"Oh, I won't."

"I'll have them send out ten pigeons. If you hit even one of them you'll be doing very well indeed and can count yourself as having the makings of a future markswoman."

As Deeping hurried off to make arrangements for the clay pigeons, Jake stood back and watched while Susan lifted the shotgun and pressed the recoil pad to her shoulder. She was looking particularly fetching today in a long burgundy-wool skirt that swirled around her leather-booted ankles. A matching roll-neck sweater and houndstooth check jacket completed her outfit. The wind riffled her silky blond hair and she'd left off her glasses for a change. She looked good with them on, but better with them off—startlingly better.

Jake's own eyes narrowed. Apparently she didn't feel she needed glasses for shooting. In that case, just what did she need them for, anyway?

"You surprise me," he said to Susan.

"Why?"

"I got the distinct impression that you didn't approve of Winston's name-dropping and high-society pretensions."

"I don't."

"Then why are you willing to give him the satisfaction of crowing over you if you don't hit those damn flying clay targets? I certainly wasn't going to."

"Maybe I'm more adventurous than you are."

Before Jake could answer, Deeping hurried back toward them. "All set. Now relax, my dear. Remember, this is all in fun."

"I'll remember."

Jake watched while Susan took up a square stance and squinted down the length of the shotgun. It suddenly occurred to him that she didn't look like a novice with that gun. In fact, she looked like a woman who knew exactly what she was doing.

In that moment Jake knew what was going to happen. After the first pigeon flew out it didn't surprise him when Susan squeezed the trigger and made the thing explode in midcourse. Apparently, though, it did surprise Deeping, who gave a game little cheer. His cheers strangled in his throat after the fifth clay pigeon exploded with machine-like precision in exactly the same spot. And when the next five repeated the performance, he fell silent altogether.

As Susan lowered the rifle, Jake folded his arms over his chest and stared at his executive assistant's slender back. The woman was a regular Annie Oakley. Now where, he asked himself, had she learned to be such a crack shot—and why?

CHAPTER THREE

INSIDE JAKE'S MERCEDES a weighty silence oppressed Susan's spirits.

"That was quite a performance," Jake murmured.

His tone might be casual, but Susan wasn't fooled. When Jake's curiosity was piqued, he had the tenacity of a bloodhound. "What performance?"

He shot her a raised-eyebrow glance. "You know what I mean."

"Not necessarily. For instance, you might be talking about Winston Deeping's snob act."

Jake grinned. "There are times when Winston can be rather overpowering. You have to know him better to understand why. For instance, you're right about the Lord-of-the-Manor bit. It really is an act. Winston's upper crust accent is acquired."

"Ha!" Susan snorted.

"He comes from a family of Yorkshire coal miners. But just because he likes to dramatize himself, never under-estimate the man. He's made his way to his present top-lofty perch in life by being tough, shrewd and lucky."

"And by marrying the right sort of woman," Susan added cynically.

Jake grinned. "Yes, Tabissa does add a certain luster of authenticity to Winston's aristocratic pretensions. But it's not Deeping I want to talk about, it's you. I had no idea my executive assistant was a sharpshooter. Where did you learn to handle a gun like that?''

Susan sank a little deeper into her seat. Since the scene with the clay pigeons she'd been mentally kicking herself. She'd been so irked by Winston Deeping's patronizing attitude that she hadn't been able to resist showing him up. But it had been stupid vanity to reveal herself like that. Now she was going to have to lie to Jake again, something that was beginning to bother her more and more. But she could hardly tell him the truth—that she'd once been at the top of her class in marksmanship at the Boston Police Academy.

''When I was a kid I had an uncle who liked to take me shooting.''

''Well, he must have been a hell of a good teacher.'' Jake shot Susan another curious glance. ''Your résumé said you grew up in this area. Whereabouts? City? Country?''

Susan thought of the squalid trailer park that had been her last foster home other than Maudie's. Images of her truck-driver foster father in his usual outfit of ragged T-shirt and grimy jeans drifted through her mind—drunk, abusive, coming at her with his beefy arms outstretched. *Don't give me that look, Miss High and Mighty! I'll teach you to turn your nose up at me!''*

''I grew up in the country in north Massachusetts,'' she lied. ''We lived in a beautiful old whitewashed farmhouse surrounded by meadows and orchards.''

''That sounds nice.''

''Yes, it was lovely, idyllic.'' Susan cleared her throat and half turned in her seat. ''Tell me more about Winston Deeping. Now that I've finally met him, I'm fascinated. How did he get hooked up with Byrnside Enterprises in the first place?''

Jake shrugged. "I believe in his early days Winston wanted to be a musician himself. Wore his hair in ringlets and played drums with some British group nobody ever heard of."

Susan choked back a giggle at the image of Winston Deeping in ringlets. "I gather that means he didn't succeed in his ambition."

"No, but he did become thoroughly familiar with the music world. He was stranded over here at some point and hustled himself a job doing talent scouting and P.R. for whatever record companies would pay him a fee. From that lowly beginning he hooked up with Byrnside Recording and since then he's risen like a cork. Until just lately, Owen's pretty much let him have his way. But all that's going back a long time, and I don't know the whole story. I've only been Owen Byrnside's attorney for the last five years."

Susan was silent for a moment, mulling this over. "Where would I go to learn more about Deeping than is in our files?"

"The man really struck a nerve with you, didn't he? Why are you so curious about him?"

"I don't know. I just am." She moved restlessly. "It occurs to me that since Gloria Dean was a pop singer and Christopher Byrnside floated around in that world, too, Deeping may have known them both."

Jake gnawed his lower lip. "I'm sure he did. I haven't questioned Deeping about it because Owen wanted this whole orphan search kept as quiet as possible. But in fact, if I've got the dates right, Deeping was still working in the States around the time of Christopher's death. Of course, that would be true for a lot of other people who remain in Owen's employ."

Susan thought of Owen Byrnside's rather forbidding private secretary. "Like Loretta Greene and Owen Byrnside's chauffeur?"

Jake nodded. "You know, if I remember correctly, there are several boxes of twenty- and thirty-year-old files stuck away somewhere in our storeroom. They came to us when Owen changed law firms. If you're really interested, you're welcome to dig through them."

"Maybe I'll do that," Susan murmured thoughtfully.

TEN MINUTES LATER Jake sat behind the steering wheel and watched as Susan ran up the steps of her brownstone and disappeared inside. Their lunch at the shooting club had lasted so long that it hadn't seemed worthwhile to go back to the office. Besides, he'd been curious to see where Susan lived.

Actually, as he'd pulled the car over to the curb, he'd shot several glances at her silky blond hair and racked his brain for an excuse to get her to invite him in for coffee. But he hadn't been able to come up with anything plausible. A pity, since he was intensely curious to see her place. The way an apartment was put together could tell you a lot about the person who lived in it.

Jake tried to imagine what Susan's apartment would be like. Would she have furnished it with antiques from that whitewashed farmhouse she'd mentioned?

What would his town house say to a stranger? he found himself wondering as he guided the Mercedes back into traffic. Did the fact that it was so obviously unchanged from the way his wife had decorated it indicate that he hadn't yet recovered from her loss? He remembered that a woman he'd dated not too long ago had said as much to him. She'd stood fingering a piece of the Japanese cloisonné collection that had been Janet's passion and remarked solemnly, "You're just going through the motions, aren't you, Jake?"

"What?" He'd been so startled that he'd almost dropped the sherry he'd just poured.

"You're a fatally attractive man and a charming companion, but you're not really interested in me, are you? I can tell when a man wants to get something started. You're just going out with women like me because you think you ought to."

At the time he'd been too polite to agree. Yet she'd been right. Since Janet's death, no other woman had truly interested him. But now one definitely did. Susan.

Oh, from the beginning he'd found her attractive. He'd been irritated when she'd resisted his attempt to socialize with her. But he'd been spending so much time traveling and at first it had been a case of out of sight, out of mind. Not lately, though. Lately he seemed to think about her all the time. And lately he found her reserve more and more frustrating—as well as more and more intriguing. What was it with her, anyway? She said she didn't believe in dating the boss, but surely she knew he would never take advantage of her subordinate position or pressure her in any way. He knew she wasn't involved with anyone else. Was it just him she disliked, or men in general?

Instead of heading back to Beacon Hill, Jake drove to his athletic club where he spent the next two hours working off some of his frustration in the weight room and on the racquetball court. Then, after a shower and sauna, he redonned his business clothes and drove to his sister's place.

"Uncle Jake," his newly engaged niece, Molly, cried. "Finally you're here!" She'd thrown open the front door before he'd even mounted the brick porch's second step. "I've been positively panting at the window waiting for you! Oh, don't you look super, just like always! Let me give you the biggest, juiciest kiss in the world!" Before Molly had even stopped speaking she'd tripped forward on her fashionable Italian leather heels, thrown her arms around her uncle and bussed him enthusiastically.

Jake patted her smooth cap of blue-black hair. "Wait! Wait! You're smothering me with lipstick." Laughing, he pushed Molly away and grinned down at her. He'd always had a soft spot for his bouncy niece. How humorless Freddie and her dull stockbroker husband, Howard, had managed to produce such a live-wire offspring was beyond him. But he was glad they'd gone to the trouble. Molly, with her endless and ever-changing enthusiasms, had always been a bright spot in his life.

"Come in and meet Todd," Molly demanded as she linked her arm through her uncle's and hurried him through the door. "The poor guy's been quaking in his shoes all day dreading this moment."

"Oh? Why would that be?"

Molly laughed up at Jake. Her green eyes glinted with mischief. "Because I told him I trust your judgment implicitly and if you don't put your seal of approval on him the wedding is off."

Jake rolled his eyes. "Oh, Molly, what am I going to do with you?"

"Well, for starters you could buy me a very expensive wedding gift. Something in Irish crystal might do," Molly joked. "Seriously, Todd really is a dear. I know you'll adore him!"

Jake didn't react quite so enthusiastically to the pleasant-faced, nervous-looking young advertising executive Molly brought forward, but he received no negative impressions, either. Obviously Todd worshipped his vivacious little fiancée and just as obviously he was outmatched and was going to spend the rest of his life allowing her to lead him around by the nose, Jake thought with wry amusement.

While Howard buried himself in the evening newspaper and Freddie flitted back and forth between the kitchen and the dining room, Jake sat chatting with the engaged couple. As they burbled about their wedding plans, Jake found himself remembering his own engagement.

He and Janet had met at Harvard and married almost immediately after graduation. It had seemed a perfect match. They had come from the same type of background, shared many of the same interests and ambitions. And they had been crazy in love with each other.

Their love had been strong enough to weather a lot of stress. It had withstood the pressures of his blossoming career and seen them through their crushing disappointment when Janet had learned she would never bear children. But it had not been able to weather a freak storm in the Caribbean.

As an image of lightning and wind blew through Jake's memory, he braced himself for the hammer blow of pain he knew must inevitably follow. But it didn't come, or at least not with the violence he'd learned to expect. Suddenly Jake knew the reason why. He was getting over it. Not forgetting Janet and how much he'd loved her—he would never do that—but moving past the loss of her. Yes, at last that time had come. And Susan Bonner had something to do with the fact, though as yet he wasn't exactly sure what.

The pad of his right thumb touched the wide gold band that circled his ring finger. As if it had the power to capture and hold the past, it was warm with memories as well as the heat of his body. But it was time to take the ring off. Tonight he would do that.

"What are you thinking about, Uncle Jake? You have the strangest expression on your face."

"What? Oh, sorry. My mind was wandering, I guess."

"Well, make it wander back here," Molly said with a laugh. "Mother's just announced dinner."

"You should treat your aging uncle with more respect," Jake joked after Freddie had bustled about seating them.

As Howard prepared to carve the roast, Molly forked a pickled cauliflower off the relish tray. "Oh, pooh! I'm twenty-six. I bet some of the women you date are younger than me."

True, Jake acknowledged. He thought again of Susan and cleared his throat. "That reminds me, Moll. My executive assistant studied at Radcliffe the same years you were there. I wonder if you remember her? Her name is Susan Bonner."

Molly's fork hovered over her plate. "The name doesn't ring a bell. What's she like?"

"Oh, blond, pretty, cool and competent."

"Well, she sounds like someone I should remember, but I don't think I do."

"Maybe she's lying about the school she went to," Freddie suggested. She began to load steamed carrots onto the plate Howard had passed down.

Jake shot his sister a startled look. "Why would she do that?"

Freddie sniffed. "A lot of people lie about the school they went to—you know, put down an ivy-league one on their résumé to make themselves look more impressive on paper. Employers hardly ever check it out. I bet you didn't."

"No," Jake admitted, "but I'm sure Susan didn't lie about her education. She's just not that sort of person."

"For a big-time lawyer, you can be very naive," Freddie commented. "I'll bet your Miss Bonner never set foot in Radcliffe. If she had, why would she settle for a job as your assistant?"

For years now Jake and Molly had been sympathizing with each other about Freddie's abrasive ways. Now they exchanged meaningful glances. Molly grinned. "Tell you what, Unc, Mom's been insisting that I sort through some of the junk still stashed up in my room. When I unearth my college yearbook, I'll look through it for you. If Susan Bonner was at Radcliffe the same year as me, she'll be in it."

"HI, SUSIE Q. Coming in just when everyone else is going home? You've got things backward, haven't you?"

"Jake and I had a long lunch with a client. But there were some files I wanted to look over before dinner." Susan smiled sheepishly at Mr. Foster. Swinging an Italian leather briefcase in one plump, carefully manicured hand, the balding senior partner in Foster, Brighton and Caine was headed out the office door along with a string of secretaries and other office workers.

"Well, don't stay too late. This place turns into a tomb at night, and all work and no play, you know—"

"Yes, I know. Don't worry."

When the door closed behind him, Susan glanced around. Hallelujah, it looked as if she were going to have the place to herself. Jake kept a set of keys to the storerooms hanging just inside his office door. Briskly she walked in and reached for them. But as her hands closed around the metal ring, her gaze fell on his desk and she paused.

As always, Jake's desk was neat. He was such an orderly man, a real conservative in every sense of the word.

A place for everything and everything in its place. Did he keep his personal life just as carefully pigeonholed, she wondered. Sometimes he struck her as lonely, though certainly a man as appealing as he needn't be lonely. It wasn't anything concrete, just a sadness she saw in his expression sometimes when he thought no one was watching. It probably came when he thought of the wife he'd lost so cruelly, she supposed.

Something squeezed inside Susan's chest and she moved forward and ran her hand along the smooth leather edge of Jake's blotter. For a second or two this afternoon she'd considered asking him up to her place for a cup of coffee. But she'd thought better of it. He would only pepper her with more questions about her life, and she didn't want to have to answer any more of those—especially when most of the answers had to be lies.

What would Jake think of her when he found out that she was really the last of Owen Byrnside's three orphans? she wondered. Jake would know that all this time she'd been deceiving him, and he was not the type to take a lie lightly. Susan pressed a hand to her heart, jolted by the pain which shot through her.

But she wouldn't have to face the consequences of her deception until she could be sure it was safe to reveal her true identity, she comforted herself. And it was always possible that she'd decide to opt out of this situation altogether and never reveal herself. After all, not for a moment did she believe that she could be the real Byrnside heiress. It had to be one of the other two. So what was the point in risking her neck when there was someone out there who wanted to treat Owen Byrnside's orphans like ducks in a shooting gallery?

I could drop out of this life just the way I dropped out of my other one, Susan told herself. Trouble was, this time it wouldn't be so easy. She'd gotten to like a lot of things about her new existence. And working so closely with Jake Caine, seeing him every day, was definitely one of those things. With a sigh, Susan turned away and headed down the hall toward the storage area.

Twenty minutes later she pried open the last of four rather grimy cartons. When Susan got the last box open and studied the dates on the yellowed papers inside it, her eyes widened. These were records made before the days of computerization, and this particular box contained Byrnside Recording files. It held letters and contracts that went back more than twenty years—to the period when the three orphans who might be Owen Byrnside's granddaughter had been abandoned, in fact. And many of these documents had been signed by Winston Deeping.

Anxious to investigate her find, Susan dragged the carton out of the closet, pushed it down the hall to her desk and then settled back to read. *It's like a time capsule,* she thought as she perused letters about the foibles of recording stars of the late sixties. Some of the people under contract to Byrnside Recording during those years were still around and still big names that she recognized. Others, luminaries who had been equally well known in that period, had long since faded into oblivion. Still others were dead from motorcycle accidents, or plane crashes, or—like Gloria Dean—drugs.

Susan tapped her chin thoughtfully. Was there any possibility that Gloria Dean could have been her mother? No, she refused to believe it. And anyway, what kind of mother would abandon her newborn baby like a sack of dirty laundry? What would have motivated her to do such a callous thing? And how many times had she asked herself that same agonizing question? *Too many,* Susan told herself and turned her attention back to her reading.

As she made her way through the faded documents, Winston Deeping's rise to power within the Byrnside infrastructure began to get clearer. Around the time of Christopher Byrnside's death, Deeping had assumed a position of real consequence in the company. As Susan studied the letters and contracts he'd drawn up, a fascinating map of his activities took shape. Clearly, he'd had a nose for talent and for anticipating the coming trends in popular music. He'd steered the company off its formerly conservative track, and for the most part his instincts for experimentation and risk-taking had paid off handsomely, Susan conceded.

Her hand froze when she unearthed a contract bearing an all-too-familiar name—Gloria Dean. Unconsciously holding her breath, Susan began to read the yellowed document. Its date interested her as much as anything else. It was a recording deal offering Gloria very generous terms and it was dated only a few days after the Broadstreet Foundling Home had burned to the ground.

When Susan finally left the office the streets were dark. A sharp wind cut through her coat and she was grateful when her bus finally lumbered up to the stop where she stood shivering. She was tired and anxious to get back home to think about the day's discoveries. What, if anything, did that contract Winston Deeping had offered Gloria Dean mean? Gloria had been on the music scene at the time, but she had never before commanded such lucrative terms. Was there some mystery there worth investigating?

As always, Susan knocked on Mrs. Crumper's door to check on her. However, when the old lady invited her in, Susan apologetically declined. "Not tonight, I'm afraid. I'm bone tired. All I want right now is a hot bath and then early to bed."

"You do look tired, dear," Mrs. Crumper sympathized. "Hurry along then and we'll have tea tomorrow night."

With a weary smile and a salute, Susan climbed the worn stairs that led to her apartment. She was on the top step when she heard her phone begin to ring. Hurrying, she dug into her pocket, unearthed her door key and jammed it into the lock.

"Oh, thank the Lord it's you. I was about to give up." The voice on the other end of the line was Maudie's.

"I just got back." Susan loosened her scarf and then opened the top button of her coat. "What's wrong? You sound as if you just found a rat on your dinner plate."

"Well, you're not far off. I think a rat may have something to do with what's happened. Patsy's gone."

"Gone?" Susan pictured the sulky teenager who'd helped cook her dinner the previous night.

"Up and disappeared. And it's my guess, though I hate to think it, that that no-good boyfriend of hers is the cause. I think I mentioned that Bucky's been hanging around here. Oh Lynn, I'm afraid he's talked her into going back on the streets with him. And if he has, God help the poor girl. She won't last long in that kind of life. And she's still just a bewildered child, really." Maudie sniffed.

Susan could easily picture the tears in the older woman's eyes. Maudie really cared for the unfortunate strays of this world. *I ought to know,* Susan thought. *I was one of them myself.*

"Listen, Maudie, don't get yourself all worked up over this."

"Oh, how can I help it? That poor, poor kid. And just when she was beginning to get her head together a little bit."

"How long has she been gone?"

"Just since this morning. But I know she hasn't simply gone out for a while. Her things are missing, too."

"Well, that's not much time, really. Maybe it's not too late to find her and talk some sense into her."

"Yes, yes, but how? Where?"

"They must have headed back to Boston. That's this creature Bucky's territory, isn't it?"

"Yes, he's a city rat, with the emphasis on rat."

"Well, I used to be a city rat-catcher, remember? What if I could track the two of them down?"

"All by yourself? How could you do that? Listen, I suspect Bucky can be pretty darned dangerous—especially where women are concerned."

Susan rubbed her forehead. "I know how to take care of myself. And we haven't much time if we're going to do something for Patsy, because she *doesn't* know how to take care of herself. Maudie, I'll see what I can do, okay?"

"Oh, honey, I don't know. I don't know. This is such an awful situation, and it's my responsibility, not yours." Maudie sounded close to hysteria.

"Now, listen, stop making a wreck of yourself and leave this to me. Maybe I won't be able to do anything. But to help a messed-up kid like Patsy I think it's worth a shot. As soon as I know something, I'll phone you."

"Are you sure?"

"I'm certain." Susan tried to make herself sound confident, though that was far from what she was feeling. "Now hang up and fix yourself a nice soothing cup of cocoa. I've got to make some calls."

When the line went dead, Susan stood holding the receiver. Then she replaced it and, deep in thought, paced back and forth in front of the telephone stand. What to do, what to do? From her own days as a runaway and her time on the police force, she knew the sleazy areas of the city where Bucky might have taken Patsy. But since she'd changed her identity and become involved in the Byrnside investigation she'd lost contact with that work. Also, Maudie's "rat" image had been apt. There were a thousand rat holes, dark alleys, abandoned warehouses, flea-bag hotels where Bucky could have taken Patsy. *What I need is some inside information,* Susan thought.

Reluctantly, she sat down in front of the phone. For several seconds her finger hovered over the number pad. Then, with decision, she punched out a set of digits that she hadn't used in well over a year.

"Garrity here."

As Susan heard the familiar gruff male voice, her expression softened and an affectionate smile sprang to her lips. "Garrity, you old creep, it's Lynn."

"Lynn. Lynnie?"

"The same."

There was a long pause. "Well, whaddaya know! So you're alive, are you? Listen, girl, all this time the way you dropped off the edge of the earth, I thought you might be dead. Gave me some bad dreams, it did."

The corners of Susan's mouth quirked. "Knowing how many beers you usually have under your belt before you hit the sack, I'm touched. But you can relax. I'm still alive and still kicking."

"Glad to hear it. No lie, I've been worried sick!" Garrity was beginning to recover from his obvious surprise and sounded like his usual irritable and argumentative self. "A private eye came around to talk to me about you. It hurt my pride to have to confess my ignorance. Mind telling me why you disappeared like that? No word, not even a postcard after all we've been through together! It's downright insulting, it is!"

"Garrity, for heaven's sake. All we ever did when we were on patrol together was argue. You once told me you hated my guts!"

"That was just a little joke. You know what a humorous old curmudgeon I am."

Susan rolled her eyes. "Okay, some day I'll tell you the story of my mysterious disappearance. But not now. Now I need a favor."

"What kind of favor?"

"Some information about a street character named Bucky Reynolds."

"Oh, really? So it's a favor you want, is it? Well, Lynnie, I figure you owe me an explanation, so you're not going to get anything out of me until you come clean about what you've been up to."

"Honest, Garrity, I can't talk about it over the phone."

"Then you'll have to talk to me face-to-face, won't you? Are you in the city?"

"Yes," she admitted.

His voice hardened. "Forty-five minutes from now I'll be in a back booth at O'Toole's. If you want any favors from this old boy, me girl, you'll be there, too."

AN HOUR LATER Susan walked into O'Toole's. It was one of Garrity's favorite haunts, and in the old days when they'd been together on patrol Susan had often had a beer with him there after work. Now as she sniffed the bitter fragrance of hops and stale tobacco, a wave of nostalgia swept over her.

When she made her way to the back of the bar she spotted Garrity's broad, humped shoulders and grizzled head. He was hunched over a mug. A half-empty pitcher of dark ale stood at his right elbow. He wore his usual off-duty uniform, a grimy windbreaker over a ragged sweatshirt and baggy pants.

Though he looked as if he'd been pickled in brandy at the age of fifty, Susan knew he was somewhere in his early forties. Ignatius Aloysius Garrity had been divorced twice, and that was because he was such an ornery cuss, staying out to all hours, running around with any female who happened to catch his eye, that no decent woman could tolerate him for more than five years running—the truth being that police work was, and had always been, his only true love. He was a full detective, the same position Susan had aspired to, and would have attained if she'd stayed on the Force.

She strode up to him and stood where she judged he could see her best through the bar's gloom. "Dressed for company, I see."

Garrity stared up at her. A puzzled expression came over his heavy-jawed Irish face.

"It's me, Garrity. Lynn."

"Lynn? My gawd! Can't be. What happened to your ugly mug?"

"I've got a new one now."

"I'll say." He blinked rapidly and then brushed at his eyes as if trying to get rid of cobwebs. "You're a raving, tearing beauty. If it weren't for those yellow cat eyes I wouldn't recognize you no matter what you said." He pointed at the chair and the empty glass across from him. "Sit yourself down and tell me how this miracle came about. After that we'll talk business—maybe."

CHAPTER FOUR

GARRITY SLAPPED the flat of his large hand against the barroom table. "You're telling me that on the strength of an anonymous letter that any kook could have sent, and we both knew there are plenty of those out there on the streets, you dropped a good job and your chance at detective and took off for Switzerland?" He rolled his eyes and made a metronome of his shaggy head. "Lynnie, Lynnie, Lynnie. And I thought you had a working brain to play with."

"It wasn't just a letter. There was a bona-fide round-trip ticket to Switzerland in that envelope—with a stopover in Paris that I was able to extend to four days. There were hotel reservations and an appointment with a plastic surgeon at a famous clinic. I checked all of those out and they were legitimate. Besides, the letter was very convincing." Susan began to quote from memory. "'You don't know me and never shall, but I know enough about you to feel responsible for some of your misfortunes in life. Enclosed is the only way I have of making amends.'"

"Who did you think might have sent that?"

"I thought—" Susan swallowed. "I thought it might have been my mother."

"Lynnie—"

"I know, I know," Susan flared. "What I did was crazy. But you haven't gone through life disfigured by a burn scar. You don't know what it's like to be laughed at and shunned from the time you were a little kid, to have people's eyes turn away from you because you're so ugly they can't stand to look at you.''

"It was never as bad as that," Garrity protested, studying her with more sympathy. "Anyone could see back then that if it weren't for your scar you'd be a good-looking girl."

"Oh, really? That was never how people treated me. You can't know what kind of childhood I had, what kind of an adolescence!"

"Bad, was it?"

"Awful," Susan declared. "The way I looked, no one wanted to adopt me. And at all my foster homes I was treated like an outcast. I don't remember a time when I didn't feel rejected. Or a time when I didn't dream that my mother would find me and rescue me."

Garrity rolled his buffalo-thick shoulders. "Well, rejection doesn't seem to have done you much harm. You were a tough cookie when we worked together, but you were smart and fair and decent. When people ragged you about your looks, you never seemed to mind."

"Oh, Garrity, that was an act. Inside I was shriveling up. I hated that scar. To me it represented everything that was wrong with my life. As soon as I got a job I started saving up for plastic surgery to get rid of it. But it would have been years before I'd have been able to put enough money together. When I opened that anonymous letter offering me a world-renowned surgeon at a ritzy private clinic in Switzerland, I thought I'd died and gone to heaven."

"You really believed it came from your mother? You weren't suspicious?"

"Of course I was suspicious. But what did I have to lose? I decided to take a chance."

Again, Garrity shook his head. He took a deep swig of beer and wiped the foam from his mouth with the back of his hand. "Nobody ever gets something for nothing. There had to be a catch."

"I know, but at first everything seemed to go smoothly. As I said, the plane tickets were legit. All the reservations were at good hotels. When I arrived at the clinic I was treated like royalty. It wasn't until after I'd had the surgery and was recuperating in my hotel room that I ran into trouble."

"What happened?"

"Someone tried to kill me."

Garrity listened closely while Susan described that night in Switzerland before her bandages were scheduled to be removed. Luckily, she'd been too nervous and excited to go to sleep. She'd been lying in bed at her hotel wondering what the mirror would reveal in the morning when a stranger dressed head-to-toe in black had climbed through her open window and into her darkened room and attacked her. There'd been a scuffle, but the self-defense skills she'd acquired in police training had stood her in good stead. Those and her vigorous screams had frightened him off. But not before he'd dropped a wicked-looking knife, a knife she was convinced had been meant for her.

"So then what did you do?" Garrity questioned.

"I packed up my suitcase and got out of there."

"Covered with bandages like a mummy?"

"No, I took the bandages off first."

Garrity cocked his head and eyed her smooth profile. "You must have been pleased as punch with what you saw when you lifted them."

"My face was still swollen, so I didn't look exactly like this. But yes," Susan admitted, "I was pleased and so shocked I felt as if someone had hit me with a tire iron. I looked so different, like somebody I'd never met. The surgeon didn't just remove my scar, he straightened my nose as well."

"I remember you told me your foster father broke it."

Susan nodded. "Honest, Garrity, I'm just now beginning to get used to the new me."

"So am I." Garrity swung into the fake Irish accent he liked to affect. "And, me girl, I hope the new you isn't so different from the old you that she never tried to find out what the connection was between the anonymous letter, the free cosmetic surgery and this knife attack."

Susan sipped her beer. "You know me better than to have any doubts about that. Before I took the next plane out of there, I sneaked into the clinic and looked at my file."

Garrity guffawed. "Did you, now? What did it tell you?"

"Not much. Whoever arranged and paid for my surgery kept it anonymous. But the stationery they used was expensive and postmarked in a little town in New England named Lowerton. As soon as I got back to the States I climbed on a bus, got off in Lowerton and checked the stationery out with the local printer. He told me it was a special stock and the only person who ever ordered it was a mogul named Owen Byrnside. Ever heard of him?"

Garrity's bushy brows flew up to his hairline. "Everyone's heard of him! He's rich as Croesus! Now that really is something!"

"I was pretty interested myself. So I did a little more digging and found out about the Byrnside quest."

"The Byrnside quest? What in hell is that?"

While Garrity's eyes widened, Susan explained about Owen Byrnside's search for his lost granddaughter.

"My gawd, girl," Garrity finally burst out, "you've got yourself a corking great melodrama there! And all this time you've been keeping mum about who you really are and working with this lawyer just to get the lay of the land?''

"Yes. After my experience in that Swiss hotel, I decided it would be plain stupid to admit to being the third orphan before I knew who was behind these murder attempts. I figured at least that way I'd be able to sleep at night until I found out what was really going on." Susan toyed with her glass. "I admit I didn't think it would take this long to get the scoop. Garrity, I could use some advice. What do you think about all this?"

The detective downed the last of his beer and then slouched back in the wooden booth. "What if it turns out that you're the one Byrnside's looking for? What if you're his true granddaughter?"

"I'm not."

"How can you be so sure?"

"Garrity, I'm nothing like the man."

Garrity cocked his head. "Oh, I don't know. I've heard he's a tough old bird. And you're a tough young chickadee."

"That's not heredity. I've had to develop some defenses to survive."

"Well, that's a likeness, isn't it? You're both survivors."

Susan shrugged that off. "Now that I've told you the story of my mysterious disappearance, will you give me some help?"

"You want me to help you with the Byrnside business?"

"No, it's something else altogether." Susan explained about Patsy and Bucky. She made it brief and dispassionate. Garrity was too hardened by years of dealing with the seamy side of life to be moved by Patsy's hard-luck story.

When Susan finished, Garrity looked disappointed. Obviously the Byrnside quest intrigued him a lot more than a runaway teenager who'd become entangled with a street tough. "I'll put some feelers out, see what I can do."

"Oh, thank you, Garrity. And make it quick, will you? Time is important here."

"I'll do me best, Lynnie. But don't hold your breath. In cases like this, as you know yourself, it's eighty percent luck and twenty percent knowin' the right people. Well, I know the right people, but that still leaves it mostly up to luck."

"IT'S ALL A MATTER of knowing the right people," Jake said the next morning. He tossed a pair of pale gray tickets down on Susan's desk. "These are a gift from Winston Deeping. He's invited us to go as his and his wife's guests. Tabissa's flying in for the occasion."

Susan picked up one of the tickets and studied it. "The Art League Ball? Isn't that the fancy charity affair your sister helps organize?"

"The same." Ruefully, Jake chuckled. "Sometimes I think it's Freddie's one passion in life. Every year from September until spring it's all she lives for."

Susan ran a fingertip over the engraved date. "The ball's this Friday. Haven't you already got a date for it?"

"No, I haven't. As it happens, I was planning to pass on the ball this time around. Deeping's invitation changes things, though. He's too important to the firm to turn down. So you see, you needn't regard this as a date, but as a business obligation." Jake flashed his charming smile. "Since you're all business, that ought to make you happy."

Susan lowered her eyes. What would it be like to spend an evening with Jake, to dance with him and be held in his arms? The prospect was so alluring that she pulled back from it like a determined dieter confronted with a rich dessert. "Really, I don't see how I can go to something like this."

"Why not? Look at it as the perfect excuse to spend money on clothes."

Susan seized on that. Jake's cavalier attitude toward money was one of the many uncrossable gulfs yawning between them, she told herself. How could a person with a background like hers ever really have anything in common with a man who had been born never needing to give money a second thought?

"That's my point. This is a fancy-dress affair. All the women will be wearing designer ball gowns. Unfortunately, there doesn't happen to be one of those in my closet, and I can't afford to go out and splurge on one."

"Don't you know someone you can borrow from? I thought all women traded clothes with their friends."

That suggestion only deepened Susan's irritation. Did Jake think she had nothing better to do than go around begging for clothes in order to rub shoulders with his hoity-toity business pals? "Not this woman. Not a single person of my acquaintance happens to have a closetful of designer ball gowns they're itching to lend out." She pushed the tickets back at him. "I'm afraid this Cinderella will have to pass up the ball."

Frowning, Jake went away to his office. But he wasn't gone long. Just before noon he reappeared with a smile once again wreathing his handsome face. "I've solved the problem of the dress."

"What do you mean?" Susan was just opening her lunch bag, which contained a yogurt, an apple and a plastic spoon.

"My sister and her daughter have been attending these functions for years. Between the two of them they have enough ball gowns to open a boutique. I called Freddie and explained that accepting this invitation is important to the firm, so she's agreed to lend you one of her outfits.''

Susan stiffened. "I doubt your sister and I are the same size.''

Jake ran an assessing eye over Susan's upper body. His appraisal made her go uncomfortably warm under her sweater, something that had been happening more and more lately when she caught him looking at her.

Jake's aristocratic features lit up in a warm smile. "Maybe you and Freddie couldn't exchange clothes, but you appear to be built a lot like my niece Molly, and there are dressmakers who can do alterations on short notice. Let's buzz out to Freddie's place right now and find out.''

He motioned Susan toward the door, but she resisted. Wasn't Molly the niece, who'd graduated from Radcliffe? *The last thing I need,* Susan thought, *is a run-in with someone who might start asking awkward questions about the college I put on my bogus résumé.* "Will Molly be at your sister's?''

"No. She's got her own apartment now. C'mon, no time to lose. You can eat your yogurt in the car.'' Jake whisked Susan out from behind her desk and hustled her to the closet where her coat was hung.

HALF AN HOUR LATER they pulled up in front of a huge Georgian-style brick house set well back from the street. It was the sort of building that fit seamlessly into its prestigious neighborhood and reeked of old money, riding lessons for the children and a summer cottage somewhere on the coast of Maine.

"Freddie's waiting for us,'' Jake said as he escorted Susan to the front porch.

We wouldn't want to keep dear Freddie waiting, Susan thought rebelliously and then pulled herself up short. Why was she so filled with roiling emotions at the prospect of meeting Jake's sister? It wasn't just that she resented being bullied into borrowing a dress from a woman she'd never met. She was nervous, truly nervous. *Why should I care what some total stranger thinks of me?* she asked herself. But since this stranger happened to be Jake's sister, she did care.

Susan's first encounter with Frederica Ashmore did nothing to soothe away her anxieties. Tall, dark and angular, Freddie looked like an older, sterner version of her brother. But where Jake's well-bred features were gentled with humor and leavened by intelligence, Frederica radiated hauteur and an air of imperious command.

"Oh, she's much too short for anything of mine," Freddie pronounced after casting a critical eye up and down Susan's modest length.

Susan managed to keep the smile on her mouth pinned in place, though it now felt like cardboard.

"Can't dresses be shortened?" Jake questioned.

"That's just like a man." Frederica shook her carefully coiffed head. "Ball gowns are designed to make a certain kind of impact. To shorten one of mine would simply ruin it."

Susan, still smiling determinedly, said, "Well, I guess that's it. Thanks anyway."

"What about one of Molly's outfits?" Jake said. "She's close to Susan's size."

"Ye-e-e-s." Frederica looked less than thrilled. "I suppose one of those might do. All right, let's go upstairs and see what we can find, shall we?"

She led Jake and Susan down the wide central hallway and up a staircase thickly carpeted in pale green. As Susan followed, she ran her palm along the gleaming, satin-smooth banister and inhaled the faint fragrance of lemon wax. This was so clearly a prosperous, well-ordered home. What would it be like to grow up in such a place? She compared it with the trailer park she'd run away from when she was a teenager and thought the two places had less in common than the earth and the moon.

Upstairs, Frederica opened a door and showed them into a young girl's room. The carpet was pale pink. A flowered quilt matched the balloon curtains on a pair of sunny windows. The walls were covered in a candy-striped paper and the top of an antique vanity skirted in white eyelet was strewn with an assortment of nail polishes, perfume bottles, eye shadows and tubes of costly brands of makeup.

"You'd never guess Molly's closer to thirty than twenty and doesn't live here anymore," Jake commented.

Frederica rolled her eyes. "She had so many things she could leave half of it behind and not notice anything missing. And as a matter of fact, that's exactly what she did. I've been begging her to come and clear some of this clutter out."

Frederica crossed the room and opened a double-doored closet. As the seductive scent of patchouli sachets drifted out, Susan's eyes widened. Molly's closet fairly bulged with clothes. The floor was covered with shoes and the top shelf held handbags and hats.

"Good grief! Surely we can find something for Susan among all that!" Jake exclaimed.

"Hmm. We'll see." His sister began pulling out gowns on padded hangers. Critically, she held them up against Susan. "Molly's coloring is different from yours, but there are a couple here that might do, if you'd care to try them on." She tossed a white lace sheath, an aqua chiffon confection and a midnight-blue silk out on the bed. "Now

Jake, let's go downstairs while she changes. There are several last-minute legal questions that have come up in connection with this year's ball, and I want to discuss them with you.''

Twenty minutes later Susan came down the staircase and into the front hall. She heard the murmur of Jake's and Frederica's voices through the archway to the right.

"Don't be so stodgy!" Frederica was exclaiming. "Honestly, no wonder our mother had such a time delivering you. You were born resisting change!"

"I don't mind change if it's for the better," Jake protested.

"Ha! Then why have you worn the same style of suit and the same three necktie patterns since you were in prep school? It used to drive Janet crazy! That's why you've had such a terrible time adjusting to her death, you know. You get your mind set in one groove and it takes a hurricane to blow you out of it."

Sympathizing with Jake, Susan coughed discreetly and then walked in. As she entered the room, brother and sister dropped their conversation and looked up expectantly.

"Each of these dresses fits very well," Susan said of the two she'd brought down with her.

"Oh, good. Well then, just take whichever one you like." Frederica laced her fingers over her knee.

"I feel a little awkward running off with your daughter's dress when I haven't asked her permission."

"Oh, Molly won't mind. She won't wear either of those again. They both must be at least two years old."

Out in the hall, the front door banged and heels beat a quick tattoo on the polished wood floor. "Hello, anybody home?" A pretty, dark-haired young woman wearing a smart hat and a voluminous ankle-length raincoat swept into the living room. "Well, here I am, Mother. I've come to clear away some of the junk you've been nagging me about. Uncle Jake! What luck! I never expected to find you here.''

Frederica shrugged and said to Susan, ''Well, that solves that problem. Now you can ask Molly's permission if you want.''

While Susan stood rooted to the floor, Jake explained the situation to his niece.

''Oh, of course I don't mind!'' she exclaimed with a cheery grin. ''Your assistant is more than welcome to wear one of my dresses. Let me see which two she's picked.'' She turned to Susan and cocked her head to one side. ''Oh, the blue and the aqua. Yes, either of those will look great on you.'' As Molly spoke, she gazed at Susan curiously. Then a light seemed to flash behind her eyes and she shot a glance over her shoulder. ''Uncle Jake, is this the girl who was at Radcliffe the same time as me?''

''She's the one.'' Jake strolled up behind his niece, put a hand on her shoulder and grinned over at Susan. ''You remember, don't you? I mentioned Molly was in your class.''

''I remember,'' Susan said in a choked tone. Now what was she going to do? Well, what else was there to do? She just had to brazen it out somehow!

Molly flipped off her hat and ran a hand through her chic mop of dark curls. ''What was your major?''

''Sociology.''

''Soch? That was mine, too. What a coincidence! It's amazing that we never ran into each other. We must have been in some of the same classes. Did you take Kettering's Principles of Sociodynamics?''

''Sure,'' Susan said offhandedly.

''Wasn't she funny?''

"A scream." Susan was conscious of Jake's and his sister's eyes on her. What if Molly asked about the textbook or some other detail that would be a dead giveaway she'd never set eyes on Radcliffe?

"What house were you in?"

Fortunately, when Susan had been making up her résumé, she'd spent a morning at the library with the Radcliffe catalog. Now she was grateful for her long memory. "Currier."

"Hmm, Currier. I was down by the river in Dunster, but I'm sure I know somebody who roomed at Currier. Let me see, do you remember Roberta—what was her name—ah, Roberta Wildy?"

"The name doesn't ring a bell. Sorry."

"Well, maybe I haven't got it right. I do have the most wretched memory."

"So do I, actually," Susan agreed enthusiastically. "Those years are just a blur now. Listen, thanks for the loan of the dress. If it doesn't make any difference to you, I think I'll take the aqua."

"That's fine. In fact, if you can wear a size six, I have shoes to match it."

"Oh, really, I . . ."

"You're welcome to them. I'll just run up and dig them out for you."

When Molly hurried from the room, Susan felt like collapsing with relief. Now if she could just get out of here with no more inquisition—

"It does seem strange that you and Molly were at the same school, majoring in the same subject and never ran into each other," Frederica said from the couch. Her dark eyes were narrowed.

Jake turned toward his sister. "Oh, c'mon, Freddie, Radcliffe's a big school, and it was all a long time ago."

"Six years isn't so long. It's been almost thirty years since I was there, and I still remember all my chums."

"That's because they all live in this neighborhood and belong to your bridge group."

"Oh, they do not. Only Doris Percy. Honestly, Jake, I had more friends than could sit around a bridge table! Why, there was . . ."

While Frederica began to count off names on her fingertips, Susan waited nervously for Molly's return. A moment later she came clattering back down holding a pair of aqua silk slippers.

"The heels are more scuffed than I remembered, but maybe you could redye them."

"Honestly, they look fine."

"Do you want to try them on now?"

Susan glanced at her watch. "There isn't time, I'm afraid. Jake, I really have to get back to the office." She thanked Molly for the loan of the dress and shoes and then turned to Frederica. "You've been very kind. Thank you for all your help."

"Oh, it's nothing," Frederica replied coolly. "I'm looking forward to seeing you at the ball."

"Yes," Molly chimed in enthusiastically. "I can't wait to see how that dress looks on a blonde!"

"Neither can I," Jake said, after he and Susan were back outside and settled in the car.

She shot him a puzzled glance. "Neither can you what?"

"Wait to see how that—" he indicated the gown draped across Susan's lap "—looks on a blonde."

"I'm sure not as good as it looked on your niece. She's very pretty."

"Yes, but so are you."

Susan averted her head.

Jake studied her flushed profile in surprise. "Hey, don't tell me you haven't peeked into a mirror lately. You can't be totally oblivious of the way men turn and stare when you walk past."

"Do they?"

"You know they do."

Susan swallowed. How could she tell him that for most of her life mirrors had been her worst enemy and that even now, a year after her surgery, the person she saw reflected back in the bathroom still seemed like a masquerader? How could she explain that the way men turned and stared was more upsetting to her than flattering? Sometimes she felt as if she were just wearing a mask and that the real her, the ugly her, still lurked behind the pretty new surface that had been bestowed by a doctor's skill and the mysterious motives of a donor who wished to remain anonymous. "I don't think much about my looks," she muttered.

"Then you must be a very unusual woman."

"Not all women are vain."

As he started up the car, Jake turned to Susan. "Not all women have cause to be." His gaze lingered on her profile with its slim, upturned nose and firm chin, its silky sweep of short, fair hair. Then his eyes dropped to the soft thrust of her breasts beneath her coat, which she hadn't bothered to button in her haste to get out of his sister's house.

Suddenly he remembered Susan the way she'd been in Barbados, with golden shoulders revealed by a sundress and long slim legs bared. Back in the Caribbean where memories of Janet's drowning had preyed on his mind, he'd been too disturbed to pay more than passing attention to Susan—or any woman, no matter how attractive. Now, however, Jake felt differently.

"Well, I'm looking forward to the ball and to seeing you in something other than a sensible tweed jacket. Oh, and leave off the glasses, will you? Horn-rims and aqua chiffon don't mix.''

ON FRIDAY EVENING Susan zipped up her dress and then eyed her reflection. The aqua chiffon dress, with its one-shouldered diagonal drape, floated around her body in a cloudy caress, emphasizing her slender femininity, bringing out the gold of her hair and the porcelain creaminess of her skin. The feeling Susan had as she gazed at the lovely woman in the mirror was much the same shocked bemusement she'd experienced a year earlier when she'd first removed her bandages and realized just how total her transformation had been. Now, in her borrowed finery, Susan felt like Cinderella all over again.

"Oh, my dear, don't you look lovely!" Mrs. Crumper exclaimed a few minutes later when Susan came down and twirled about in her elderly friend's tiny living room. When the old lady had learned that Susan was going to a ball, she'd begged her to stop in before she set off. "Oh, child, you're simply scrumptious! But you can't mean to ruin that beautiful dress with a tweed coat!"

"This is the only winter coat I've got, and it's too cold to go outside with nothing on but a bit of chiffon."

"But tweed—oh no, no, no!" Rubbing her hands together excitedly, the old woman scampered into a back room. Minutes later she reappeared bearing a fur jacket. "Here," she said with the air of a queen presenting the crown jewels, "this will be just the thing. It was my older sister's and Bea was such a fashion plate. Oh, my, my! It's real mink, you know. Now hurry and try it on so I can see how it looks."

Susan accepted the garment with a sinking heart. Perhaps at one time in its long history Mrs. Crumper's sister's jacket had been beautiful. Now, aside from its old-fashioned style, it was moth-eaten and smelled slightly moldy. But it would cut Mrs. Crumper to the quick to tell her so. Smiling bravely, Susan slipped her arms into the threadbare silk lining.

"Perfect! Perfect, my dear! Sheer perfection!" The old lady clapped her palms together with a three-year-old's delight. "There's just one more thing you need."

"What's that?" Susan queried warily.

Mrs. Crumper dug into a pocket and brought out a blue box, the top of which had been worn shiny. "These were my Great-Aunt Francy's." With fingers stiffened by rheumatism, she pried the box open. Two of the most beautiful earrings Susan had ever seen lay on a bed of cream satin.

"Why—why, they're lovely." Susan lifted one out and held it up to the light. From its diamond-and-seed-pearl center, petals carved from ivory flared out in the delicate shape of a half-opened rose.

"And ever so much nicer than those fake pearls you're wearing. Really, dear, between Aunt Francy's ivory roses and my sister's mink, you'll make a splash when your beau comes to pick you up."

"He's not my beau, he's my boss, Jake Caine," Susan demurred as she began to remove her pearls, which she'd bought with her Christmas bonus and which were not fake.

"Well, after he sees you tonight he'll want to be your beau," Mrs. Crumper insisted. "Any man in his right mind would."

CHAPTER FIVE

THE ORCHESTRA had settled into nostalgia mode. While the strains of "Stranger in Paradise" throbbed softly through the crowded ballroom, gowned and tuxedoed couples revolved slowly beneath glittering chandeliers.

"You're a good dancer," Jake murmured. His breath stirred the fine tendrils of Susan's hair.

Actually, Susan thought she was a rotten dancer. In foster homes and on the street, she'd had no opportunity to learn how to dance. "There isn't much to this kind of dancing. All we're doing is swaying back and forth."

Jake chuckled, the sound reverberating deep in his chest. "True, but you're swaying very nicely."

Through the thin fabric of her dress, Susan luxuriated in the warmth of his palm on the small of her back. It was Jake who danced well, she thought. He moved with lightness and grace, and yet with the authority that characterized everything he did. Any partner he took would have to have no sense of rhythm whatsoever not to follow his lead easily. From the moment Susan had stepped into Jake's arms their bodies had seemed to meld.

Through her lashes she glanced up at the firm structure of his jaw. His eyes were hooded so she couldn't quite catch their expression. Above them, his dark hair with its few threads of silver lay close to his well-shaped head. In his evening clothes which seemed only to accentuate his height and lean, athletic build, she thought him easily the most attractive man in the room. But then she almost always thought that.

Her hand tightened on his shoulder, absorbing the strength beneath the immaculately tailored jacket. Then, aware of her possessive gesture, Susan loosened her grip and pulled away slightly.

"It's all right. When you're dancing with a man you're supposed to hold on to him." Adroitly, Jake hauled her back so that the tips of her breasts brushed the crisp front of his pleated shirt and their knees and hips came into sensuous contact. Ripples of awareness coursed through Susan's body and she felt herself blush.

"You're even lovelier in that dress than I imagined." Gently, Jake touched the lobe of her ear. "You're like these ivory roses, only much softer and sweeter.'

Susan still wasn't quite sure how to react to a man's compliments, especially Jake's. He was so attractive to her, yet because of her deception and the gulf between them, he was forbidden. "Mrs. Crumper, my downstairs neighbor, lent them to me," she said.

"Along with her historic fur jacket?"

"Yes." Susan had already explained to Jake about the jacket. She'd had to say something because on the drive over in the closed interior of his car the smell of mothballs and mold had all but overwhelmed both of them.

"Well, that's one out of two," he commented with another wry chuckle.

His hand slipped around to Susan's back again, only this time he placed it high enough so that his fingertips caressed the bare skin between her shoulder blades. Susan couldn't control the delicious shiver that rippled through her and, chagrined at how transparent she was making herself to Jake, she stumbled slightly.

"Are you all right?"

"I'm a little tired, actually. Too much champagne, maybe. Do you mind if we go back to the table?"

"I do, actually. I'm enjoying dancing with you immensely. But if you're tired, of course, we'll go back." He began guiding her through the swaying crowd toward the table where Winston Deeping and his wife held court.

When they were within a few feet of reclaiming their chairs, Tabissa Deeping called out, "Oh there you are, back at last!" Tabissa was a regal blonde in a rich green velvet dress and diamonds that sparkled with unmistakable authenticity. She had a great deal of confident charm and had quickly taken command of all her husband's guests.

"I can't tell you what a divine couple you two make out on the dance floor. Loretta and I were just remarking on it," she said, glancing across the table at Loretta Greene. "Positively makes me itch to be young and fancy-free. What do you think of that, darling?" She turned to her husband, but Winston was engrossed in business talk with the balding Byrnside executive seated next to him.

"Obviously your husband is happy with the status quo," Jake said gallantly.

"Oh, you sweet thing. But you know, I've observed that men almost always are. They are the dullest creatures! Don't you agree, Loretta?"

The expression on Miss Greene's narrow face was closed. She shrugged. "I wouldn't know, since I've never been married. But I must say my boss, Owen Byrnside, has never been satisfied with the status quo."

While this inane chatter swirled around her, Susan wished she'd stayed out on the dance floor with Jake. It was better to be here, she remonstrated with herself, where she could learn more about these people. After all, any one of them might be her mysterious benefactor or her equally mysterious assailant. Yet she felt awkward and out of her depth in their midst, and ten minutes later she found herself making excuses to head for the ladies' room. Anything for a bit of breathing space.

The powder room was no oasis of privacy, however. Clusters of gossiping socialites formed and reformed in front of its bank of shell-shaped marble sinks. Determined to bathe her eyes and repair her makeup before returning to the fray, Susan waited her turn patiently.

"What a throng," a familiar voice complained just as Susan finally achieved her goal and grasped a heavy brass tap.

She looked up and saw Loretta Greene's reflection behind her own. In her crimson silk dress with its gores of shrimp pink, the woman made Susan think of a lit firecracker ready to explode. "Oh, I didn't realize you were in line behind me."

"I wasn't." Loretta's bright red mouth curved like a scimitar. "My dear, by the time you're my age you'll have learned that getting where you want to go in this world without always waiting your turn is merely a matter of learning how to maneuver."

"Yes, I suppose so." Susan's gaze dropped away from Loretta's and she busied herself with washing up. Again she was aware of a feeling of antipathy between herself and this woman. It wasn't anything she could put a name to, just some sort of negative chemistry.

"Have you been dating Jake long?" Loretta asked. She'd now taken over the washbowl next to Susan's and was opening a tapestry bag.

"We don't date at all. Tonight is strictly a business outing."

"Really? It certainly didn't look like business when the orchestra was playing. Though I don't agree with half of the idiotic things that shallow twit Tabissa says, she's right about the two of you. Out there on the dance floor you could have stood in for Cinderella and Prince Charming." Loretta shrugged. "But then, Jake Caine makes any woman he's with look good. And he certainly has been with quite a few in the past couple of years since he lost his wife. Not that any of that means anything." Loretta unscrewed a tube of bloodred lipstick and despite herself Susan stopped to stare as the tall brunette women applied it to her already brilliantly colored lips.

"I hate to sound naive, but why doesn't it mean anything?"

Loretta glanced at Susan sideways and then reached for a tissue. "Everyone knows how devastated Jake was when Janet died. He's never gotten over her, and I doubt he ever really will. For Jake, women are just a diversion now, a way of passing the time."

Susan backed away from the washbowl. "Maybe now, but sooner or later Jake will recover from his grief," she said tightly. "That's human nature."

Back at the table, Susan stared hard at Jake. He certainly didn't look racked by grief. Despite what Loretta had said, it was impossible to see him as anything but gallant, handsome, and completely in control of whatever situation fate handed him.

"Feeling better?" he asked.

"Oh, yes."

"Up to another dance. They're playing our song."

Susan cocked her head and caught the strains of "Some Enchanted Evening." "Since when is that our song?"

"A man can always hope, can't he?"

Once Susan stepped into Jake's strong arms Loretta's words stopped troubling her. All of Susan's problems and doubts seemed to recede into a shadowy limbo. The only reality was the music and the slow, heated rhythm of Jake's body moving against hers. There'd been so little romance in Susan's difficult life. Surely, she rationalized, it wouldn't hurt just this once to forget her troubles and enjoy herself.

With the exception of one puzzling incident, the rest of the evening passed in a pleasant dream. Around midnight, as Jake drove Susan home, she sat next to him thinking about that incident. An hour earlier back at the hotel and feeling in need of fresh air, she'd stepped through French doors out onto a flagstone terrace overlooking a garden.

She'd spotted a stone bench behind a row of potted hollies and dropped down onto it. Since the night was chilly, she'd planned to sit for only a moment. But the muffled throb of angry voices and the sudden appearance of Loretta Greene and Winston Deeping from around a corner changed her agenda.

It would be embarrassing for them to know she'd caught them in what was obviously a private argument. What's more, Susan was intrigued. All evening Loretta and Winston had treated each other like polite strangers, and she'd imagined that they were barely acquainted. But clearly they knew each other very well.

"Why should I believe a word you say?" Loretta hissed as she strode past the potted hollies. "For twenty years you've done nothing but lie to me."

"Have it your way," Winston replied curtly. "God knows you always do!"

Loretta disappeared through the French doors and Winston stayed outside, puffing angrily on a cigarette. Then, in a flurry of fiery sparks, he hurled it away and stalked inside, too, leaving Susan alone on the terrace.

Though she knew that Jake would be looking for her by now, she stayed hidden behind the hollies for another quarter of an hour. She didn't want Winston and Loretta to realize she'd overheard them. But what exactly had she overheard? And what exactly was the nature of their real relationship? Perhaps, she mused now in Jake's car, it behooved her to try to find out.

"Penny for your thoughts," Jake said after he'd parked across the street from Susan's brownstone.

"Oh, nothing. Just thinking about the evening."

He laid his arm along the top of the seat behind her head. "I hope coming to this thing with me wasn't too much of a chore."

Suddenly she was powerfully conscious of his fingers, inches from the back of her neck, of the dull gleam of his crisp white shirt cuff. "Not at all. I enjoyed myself." She'd made that plain, slow-dancing with him all evening, she thought.

"Well I certainly had a good time. But then I almost always do when I'm with you." He studied his neatly pared fingernails. "My only regret is that I didn't take the time to have a cup of coffee before we left."

"But you didn't have much to drink," Susan pointed out.

"No, but it's late and I could use a little waking up. I do have to drive back to my place through the city."

Jake looked at her expectantly. His hint couldn't have been plainer. Susan hesitated. She could still pretend that tonight had been nothing but business. But if she invited Jake in for coffee, things were bound to be put in a different light and that, her brain told her, wasn't wise.

Jake looked at her steadily, waiting for her answer and not giving her any room to wriggle free of the decision— and the challenge—easily.

The evening's romantic spell still affected Susan, and in the street lamp's silvery light, which filtered in through the car window, Jake looked so handsome, so utterly the perfect Prince Charming to her Cinderella. "Would you like to come up to my place for a cup of coffee?" she heard herself murmur huskily.

"Yes, I would. I'd like that very much."

As soon as the invitation was out, Susan regretted it. But it was too late now. Already, Jake was striding around to her side of the car.

"At least I hope that fur is warm," he said as they mounted the stone steps.

"It is, but I'll be glad to give it back to Mrs. Crumper in the morning."

"I'll bet if you could you'd slip it under her door tonight."

"You never know. She might still be up. She keeps rather surprising hours, and she adores Johnny Carson. Care to meet her? I could try tapping on her door."

"Thanks all the same, but . . ."

Mrs. Crumper threw open her door and poked her fluffy dandelion-seed head out. "Oh there you are, dear. I've been waiting up for you," she chirped.

Susan caught the expression on Jake's face and stifled a giggle. "You shouldn't have," she managed as she slipped off the moth-eaten mink and, with thanks, handed it over to the old lady, who was eyeing Jake with deep interest. "This is my boss, Jake Caine. Jake, my neighbor Mrs. Crumper."

"Would your handsome beau like to come in for a glass of port?" Mrs. Crumper asked after Jake had politely acknowledged the introduction and shaken her hand.

As diplomatically as possible, Susan refused, and a few minutes later, as she slipped her key into her front door,

Jake whispered his thanks. "You've really got a watch-dog down there, haven't you? Does she check out all your dates like that?"

Susan flicked on the light in the hall and then stood aside while Jake ambled past her. "Not usually." Susan didn't explain that her dates were few and far between. She was still leery of the men who were attracted to her new face and uncertain of how to behave with them—just as now she was uncertain of how to behave with Jake. Only in his case it was much more of a problem because the attraction was mutual and getting stronger by the minute.

"Nice place," he said, stationing himself in the living room and glancing around. "Really, when it comes to character these old buildings can't be beat."

"I love old houses. I'll trade a fancy bathroom for a twelve-foot ceiling any day." Susan was proud of her apartment. It had only two rooms, and the railroad-style kitchen with its metal cabinets and chipped porcelain sink wasn't about to appear in any decorating magazines. But the hardwood floors and elaborate ceiling moldings were from an era when craftsmen took pride in such things, and from the couch the night view of the city's twinkling lights was breathtaking.

"Is this an heirloom?" Jake questioned, running a hand along the carved arm of the Victorian sofa that had been upholstered in worn plum velvet.

"No, I picked it up in a secondhand shop for practically nothing."

"And that?" He pointed at a claw-foot table.

"Same story. I got it at an auction. I'm a sucker for auctions and secondhand stores and thrift shops. It's the ragpicker in me, I guess. I love to find beautiful things that other people have overlooked or undervalued and then bring them back into their own."

"Admirable, but do I detect a streak of reverse snobbery there?"

"What do you mean?" She gave him a startled look.

"Only that finding treasures others have passed up has to make you feel just a little superior."

"Maybe," Susan acknowledged. She felt jarred by his insight. Really, she'd just handed him the story of her life in a nutshell. Disturbed, Susan crossed to the open bar of the kitchen. "I'll fix us some coffee. It won't take a minute."

"I'm in no rush." He followed her and stood leaning against the counter in a pose of unconscious male elegance. Jake had a way of moving that was a pleasure to the eye. So often in the office when Susan knew he wasn't aware of it, she'd allow her gaze to rest on him, to enjoy the sight of his masculine grace. Resisting the temptation to do that now, she busied herself pouring and measuring.

He was the first man Susan had invited up to her apartment, and a few minutes later as she prepared a tray and then carried it back out into the living area, she was very conscious of this fact—and conscious of Jake following at her heels and of his smoldering gaze pinned to the low-cut back of her gown. It was as if she had a special set of radar where he was concerned. The closer he got, the more her skin tingled. And, right at the moment, she had a lot of tingling skin on view.

She set the tray down on the glass table in front of the couch and turned to face him. "That ballroom was warm, but it's a bit chilly in here. I think I'll slip on a sweater."

"I suppose it would be ungallant of me to tell you not to, but seeing you cover those beautiful shoulders is going to break my heart."

"Oh, I doubt that." Recalling Loretta Greene's remarks about Jake's women, Susan shot him a brittle smile. "I'm sure you've seen a lot of bare shoulders in your day."

"I have," he agreed calmly. "But this is only the second time I've set eyes on yours. And the view is doing more for me than any other has done in a long, long time. I think you know that. I think you must have realized that when we were dancing together this evening."

She was taken aback by his directness. "I...I don't know what you mean."

As Jake studied Susan, his mind juggled a new and complicated equation. He was seeing a different side of Susan Bonner, a side that intrigued and puzzled him. In the office she was always so cool and competent, so much in charge of herself and her work. Never in a million years would he have described her as shy or uncertain. Yet that was exactly how she appeared now.

It was almost as if she were insecure about dealing with a man in a potentially intimate social situation. But how could that be? By now, a woman as attractive and intelligent as she must have had plenty of experience with the opposite sex. Yet Jake was picking up unmistakable signs of female vulnerability.

Jake wanted Susan badly. His aggressive male instincts prodded him to test the frailty he detected, to sweep her into his arms and crush her lips to his.

But what if she rejected him? Where would their relationship go from there? And was it fair to maneuver a woman who worked for him into a situation like this, as he knew he'd done when he'd insisted that she accompany him tonight, and then take her by storm? In that split second Jake's sense of fair play won out over his male urges and he decided to bide his time—though he was still hopeful that his time might be tonight.

"You don't know what I mean? Then maybe I should explain," he said evenly. He gestured at the couch. "Why don't we sit down and have that coffee? Oh, and you'd better go and get your sweater. The last thing I want is for you to be uncomfortable."

"Yes, uh, certainly. I'll only be a minute."

When Susan returned from the bedroom she said, "I know red wool looks silly with your niece's beautiful aqua chiffon, but this is the only cardigan I have."

"It isn't any sillier than some of the outfits I saw tonight. I thought that black-and-white thing Freddie had on made her look like a chessboard."

"Oh, but it was very striking. I thought all the women looked terrific. Your niece was very pretty in her pink lace gown and Tabissa Deeping's green velvet was absolutely stunning."

Jake answered easily. "Tabissa always makes a splash. She makes Winston quite a showpiece."

"Showpiece. That's an odd way of describing a man's wife." Susan sat down next to Jake on the couch and, vibrantly aware of the intimacy of the situation, poured them each a cup of coffee.

"Perhaps, but I think if you get to know the Deepings better, you'll agree that it fits. I don't think either one of them married the other because they were starry-eyed with love."

"They haven't been married all that long, have they?" She lifted her cup to her lips.

"No, only a couple of years."

Susan thought of the terrace scene she'd witnessed between Winston and Loretta Greene. "Who was he involved with before he met Tabissa?"

"I don't know. I haven't been handling legal business for the Byrnside corporation that long." Jake crossed his long legs at the ankles and sighed. "Owen's really getting antsy about the stalemate we're in. I got another call from him this afternoon demanding that we stop dillydallying and come up with something on this third orphan."

Susan felt herself going pale. Carefully, she put down her cup. "What did you tell him?"

"That I'm expecting a break from my detective any day now. I know the man's onto something. He just isn't ready to tell me what it is yet."

Susan's alarm deepened. Had Jake's detective discovered her true identity? But surely that was impossible. She'd covered her tracks too well. Hadn't she?

Jake put down his own cup and turned to her. "Have I told you what a help you've been to me through all this?"

"I—I've only done my job."

"You're done it superbly, Susan. It's you, really, who's responsible for tracking down those first two orphans. Without your help it would have taken me much longer to find Kate and Maggie. But you're good at everything you do, aren't you?"

"Not everything." Susan's gaze skittered away. She was thinking what a mess she'd made of this whole situation. A year ago, changing her name and getting a job with Owen Byrnside's lawyer had seemed a perfectly reasonable plan. Fresh from the clinic in Switzerland, she'd been a new person with a new face. And there'd been a mystery to investigate, a mystery that might affect her in the closest, most personal way.

How could she have imagined that her boss would turn out to be a man like Jake, a man she hated to deceive? How could she have known that having a new face didn't necessarily mean she'd be able to leave her old self behind? Underneath this pretty new exterior, the old badly scarred Lynn was still there—still frightened of rejection, still shrinking away from being hurt.

"Name one area in which you're not at least twice as competent as anyone else," Jake said with a grin.

"Well, unlike Tabissa Deeping, I'm not some rich man's showpiece." She'd meant it to sound like a joke. But somehow it hadn't come out that way.

Jake cocked his head. His eyes searched hers. "Would you want to be? I thought you were far too independent for that."

"No woman is too independent to want love." Again, Susan's gaze avoided his.

"Love and being a man's showpiece—those are two different things."

"I know, I know. I don't know why I said that. It was stupid. Please forget it."

"How can I?" Jake reached out and lightly touched her cheek, guiding her face back toward his. "Susan, we've had this discussion before, but I think it's time we had it again. I forced you into coming out with me tonight. I told you it was strictly business. But when we were dancing, I felt—"

Through the gilded screen of her lashes Susan glanced up at Jake, and he stopped speaking—jolted by the electric charge which shot between them. There was a time for talking. But there were also times when words stopped being the appropriate way to communicate, he thought. The expression in Susan's eyes told him that this was one of those moments. She looked like a little kid contemplating a penny theft in a candy store. She was frightened, but she was also yearning. And when a beautiful woman looked at a man like that, well—what else could he do? Fair play be damned!

Jake's hands went down to Susan's shoulders and, as he drew her closer, his head bent and their lips touched. At first the contact was gentle, exploratory. Badly as Jake wanted this, he was too much the gentleman to force it. But Susan didn't pull back. At first she seemed merely confused, startled. Then her lips softened under his and Jake knew she was willing—willing enough. With a rough little groan, he tipped her head back and his hungry mouth touched her throat.

Susan had been sitting rather stiffly next to him on the couch. Just being hip to hip with Jake unnerved her. When he'd first kissed her she hadn't known what to do. Her brain had seemed to freeze solid.

Yet his caresses seemed to make her bones liquefy. Her hands fluttered out and slipped under his suit jacket to lie flat against the smooth material of his shirt. Beneath the fabric, under her fingertips, she could feel the hard ridge of his collarbone and the strong, steady drumbeat of his heart. As Jake nuzzled the pulse point in her throat, her own heart thrummed double time.

When his mouth slid sensuously to the underside of Susan's jaw, she drew in her breath. As she inhaled the spicy fragrance of Jake's after-shave and the clean, masculine aroma of his skin, she felt like a swimmer surfacing after a long dive. Instinctively, she shifted closer to him and the silken material covering her thighs rubbed against the rougher material that sheathed his.

The contact excited them both. Jake's hand curved around Susan's hip and tightened. Lightly, his thumb stroked along the indentation of her waist. At the same time, his lips abandoned her jaw and once again claimed her mouth. One of his palms cradled the back of her head, his long sensitive fingers tangling possessively in the silky blond mass of her short hair.

Like a hungry man who'd stumbled on a rich cache of honey, Jake plumbed the sweetness of Susan's mouth. Susan quivered beneath him. She'd never been kissed like this before and her response quickly escaped her control. She, too, was starved, starved from years of denial. From the first, Jake had drawn her. Lately, she'd been dreaming about him, and those dreams had been disturbingly erotic. Now her body couldn't refuse the delightful sensations he offered.

Jake's lips vanquished the yielding barrier of hers. At the same time his hands ran lightly up and down her sides and then grazed her breasts with sure, tantalizing strokes. Susan had slipped her hands further beneath his jacket and wrapped them around his back. When Jake felt the excited movement of her fingertips against his spine, he lifted his head long enough to smile down at her.

"You're so lovely. I've been wanting to kiss you like this for weeks."

Susan gazed up at him dazedly. This was crazy, her stupefied brain told her. But there didn't seem to be a thing she could do about it.

She was jarred when Jake shrugged out of his jacket and then loosened his tie. It occurred to her more forcefully that she ought to put a stop to this. But when Jake's lips found hers again, the thought flew out of her mind. His hands went to her breasts, and through the soft aqua chiffon that covered them she could feel him trace a delicate erotic line around her hardening nipples. In reaction, she arched her back, which only thrust her sensitized breasts more completely into his hands.

He made a sound of pleasure and then, holding her tightly, stretched his long length out against the back of the couch and drew her up against him. As their bodies meshed, Susan realized just how aroused Jake actually was. The fact shocked her from the sensual fog that had been governing all her reactions.

"This feels just right," he was whispering into her ear. One of his hands had strayed from the curve of her breast to the swell of her buttock. She shivered, conscious that his other hand was sliding the zipper of her dress open.

Her golden eyes flew open and met the smoky depths of his gray ones, which were shuttered behind his long black lashes.

"Susan, let me make love to you," he murmured while his hand stroked the bared flesh of her lower back.

The fact that he'd asked and was now holding back to wait for her answer gave her a chance to try to gather her wits. Excitement, desire and fear warred inside her. This was crazy, crazy! It would ruin everything if she let Jake make love to her!

"No!" she whispered hoarsely. "No, I can't!"

Jake's mouth went still on the sensitive skin of her shoulder. Then he lifted his head and stared at her, frowning.

"What is it, Susan? What's wrong?"

Refusing to look at him, she struggled to extricate herself from his embrace. Her high heels had fallen off, her skirt had ridden up to her thighs, and the unzipped bodice of her dress dropped away from her breasts.

As Jake's gaze focused on them, the hard flush that lay along his cheekbones darkened.

Thankful for her cardigan, Susan sat up, drew its edges together and with her free hand pushed frantically at her skirt. She knew her face was as red as her sweater. Her tongue felt twisted into a corkscrew and she couldn't think of a single reasonable thing to say.

"Let me help you." Jake sat up and swung his feet onto the floor. Then, impassively, he pulled her dress back up around her shoulders, flipped up the back of the sweater she clutched and tugged her zipper into place.

"I'm sorry," she muttered. "This was my fault."

"Why do you say that? You didn't start it, I did. Fortunes of war."

Jake tucked his shirt into his waistband and then straightened his tie. "What made you change your mind?"

"My mind? I wasn't using my mind."

Jake's mouth quirked. "No," he agreed ruefully, "neither of us was exactly thinking. But even if I had been in a state to think about what we were doing, it wouldn't have made a difference to me. Obviously, it did to you." He picked up his jacket. "I'd better go. Good night, Susan."

CHAPTER SIX

SUSAN HUDDLED ON the couch cursing herself. She couldn't believe what had just happened. How could she have been so foolish? It was bad enough that she was deceiving Jake and that sooner or later he would find out. After this episode, it would be a hundred times worse. Where had all her good intentions flown? And what must Jake think of her? Even more daunting was the fact that on Monday she'd have to face him in the office.

Finally, Susan pushed herself off the couch and, with a heavy sigh, picked up the coffee cups and carried them into the kitchen. She wouldn't be getting much sleep tonight, she thought as she put them into the sink. As if to fulfill her prophecy, the phone rang. The clock on the stove showed that it was past one o'clock in the morning. Now who—could it be Jake?

"Lynnie? Garrity here. Sorry to call so late, but you said as soon as I had something on your runaway teenager and her boyfriend to let you know."

Susan clutched the receiver to her ear. "What have you found out?"

"I just had a conversation with an informant I use. He knows who this Bucky character is. He's seen the guy going in and out of an abandoned warehouse with a young girl." Garrity named a street in an unsavory area of the city. "Sounds to me like they've taken up residence there until they can line up something better. Listen, from what I've heard this Bucky is pure poison. You want some help?''

Susan frowned, thinking hard. Garrity had already gone out of his way for her. She knew he must have traded a favor to get this information. It wouldn't be fair to ask him to risk his neck in a part of the city where no one, including off-duty cops, wanted to go at night. "No, you've done enough. I'll handle the rest."

"You sure about that? You wouldn't be about to take a foolish risk, would you?''

"Me? Of course not. Listen, Garrity—thanks.''

"You're welcome. And don't do anything I wouldn't do.''

Susan laughed. She didn't need to give the standard reply. They both knew what it had to be.

After Garrity hung up, Susan tapped her nails on the drainboard and thought hard. If Bucky and Patsy were holed up in that warehouse, she'd be a lot more likely to find them and take them unawares at night then during the day. What's more, time was precious. The longer Bucky had Patsy in his clutches, the more trouble he could make for her.

"I wasn't going to get any sleep anyway," Susan muttered as she headed for her bedroom. There she rapidly shrugged off her sweater, stepped out of Molly's dyed silk shoes and stripped off the matching gown. Since Jake had already half undressed her, that was easy to do.

Flushing slightly at the thought, and wearing nothing but white lace briefs, Susan pulled on a pair of close-fitting black slacks and a thick black turtleneck sweater from the back of her closet. When she'd donned these practical garments and laced her feet into matching leather running shoes, she topped the outfit with a leather jacket. She crossed to her bureau, opened the top right-hand drawer, pushed a layer of silky underwear to one side and hesitated. Her old police revolver lay at the bottom. Should she take it? *Better safe than sorry,* she thought, slipped it into her pocket and headed for the door.

The night had turned bitterly cold and at this late hour the streets of the city were deserted. A subway and cab ride later, Susan prowled down the dark alley where she expected to find the warehouse Garrity had told her about. She kept a sharp lookout. Other vagrants were sure to have taken shelter in the rotting, abandoned structures that loomed on all sides. Most would be harmless, but not all. You never knew what kind of situation you might stumble into around a derelict neighborhood like this.

A mangy black cat crossed Susan's path, but there was no other movement and a few minutes later she stood in front of the brick building Garrity had described. In the moonlight she could make out the remnants of painted signs that previous tenants had left—L&F Hosiery, Brent's Tires. Though the windows had been boarded up, a corrugated metal door gaped open, half falling off its hinges.

Keeping to the shadows, Susan slipped through the door. Inside, since half the roof had tumbled away, the moon provided enough light for her to see without a flashlight. As she stood trying to get her bearings, she took stock of her options. It would be stupid to call Patsy's name, especially if Bucky was around. Better to try to find them without alerting them first.

A cold wind whistled through the lower half of the building, but on the other side of a pile of trash Susan could make out a staircase that appeared to lead up to a second floor. If this rose-covered cottage were her abode, heaven forbid, that would certainly be where she'd prefer to camp out. Silently, Susan threaded her way to the staircase and then climbed it.

It led to a loftlike area, which had been partitioned into small storage units. Many of the partitions had long since fallen apart and lay in pieces. Someone, probably desperate for warmth, had recently used the wood from one to build a fire. Susan could smell the ashes. Gingerly, she picked a path through the debris.

Ahead of her the floor creaked and she heard a faint moan. It sounded female. With even greater caution, Susan veered toward it. On the other side of a tumbledown wall she spied a small mound of blankets. On closer inspection it turned out to be a sleeping Pasty—and, oh happy day, she was alone. Susan tapped her shoulder.

"Uhh, ohhh, wha-at!" Patsy jerked upright and stared through the gloom at Susan, who'd hunkered down next to her.

"Don't scream. It's me, Susan."

"Susan?"

"Maudie's friend from Hull. I'm here to take you home."

The girl rubbed her eyes in disbelief. "Home? What home? How'd you find me?"

"Wasn't easy." Susan glanced around. "This isn't exactly one of the better addresses in the social register."

Patsy's mouth turned down. "Yeah. Well, you shouldn't be here. Go away and leave me alone."

"Not until I've had a chance to talk some sense into you. Where's your boyfriend?"

"I don't know, out doing a job somewhere."

Just what kind of job might that be? Susan wondered. Doubtless nothing legal. Lucky thing he wasn't around. But he might be back at any minute, so she'd better make this as quick as possible.

"If you know what's good for you, you won't let Bucky find you hanging around here," Patsy threatened sullenly.

"Why? What do you think he might do to me?" Now that her eyes had adjusted to the gloom, Susan was able to see Patsy's face a little more clearly. Dark shadows cupped her eyes and there was a mark on her cheek that looked as if it might be a bruise.

Patsy's eyes avoided Susan's. "There's no telling what Bucky might do."

"Oh? Well, let me guess. Does he like to knock women around?"

"I don't know what you mean."

"Sure you do." Susan flicked on her pocket flashlight and gently touched the discolored area on Patsy's cheek. "Did he hang that on you?"

"No."

"How'd you get it, then?"

"Bumped into something."

"C'mon, Patsy. Don't lie to me. Bucky did it, didn't he?"

The girl pulled her moth-eaten army blanket up around her chin. "Okay, he did it. So what?"

"Why'd he hit you?"

"Just something I said. I said something wrong." A tear oozed from the corner of Patsy's eye and she rubbed her nose with her grimy fist. "Seems like I'm always saying something wrong."

"Of course it does. He's the kind of guy who gets his kicks from hurting people like you. It doesn't matter what the excuse is. But you already knew that about him, didn't you?"

"Yeah. Hey, turn that thing off, will ya? I feel like I'm getting the third degree." Patsy snuffled and then buried her face in the blanket.

Susan put away the flashlight and then reached out and stroked the teenager's hair, which was tangled and dirty. "Why'd you leave Maudie's? Don't you even know when something good is happening to you? Why'd you let Bucky talk you into this?"

"Because he's my man. He's the only one I've got." Patsy's voice was muffled by the blanket.

"You've got Maudie, and the other girls, and me."

"But you all don't love me the way a real family would."

"We care more for you than Bucky ever will. He doesn't love you at all. He just wants to use you." Susan continued the soothing stroking motions. "And as for Maudie not loving, you really underestimate that lady. Sometimes I think she has a heart big enough for the whole world. I ought to know. When I ran away from my foster father, she took me off the streets just the way she did you. I wasn't as pretty as you so, fortunately for me, I didn't have a Bucky."

"Oh, I don't believe that. You're a lot prettier than me." Patsy lifted her tear-streaked face.

"Believe me, I wasn't. Anyhow, my looks didn't keep me from learning to get into plenty of trouble. If Maudie hadn't taken me in and taught me some sense, I don't know where I'd be now. Most likely in jail." Susan's voice pleaded. "Oh, Patsy, you're so lucky to have a fine lady like Maudie care about you. And she does, deeply. She's worried sick, you know. She called me and begged me to search for you. Please let me take you back to her before it's too late."

"It's already too late. I can't go back," Patsy wailed. "Bucky said he'd kill me if I left him."

"More likely he'll kill you if you stay with him."

"I'm afraid. Honest, I hadn't been with him a day before I knew I'd made a big mistake. But I'm scared of what he'll do."

"Then come with me now before he shows up. Leave it to me. I'll make sure he doesn't bother you." Surely Garrity would help her there, Susan thought.

Patsy swallowed and then pushed her blanket aside and stumbled to her feet. "Okay, if you really think it'll be all right."

"I really think so. But let's get a move on. The sooner we're out of here, the better."

Susan took Patsy's hand and led her to the stairs. On the way down Patsy started to whimper from nerves and fear. Susan felt fairly stressed herself, but she tried to keep her voice calm. "We're not far from the docks. An hour from now you'll be buying your ticket to Hull."

"I don't have any money. Bucky takes it all."

Of course he liked to keep her powerless and dependent, Susan thought. She handed Patsy a twenty-dollar bill. "Here, now you can buy both our tickets."

Patsy had just pocketed the money when the door at the other end of the warehouse creaked and they heard a string of low-pitched curses. Both women froze and stared at each other in consternation.

"That's him. That's Bucky," Patsy mouthed.

"Let's get out of here."

"No way! He'll catch up with us and then he'll really be mad at me."

"Okay, you go ahead by yourself. I'll stay here and make sure he doesn't follow you."

Patsy goggled. "You'd do that?"

"Yes. Now get going."

"But he might hurt you. He's really mean when he's mad."

"Don't worry about me. I can take care of myself. Now get!"

Patsy hesitated. But when Bucky's rapid footsteps thudded on the concrete floor, she let out a squeak of terror and fled through an opening on the opposite side of the warehouse. At the noise of her running feet, Bucky's footsteps stopped.

"Patsy? Is that you? What the hell's going on?"

Susan debated whether to answer. But why give away her presence before she had to?

"Patsy?" Bucky brushed roughly past a pile of rotted timber and knocked a box of nails to the ground. He cursed when they made a loud crash and kicked several out of his path. As he began trotting toward the exit Patsy had used, Susan stepped out of the shadows and into a patch of moonlight where she planted herself in his path.

"Patsy's not here anymore." Though Susan had never seen Bucky before, she recognized his type. In his grimy sweatshirt, canvas jacket and stained jeans he was slightly above average height and weasel-skinny. He wore his hair pulled back into a greasy ponytail secured by a rubber band. A thin goatee decorated his chin, and a plastic bag dangled from his right hand.

"Wha-at, what the hell!" At the sight of Susan, Bucky's narrow jaw dropped. "Who are you?"

"I'm a friend of Patsy's."

"Friend? Patsy hasn't got any friends." His eyes slitted. "Are you one of those bitches she hung out with on the island?"

"You might say that." Susan sized Bucky up. He looked tense and frightened, and she could see from the way his chest still heaved and the sweat sheened his cheeks and forehead that he'd been running. What from? she wondered. And what was he carrying in that plastic bag? And just how much trouble was he going to give her?

"Yeah? Well, what are you doing poking your nose in here? Where's Patsy?"

"I already told you. She's gone."

"Gone? Gone where?" Bucky glowered.

"Someplace where she'll be warm and safe."

"Safe, hell! You mean you've talked her into going back to that damn island, don't you?"

"Bucky, give her a break. She's only a kid."

"Yeah? Well, she's old enough to know better than to cross me." Bucky showed his pointed teeth and took a menacing step forward. "And you're old enough to know it ain't healthy to stick your nose in where it don't belong, lady." Bucky glanced around. "You mean to tell me you came here all alone just to make trouble? Now that wasn't smart, not smart at all!"

Susan decided her best chance was to bluff. Bucky was basically a coward. If she put up a brave enough front, he might back off. "I wasn't making trouble, I was doing a good deed. And if you don't want to make a bad situation worse, you'll get out of my way."

"Hey, you got it wrong! You're in *my* way, lady. But you know something? Maybe that ain't such a bad thing." He smirked. "Since Patsy ain't here but you are, maybe you'll just have to be her stand-in." With his free hand, Bucky reached for Susan, but she twisted out of his grasp. As she wrenched loose, he dropped his bag. Watches, rings and glittery necklaces and bracelets spilled out of it. That explained Bucky's "job," Susan thought. Judging from his loot, he must have been out robbing a jewelry store.

She didn't linger to have a better look. With Bucky at her heels, Susan sprinted through the doorway Patsy had used. Cursing foully, he caught up with her out in the alley and yanked at her jacket so violently that her gun fell out of its pocket and onto the broken pavement. "Not so fast, bitch! You're not going anywhere yet!"

He was unprepared for the well-placed kick she aimed at his knees. Still clutching her leather jacket, he gave a yelp and staggered back. Susan was about to retrieve her service revolver and resume her flight. Bucky wouldn't follow her so easily, now. But just as she'd pulled her jacket free of Bucky's grasp, a police car rounded the corner and shone its headlights on them. Horrified, Susan started to dash in the opposite direction, but was brought up short by the appearance of another squad car. She only had time to kick her gun out of sight and into a stand of weeds before officers from both cars leaped out and homed in on her and the sprawled Bucky.

"No, Mrs. Crumper, really, I'm fine. There's nothing for you to worry about."

"But dear, you've been arrested! You're calling from the police station! What did they arrest you for?"

"Disorderly conduct."

"Oh, my, oh, my!"

"It's all a mistake, a misunderstanding. I'm sure I can get it straightened out."

"Oh, dear, oh, dear!" The old lady perched on the edge of her bed. She wore a long white flannel nightgown yellowed from age and slightly threadbare. Her snowy hair was wrapped around pink rubber curlers that stood out from her scalp like electrodes. She peered at the cracked china clock next to her beaded milk-glass lamp. "It's five o'clock in the morning."

"Yes, I know, Mrs. Crumper. And I'm so sorry for waking you. But I need some help here. I've tried to call my friend Maudie Walters, but for some reason her line is busy. Maybe one of the girls who lives with her left the phone off the hook. Anyhow, since it's going to be difficult for me to use the phone here at the station for the next few hours, I wonder if you'd try calling Maudie a little later this morning and telling her where I am? I need to talk to her.''

"Oh, but dear, you mustn't spend the rest of the night in a police station!''

"It's all right. I'll be fine. If you would just get in touch with Maudie for me—''

"But of course I will. You can count on me.''

"Oh thank you, thank you. You're a peach!''

When the line went dead the old lady sat frowning. Her mouth drew down into a pleated O. Dear, dear—to think of that sweet child locked up in a police station with criminals and scarlet women and who knew what other sort of riffraff! Really, it was terrible! And no one there to help her!

Though Mrs. Crumper would never have admitted the fact, she was slightly jealous of Susan's affection for Maudie. Nevertheless, she tried the number Susan had given her. But Daisy Crumper had never been praised for her patience, and each time she dialed Hull she received an annoying busy signal.

"*T-s-s-k.*'' The old lady's breath hissed through her teeth like steam. What in the world could be going on in that woman's house at this hour of the morning? And what earthly good did Susan think this Maudie would do her? At times like these a young woman didn't need another female. She needed a strong man. Or at least, that was Mrs. Crumper's very decided opinion.

She fished her phone book out of the drawer and began searching for a name she'd heard earlier that evening. Jake

Caine. Now there was a man who looked as if he could help out a pretty young woman in distress. And, yes, there was his name. Mrs. Crumper smiled delightedly and then dialed the number next to it.

"WELL, ARE YOU GOING to talk to me about this or not?"

With Jake at her heels, Susan wearily mounted the last step leading up to her apartment and then stuck her key in the lock. When the door opened, she turned and faced Jake. "This is the first time I've ever seen you in anything but a business suit. I guess I thought you even slept in one."

He had on a padded ski jacket over a navy blue warm-up suit. That and the shadow on his normally clean-shaven jaw gave him quite a different look. And despite the awkward situation, Susan found it devastatingly attractive.

"I didn't ask for your opinion of my wardrobe. Susan, what the hell was this all about?"

"It's a long story, and I'm so tired."

Though it was obvious she wanted him to go, Jake had no intention of leaving until he'd heard her version of the night's peculiar happenings. He confronted her stubbornly. "Since I'm not exactly fresh as a daisy myself, I can sympathize. Your guardian angel down there called me at five o'clock in the morning."

"At least you got some sleep. I've been up all night."

So had he, Jake thought. After leaving Susan's apartment at what he'd then imagined was a late hour, sleep had been out of the question. Once he'd arrived home he'd been too disturbed to do anything but take a cold shower, and then pace and think until sometime well after three. Actually, he'd probably just dropped off to sleep when he'd been yanked awake by Mrs. Crumper's call. And it had been a real jolt to his already overwrought system.

"Oh, Mr. Caine," she'd trilled hysterically. "You have to rescue Susan. The police have locked her up!"

"That's what I don't understand," he said to Susan. "What were you doing roaming around the streets of Boston in the wee hours of the morning? Since I got up at five a.m. to testify to your good character and get you off the hook, I think you owe me some sort of explanation."

Susan sighed and motioned him in. She was still traumatized by the night's events. When she'd first laid eyes on Jake at the police station she'd wanted to sink through the tile floor. But he'd handled the situation with his usual efficiency, and now she was free—at least temporarily.

Inside her apartment it was a shock to see some of the coffee things they'd used earlier in the evening still sitting on the table in front of the couch where she and Jake had kissed so heatedly. To Susan that scene seemed to have taken place in another life. Too strung out to feel any more embarrassed than she already was, Susan dropped down on the couch and leaned back wearily.

"Not that I'm planning on replaying our last mishmash of a love scene, but I could use a cup of coffee. How about you?" Jake said wryly.

"Yes, I'll get—"

"Stay right there. You look as if you're about to fade into the walls. I'll fix it."

For the next quarter of an hour Susan slumped back with her eyes closed, listening as Jake bustled about in her kitchen. Why did the noises he made seem so comforting, she wondered, when this situation was so fraught with disaster? Though the police station where she'd been taken hadn't been in the precinct where she'd once worked, Susan had feared that she would be recognized—especially when an officer she'd known fairly well strode past her.

But her new face had protected her, and he'd shown no sign of remembering her.

The fragrance of brewing coffee wafted into the living room. A moment later, Jake came out bearing freshly filled mugs. "All right," he said, handing her a new red one and taking the chipped blue for himself, "tell me all about it."

Susan bought time with a careful sip and, as the strong brew slid down her throat, wondered how she must look. Like hell, undoubtedly. Resignedly, she began an edited account of the night's events.

Grimly silent, Jake listened. "My God, are you crazy?" he exclaimed when she finished. "What possessed you to think you could perform a one-woman rescue mission at night in the worst part of town?"

"I wasn't planning any heroics. I just wanted to find Patsy and talk some sense into her."

"No heroics? You couldn't have been so naive—not knowing you had this Bucky person to deal with. Susan, until now I gave you credit for common sense."

"Thanks a lot. I've already admitted that it was a mistake."

"Mistake? It was a piece of raw lunacy!" Jake slammed down his cup, jumped from his chair and began to pace like a frenzied wolf. "Anything might have happened. You're lucky you're sitting there in one piece."

Susan laced her cold fingers together. "All's well that ends well."

"How do you know that your little adventure has ended well?" Jake snapped. "Are you sure that Patsy's gone back to Hull at all?"

Susan swallowed a retort. "I tried to call earlier," she replied wearily, "but Maudie's line was busy. I'll try again now."

"Maybe you should."

Stiffly, Susan walked into the kitchen and dialed. Maudie answered immediately. "Oh, thank God you're all right!" she exclaimed. "When Patsy told me what happened I was so worried about you! I've been calling your number all night."

Susan slumped against the wall. Well, that explained the busy signal, she thought. And it also answered her question about Patsy. The girl must have made it to Hull all right. "How's Patsy?" she asked.

"Worn out, but she's going to be fine," Maudie said. "Oh, how can I thank you? It's wonderful what you did! You deserve a medal."

Susan decided not to tell Maudie that instead of getting a medal she'd wound up spending the night in jail. Why spoil her festive mood? "I'm glad that Patsy's okay," she declared, injecting as much cheer as she could muster into her voice. "Give her my best. I'm fine, too, so stop worrying. Oh, and you'll be relieved to hear that Bucky's behind bars where I think he's going to stay for a good long while."

Susan stayed on the phone with Maudie another ten minutes, doing her best to reassure the older woman that all was well. Nevertheless, when Susan finally hung up, she started to tremble. All the strength leaked from her legs and suddenly she felt so weak she had to support her weight by leaning her elbows on the counter.

"Susan?"

Overcome by uncontrollable shaking, she didn't answer.

"Susan?" Jake came walking into the kitchen. When he spotted her huddled over like a person having an attack of nausea he stopped short. "What's wrong?"

"I d-d-don't kn-know." Tears spurted from Susan's eyes and she gasped. She was horrified. It was if her body had been taken over. She was completely unable to control her reactions.

In one quick stride Jake was next to her. He took a look at her quaking profile and then turned her around and wrapped his arms about her. "It's all right," he said gruffly. "Stop fighting it."

"N-n-no. I d-don't kn-know..."

"Sh-h-h. It's okay. Just relax and go with it. You've had a rough time, and this is just a reaction." He tightened his arms, encircling her in the protective wall of his strength. "Sh-h-h, sh-h-h." He stroked the top of her head.

Susan closed her eyes, pressed her cheek into his shirt. For several minutes she allowed herself to luxuriate in his comfort. Then she pulled away. "I'm sorry. Really, I'm normally not the weepy type." She accepted the handkerchief he offered and dabbed at her eyes.

"I know you're not. If there's anyone I wouldn't describe as weepy, it's you."

"I'm not sure why I'm reacting this way." Susan took a deep breath, struggling to pull herself together. Of all the embarrassing displays!

"No matter how tough you think you are, sometimes life just gets to be too much for you. You're probably reacting this way because a lot of things are bothering you, not just what happened tonight."

Through her wet lashes, Susan shot him a glance. "Maybe."

"I remember after my wife died, I thought I was handling my grief pretty well. But one day while I was searching the back of the closet for a lost tie, I ran across one of her ballet slippers. When I picked it up and saw the mark her heel had made in the lining I fell apart.'' Jake's mouth tightened. ''I'm glad I wasn't in a public place.''

Susan studied his shadowed face. ''Your wife was a ballet dancer?''

''Yes, though I guess most people would have called it her hobby. If she hadn't decided on college and then marriage to me, Janet might have been able to dance professionally. But she never lost interest in dance. She took regular classes. We had season tickets with all the local companies and caught the train up to New York for performances.''

How romantic, Susan thought. She pictured a slender woman in a pale pink leotard—ineffably graceful. Then she pictured an evening of dance followed by a candlelit dinner. They'd probably stayed the night in some elegant hotel off Fifth Avenue. Probably they'd ordered a bottle of champagne from room service. She quickly closed her mind on the scene that most likely followed. It horrified her that she felt so jealous of a woman who had been dead for four years.

''I know that your wife was killed in a boating accident in the Caribbean,'' she said hesitantly.

Jake nodded. ''We were sailing off the coast of Martinique on a forty-foot ketch. It was late at night and there'd been a party on board. Our anniversary,'' he added with terrible irony. ''We'd all had too much wine to drink, including the captain. A freak storm came up and—'' Jake shook his head as if to clear it of a terrible image.

Instantly Susan's jealousy changed into sympathy. Come to think of it, she'd noticed that Jake rarely drank anything alcoholic. Was that the reason? Guilt? ''Do you blame yourself for not having been able to save her?'' she asked in a low voice.

He hesitated. "In my rational moments, no. In my rational moments I know it was an accident and that no one was to blame. But there are times when I wake up in the middle of the night, wondering." Again, Jake hesitated. His gray eyes had a haunted look. "What if I hadn't had three glasses of wine? What if I'd taken the trouble to be a stronger swimmer? It's crazy I know, but sometimes I even imagine myself back in college practicing laps in the pool. Swimming was never my sport. But what if it had been? I might have been able to save Janet."

"Oh, Jake."

"I know that doesn't make a lot of sense."

"What does sense matter? There are so many turning points in life. We all play the 'what if?' game. It's just that for you—it must be so very painful."

"And pointless," Jake replied, gazing down at Susan. "You're right about the turning points," he added. "It's just a matter of getting around that corner, emotionally, and really knowing there's no going back. After Janet died, it took me a while to do that. Oh, I knew she was gone and that my life had to go off in a new direction. But I only knew it in my head. I didn't *feel* it." Still, gazing at Susan, he touched his chest above his heart. "Just lately that's changed."

"It has?" Something in his expression, the steady regard of his clear eyes, made Susan's stomach start to flutter.

"It's because of you, Susan."

"Me?"

Jake leaned forward, stroked a finger along the underside of Susan's chin and then placed a gentle kiss on her parted lips. "I want you, Susan. Make no mistake about it. You're the first woman I've really wanted in more than four years. I don't dream about Janet anymore—not lately. Lately, I dream about you."

"Jake, I . . ." Susan's voice trembled.

"Don't say a word, not now. I know this isn't the time, not after what you've just been through. I'm going away so you can get some rest. But later, Susan, later we'll have to discuss it. Because, believe me, this isn't something that either of us can ignore. Not any longer."

CHAPTER SEVEN

SINCE SUSAN HADN'T had any sleep for over twenty-four hours, she tried to get some shut-eye. But after she stripped, showered to get the smell of jail off her and then headed for her bed, all she did was lie awake thinking about Jake and what he'd said. There'd been a challenge in his words as well as a declaration of intent.

After four hours of tossing and turning, punctuated by an occasional fitful doze, she sat up, ran a weary hand over her eyes and studied the clock. High noon. And, judging from the light which streamed through the window, a sunny day. Sometimes the best thing to do when you were in an agitated state was just to get out in the fresh air and walk.

Dressed in wool slacks, a sweater and her tweed coat, Susan left her apartment. The first thing she did was take a taxi to the district where she'd left her gun. After retrieving it, she grabbed a bus headed for one of her favorite parts of town. An hour later she sat at a small table in the window of a bistro just off fashionable Newberry Street. A forgotten piece of broccoli quiche lay cooling in front of her. From time to time she sipped from a tall glass of sparkling water garnished with a slice of lime. Though Susan pretended to admire the passing scene, she was actually still thinking about Jake.

What had he really meant by that last remark? she kept asking herself. Yes, it had been a declaration, but of what?

Liking, lust, love? At the very thought of the last L-word, Susan's hand froze on her glass and her insides turned to jelly.

Long ago she had given up on the idea of ever being loved. If her mother hadn't cared for her enough not to abandon her, then how could she expect true caring from anyone else? Though a man like Jake might be attracted to her newly acquired exterior, surely he would never actually love her. No, not love, not the real thing.

Well, then, lust, let's say. Yes, given the way he'd kissed her the night before and the way she hadn't been able to stop herself from responding, she could believe that. Oh yes, it was very believable. Susan's lips parted and her golden-brown eyes took on a humid sheen. She'd wanted Jake last night, and she still wanted him. And the desire that had sprung up between them wasn't going to go away. Hardly.

So how did all this affect their working relationship, she asked herself, sternly regrouping her rational forces. And how did it affect her purpose in passing herself off as a fictional person so she could figure out who was behind the attacks on the three possible Byrnside orphans?

"Was there something wrong with the quiche, ma'am?"

"The quiche?" Susan stared at the waiter hovering over her table. "Oh, the quiche. Oh, no, nothing wrong with it at all. I'm just not hungry. I guess you might as well take it away."

"Can I bring you something else?"

"No, just the bill."

OUTSIDE, SUSAN ADJUSTED the shoulder strap on her purse, jammed her hands in her pockets and started to walk. The afternoon was beautiful and crisp. Shoppers, students and sightseers paraded along the sidewalk. Occasionally a tour bus drove slowly past and Susan caught snippets of the tour guide's patter about Boston during the Revolutionary War.

Every now and then she paused to gaze into the window of one of the many elegant boutiques that lined the historic old street. Their prestige labels were much too pricey for her checking account, but it was fun to dream. Only her dreams quickly took a dangerous turn. As she gazed at soft-shouldered cashmere jackets and long swishy silk dresses she kept imagining modeling them for Jake. She kept seeing him striding toward her, a hungry look in his eyes as he mentally stripped them off her.

With her collar pulled up around her ears, Susan was just picturing his sexy reaction to a dusty pink Roderi ensemble when a familiar figure hurried up the steps and disappeared into the famous Italian designer's showroom.

Loretta Greene. But of course, Susan thought, she was still in town because of the Art League Ball and had probably decided to get in a little shopping before going back to Taleman Hall. If she bought her clothes at Roderi, no wonder she always looked so well turned out. But how could a secretary, even Owen Byrnside's private secretary, afford to spend so much on her wardrobe?

Again, Susan thought of the hotel terrace scene between Loretta and Winston Deeping. What had that been all about? And what was the connection between those two? Shading her eyes, Susan glanced around and caught sight of Owen Byrnside's limousine cruising down the street, evidently in search of a parking spot. But every space was full, so it turned the corner.

No sooner had it disappeared from sight when a harried-looking man ran out of a brick building two doors up, leaped into a gunmetal-gray BMW and pulled out. The spot he vacated, Susan observed, was quite large. She hurried over to it.

Just as she arrived at the curb a small pickup truck pulled up, screeched to a stop and prepared to park. Susan stepped into the empty space and waved her hands until the young man in the pickup truck rolled down his window.

"Hey lady, what are you doing?"

"You can't park in this space. It's taken."

"Taken?" He pushed back his baseball cap and scowled. "It don't look taken to me."

"I'm saving it."

"What, are you crazy? You can't save a parking space on a public street!"

"Well, I am." Susan planted herself firmly. "And if you want to park in it, you're going to have to run me over first."

Trailing a colorful string of sexist curses behind him, the young man in the truck roared off. Susan looked around anxiously. If Owen Byrnside's limousine didn't come around the block soon she was going to wind up in jail again, she thought. But an instant later it appeared and Susan waved to attract the chauffeur's attention.

"Are you signaling me, miss?" The man rolled down his window, a confused expression on his face. "Yes, I'm Susan Bonner, Mr. Caine's assistant," Susan explained quickly. "You must be Mr. Byrnside's chauffeur, but I don't know your name."

"Wrigley, miss. Wendell Wrigley."

"Pleased to meet you, Mr. Wrigley. I saw you looking for a place to pull over so I've saved this spot for you. Do you want it?"

While traffic swirled around them, the chauffeur gauged the size of the empty space. "Tight fit, but I'll see what I can do."

Susan stepped back up on the curb and watched with interest while the man maneuvered the long vehicle into the space. He'd been right about the fit. When he was finally in, there were only a couple of inches to spare on either end.

"Bravo!" Susan stepped back off the curb, peered into the limousine's open window and grinned.

Under his chauffeur's cap, Wendell Wrigley's narrow, lined face flushed with self-conscious pride and he grinned back. "Well, it's my job, you know. I've been hauling this limo—or one like it—around for the last forty years. I should know a thing or two about parking it by this time, wouldn't you say?"

"I certainly would. Forty years! Have you really worked for Owen Byrnside that long?"

"Every bit of it, miss. Though since the old man's been laid up so bad it's Miss Greene I've been driving. Thanks for saving me the space. Who knows how long she's likely to be in that shop, and it gets tiresome just wheeling around the block."

"I can imagine. Listen, I have a couple of questions I want to ask Miss Greene, but I hate to bother her while she's shopping. Do you mind if I just get in here beside you and wait until she comes out?"

"Not at all." He looked surprised. "Though, as I said before, it's likely to be a while. Miss Greene's one dedicated shopper." Wrigley got out, came around and opened the passenger door for Susan. When they were both back inside the luxurious automobile, Susan, searching for topics of conversation, commented on the fine weather, the traffic and the luxury of the limousine.

It was the last which sparked an enthusiastic reaction. "This baby's all right," Wrigley said, "but it was the '55 I liked best. That was one sweetheart of a car."

"Fins and all," Susan agreed. "But the real beauties were the old Packards and Duesenbergs."

Wrigley's face lit up. "My dream is to drive a Duesie. Closest I've ever gotten to one is at an antique auto show. But I've been behind the wheel of a Bugatti."

While Susan drew him out with questions, he discoursed on the difference between all the leading limousine manufacturers and the fine points of the vehicle in which they sat. Susan didn't have to feign interest. She knew a thing or two about cars, but Wrigley was an expert, and what he had to say was fascinating.

Gratified and much less reserved, Wrigley finally remarked, "You know, I should thank you again for saving this parking spot for me. Not many of Mr. Byrnside's friends or employees would have gone to the trouble, or even thought of it. Most of them don't even know I'm there, really. Just think it's a robot or a stick of wood in the front seat driving them around." He laughed scornfully. "If they only knew, I've got ears and eyes just like everyone else."

Susan nodded sympathetically. "Of course you do. And I'll bet you've seen and heard some pretty interesting things during all this time that you've worked for Mr. Byrnside."

"I'll say I have. I could write a book. Of course, I wouldn't do that." He shot her a guarded glance. "But I could if I wanted to."

"You know, I just thought of something," Susan said. "I'll bet you could answer some of the questions I've been sitting here waiting to ask Miss Greene."

"Oh, I don't know." Wrigley looked nervous.

"Well, let me just try you." Susan smiled encouragingly. "Do you know who Winston Deeping is?"

A subtle change came over Wrigley's expression. "Sure I do. Known who he is ever since he come to work for Mr. Byrnside, almost. Drove him up to Mr. Byrnside's just a few days ago. Heard from one of the nurses that they had a corker of an argument, too."

"Oh, really?" Susan cocked her head. "I know Mr. Deeping heads Mr. Byrnside's recording company and that they don't always agree on matters of policy."

Wrigley snorted. "That's a polite way of puttin' it. Mr. Byrnside never did like those loud rock singers with their dirty songs and their drugs. But lately the ones Mr. Deeping's all for pushing have really been stickin' in the old man's craw. Can't say I blame him, considerin' what happened to his only son."

Susan leaned forward slightly. "You must have known Christopher Byrnside."

"Sure I did. Remember him when he was just a little boy and the apple of his mama's eye." Wrigley shook his head. "Alice Byrnside, Mr. Byrnside's wife that died, was the nicest lady you'd ever want to know. But after her son was killed, the life just seemed to go out of her, and she pined away."

Susan studied the chauffeur and prayed that Loretta Greene wouldn't come out of the store for at least another half hour. "I'm curious. What was Christopher like? Was he as wild as they say?"

Wrigley tapped the steering wheel with his gloved fingers. "Oh, he wasn't bad, just spoiled and restless. He had it all—good looks, charm, money. But I tell you, maybe he had too much of everything and not enough of what he really needed. I've seen these rich kids. They live the life of Riley, but it isn't always good for them. Take Christopher, now. If he'd grown up poor and had to struggle for what he wanted he might have done all right. But it was all handed to him, so he got bored and went out looking for excitement.''

"Did he find it?"

The chauffeur pursed his mouth. "Excitement isn't hard to find if it's the wrong kind. And when you're rich you attract it like a magnet. Or at least, I've been around rich people for many years and that's been my observation.''

"By excitement, are you talking about Gloria Dean?'' Susan asked.

Wrigley grimaced. "Her and her crowd. Fast livers who didn't give a tinker's damn for anything or anybody but themselves. Once Christopher got in with them . . .'' The chauffeur shook his head.

"Did you ever meet Gloria Dean?"

"Saw her a few times with Chris. A real flashy looker. Dressed herself up in boots and skirts so short they barely covered her up decent, if you know what I mean.''

Susan had seen publicity stills of Gloria and knew exactly what he meant. "Did you see any of Christopher Byrnside's other friends?''

Wrigley shrugged. "Lots of 'em. Mr. Deeping was one."

"Deeping!"

"Sure. He's a big shot now, but back then he was just a smart-talking kid with a cockney accent who ran with Gloria Dean and her crowd. Chris might even have met her through him.''

Susan was amazed. "I knew Deeping was in the States at that time and that he knew Christopher, but I hadn't realized that they were close friends.''

"Oh yes, thick as thieves they were. It was Chris who got Deeping his first job at Byrnside Enterprises. He wouldn't be where he is today and talking as if butter wouldn't melt in his mouth if it weren't for Chris putting in a good word with his dad. Chris got Loretta Greene her job, too. Deeping and Loretta were going together back in those days, you know."

"They were?" Susan's eyes widened.

"Oh, sure. She was his girlfriend and crazy about him. Always living in hope that he would marry her and take her to England with him. But from what I've seen, he's one of those guys who knows how to sweet-talk a woman without meaning a word of it. For all he strung her along, he never wanted to have anything with her but an affair."

"Really?"

"She kept it a secret from the old man, but you can't expect to keep secrets like that when you live in a house full of hired help. We have to work for a livin' but we're human, just like anybody else. We all have ears and eyes and we can't help but talk to each other. We all knew what was going on whenever Mr. Deeping came over for business with Mr. Byrnside." Wrigley's mouth tightened into disapproving lines.

"You mean he and Loretta Greene were carrying on an affair right in the house?"

"Oh, yes—meeting in hallways, sneaking around like a couple of kids. Came as a real shock to Loretta when Deeping up and married another woman."

"I'll bet it did."

"From what I hear, he's got himself a real classy wife now, good-looking English lady with money and a fancy title."

"I've met Mrs. Deeping," Susan agreed. "She's impressive."

"Yeah, so I can't understand it."

"Understand what?"

"Why he'd want to run around on her with Loretta."

Susan's eyebrows lifted. "Is he?"

"Oh, now I can't say for sure. I'm just guessing. But there was something about the way they acted together when I drove Mr. Deeping up to see the old man. It was as if they had some kind of secret." Wrigley shot Susan a worried look. "I don't know why I've been shooting my mouth off. Normally, I mind my own business. Miss Greene sure wouldn't like it if she knew I'd been talking about her like this."

"Don't worry, I won't say a word to Miss Greene," Susan assured him. Over her shoulder she glanced back at the boutique. "In fact, since you've answered my question, I don't think I'll wait for her." Susan climbed out, shut the car door and leaned in through the open window. "Thanks, Wrigley. You've been a big help."

WELL, SUSAN THOUGHT as she hurried up Newberry Street to a subway station, this has been a most instructive afternoon. As her heels clicked along on the pavement, she consulted her watch. It was only a few minutes past two, so there was plenty of time to start going through those files in the storeroom again. Now that she knew more about Winston Deeping and his relationship to Christopher Byrnside and Loretta Greene, the documents stored away in those boxes might mean more to her.

Susan's steps slowed slightly. Was she likely to run into Jake at the office? she wondered. After last night, she still felt unprepared to see him again. But no, it was Saturday, after all, and he'd probably stayed away, too. What with their late night and then having to bail her out, he hadn't gotten much sleep, either.

Susan had forgotten Jake's iron constitution and work-aholic tendencies. Sure enough, when she walked into the office there he was, sitting at his desk in his shirtsleeves and resting an open palm on the back of his head while he carried on a brisk phone conversation. When his gray eyes lit on Susan, they darkened.

"Listen, Bob, I think I understand your point of view on this, but I can't give you an answer until I've talked it over with my partners. Tomorrow soon enough? Okay, you've got it." With his gaze still fixed on Susan, Jake dropped the receiver back into its cradle. "Where've you been?"

"You didn't actually expect me to come into the office after what I've been through, did you?"

"I expected you to stay home and get some sleep. But I've been calling your place since noon and getting no answer, not even an answering machine."

"I don't own one of those infernal things," Susan replied defensively.

"If you're going to play hooky and then make yourself impossible to reach, maybe you should consider buying one."

"I wasn't playing hooky. I was..."

"I know, I know." Jake stood, raked a hand through his thick hair and then stalked to the window and peered down at the busy street. "I'm sorry, Susan," he said quietly. "I guess we're both tired. But I did have an important reason for wanting to speak with you." He turned to face her. "There's been a break in the Byrnside case."

"There has?" Susan clutched at the lapel of her coat.

"I've finally heard something concrete from the detective who's been trying to track down Lynn Rice. He's come up with the information that a little over a year ago our mystery girl took out a passport and traveled to Paris."

"Oh?" Susan's free hand went up to her other lapel.

"You don't sound particularly impressed."

"Well, it's—I mean, it's interesting, but it's just a trip she took and you said it was over a year ago, so—"

Jake dismissed that with a flick of his sinewy wrist. "I know, it's not the answer to our prayers, but it is a solid lead, and we haven't had one of those in quite some time. I've discussed it with Owen. He's anxious that we follow up on this as soon as possible, so I've taken the liberty of booking a flight to Paris for the two of us on Tuesday."

"The two of us! Paris! Tuesday! Tuesday is just two days after tomorrow." Susan's jaw sagged.

"That's what I was calling you about. It's short notice, so I wanted to let you know immediately."

"But there are so many things to do. I'd have to pack, get my affairs in order."

"You have more than forty-eight hours. Surely you can manage it."

"Why do you want me along? Can't you go by yourself?"

"As a matter of fact, your going is Mr. Byrnside's idea. He was impressed by you and specifically asked that you accompany me." Jake studied her, his mouth tightening. "Most young women would be thrilled by an all-expenses-paid trip to Paris. You look as if I'm suggesting an overnight stay in the Black Hole of Calcutta. Why? Is it because of last night? Because of what I said about wanting more between us? Are you afraid that if I get you alone in a romantic city like Paris I might try to take advantage of the situation?"

"No, of course not."

The stern expression left Jake's face and his mouth quirked. "No? Well, you ought to be. When all this came up that was one of my first thoughts. But if my forcing myself on you is what really has you bothered, relax. I promise this will be a business trip for both of us."

Susan felt a flush creep up over the edge of her neckline. The moment Jake had announced this trip, her mind had started to race. Now it spun. What was Jake likely to uncover in Paris? How detailed was the information this detective had gleaned? Was it only a matter of days before Jake figured out that *she* was actually his quarry—in more ways than one? For only this morning he'd told her that he already thought of her that way.

Susan's flush deepened. An image of the two of them embracing on a balcony with the twinkling lights of Paris spread out before them flashed through her mind. But she forced herself to dismiss this enticing fantasy.

Jake was a proud man who placed a high value on honesty and integrity. Once he knew who she really was and how she'd been tricking him all these months, he'd probably be so angry that he'd lose all interest in her. Added to that, it didn't help that she was about to be unmasked just when she'd uncovered information about Winston Deeping and Gloria Dean, information that might take her to the heart of this mystery, which she'd already devoted a year of her life to uncovering.

"How long are we likely to be gone?" Susan asked.

"I can't say. It all depends on what we find in Paris and where, if anywhere, that new information takes us. Mr. Byrnside is prepared to bankroll an indefinite stay."

"Indefinite?"

Jake shrugged. "Probably we'll be gone no more than a week or two, but I can't promise."

Susan gazed at him, unconsciously admiring the way the midafternoon light burnished his hair, bringing out flickers of red and gold that normally remained hidden.

"All right, but I'll have to take Monday off to get ready."

Jake cracked a smile that lit up the hard edges of his face and glowed deep in his expressive eyes. "You drive a mean bargain, but I suppose it's fair. I have a certain amount of tidying up to do myself, come to think of it. If we're staying a week or more, I can't do my usual thing and travel with just my briefcase and an overnight bag," he allowed. His smile widened mischievously. "Be sure and pack some warm underwear. This time of year the nights can be chilly in Paris when you're sleeping alone."

THE NIGHTS ALONE in New England can be even chillier, Susan thought late Monday night as she finished sorting through the clothes spread out on top of her bed. She'd spent the previous two days getting her hair cut, shopping for necessities, retrieving her passport from its safe-deposit box, canceling all deliveries and putting her apartment in order. Tuesday morning, before catching her flight, she'd pay her bills and check on Maudie, Patsy and Mrs. Crumper to make sure there was nothing they needed before she left.

Susan flipped a lock of fair hair back off her forehead. She thought of sinking into a hot tub and just relaxing for a while. But before she could allow herself that luxury, she had one last important call to make. Squaring her shoulders, she picked up the telephone and dialed.

"Garrity here."

"Garrity, it's Lynn."

"Lynnie?" Garrity gave his gravelly chuckle. "I thought I recognized your dulcet tones. I hear through the grapevine you got yourself in a bit of trouble the other night and your boss had to bail you out of the slammer. He must be a helluva nice guy."

"He is."

"Well, he'd have to be to put up with your shenanigans. You were following up on that tip I gave you, weren't you?" Suddenly he sounded peeved. "Now why in glory-hallelujah didn't you take me up on my offer to come along? If I'd a been there, you wouldn't have been so butterfingered and wound up in the cooler."

"You didn't tell anyone who I really am, did you?"

"If you don't know me better than that by now, then we'd better end this conversation while it's still on a relatively civil note."

"Sorry, Garrity. But really, it was enough that you got me the tip. I didn't want to ask you to take any risks."

"Risk is my middle name. Judas priest, Lynnie, I don't make an offer if I don't mean it. Next time you keep that in your tiny little mind."

Susan grinned. "Glad you said that, Garrity. Because, as a matter of fact, this *is* next time."

Garrity sighed theatrically. "Now when am I going to learn to keep my big mouth shut? What is it you have in mind? Another night prowl through the warehouse district?"

"No, just more information. Almost twenty-eight years ago, Christopher Byrnside was killed in an auto accident. If there are any files on that accident, I'd like to know what they say."

"Why? Are you thinking it might not have been an accident?"

"I'm not thinking anything. I'd just like to know what those files say."

"Well, okay, I'll see what I can do. But that was a lot of years ago. Who knows what's in the computer now? When do you want me to get back to you?"

"I'm not sure." Susan cleared her throat. "As a matter of fact, I'll be in Paris this coming week with my boss, Jake Caine."

"Paris? You mean Paris, France?"

"That's the one. Paris, the city of light and love. And I'm not exactly sure when I'm going to be coming back, either."

"PARIS, THE MOST glamorous city in the world," the pilot announced through the loudspeaker just before the huge, silvery jet touched down on the runway. "Right now it's overcast and drizzling, but soon the sun will shine through the clouds. Enjoy your stay, ladies and gentlemen. And don't forget to fall in love."

"Paris, the city of suspicious customs inspectors and wild and crazy traffic," Jake groaned over an hour later when he and Susan finally settled themselves and their luggage into a taxi outside the terminal. He shot her a questioning look. "If you'd stayed in line behind me we would have been finished half an hour earlier. The line you picked moved like molasses."

Susan shrugged. "Sorry. Weather and the speed of lines are both pretty hard to predict." She turned her head and studied the slick street outside the window. "Anyhow, we're out and on our way, so what does it matter?" Actually, she'd deliberately slipped into a different customs check from Jake's. Her passport had an updated photograph, but it also had her real name on it. On this trip, as well as an earlier business trip with Jake to Barbados, she'd worried about that. But both times she'd managed to handle the problem and squeeze through without bringing her double identity to Jake's attention.

As the taxi approached the outskirts of the city, Susan kept her gaze on the window and remembered her first trip to Paris. At that time it had been the biggest adventure of her life. Of course, she'd instantly fallen in love with the city. A reminiscent smile quirked Susan's mouth as she remembered Le Jardin, the romantic little hotel where she'd stayed. It had had charming rooms with feather bolsters on the beds and balconies that looked out over a courtyard.

"Where are we going?" she asked Jake a few minutes later.

He took a small notebook from his breast pocket. "A hotel near the Boulevard St. Michel. It's called Le Jardin."

The smile instantly slid from Susan's mouth and a cold sweat began to gather at the back of her neck.

"According to my detective," Jake continued, "that's where Lynn Rice stayed. I'm hoping that the desk clerk or one of the chambermaids will be able to tell us something about her, maybe even give us a solid lead."

What if one of them recognizes me? Susan thought. She'd spent four days in that hotel, plenty long enough to make an impression. And though it had been many months ago, the French were a very observant people. Was her changed appearance enough of a disguise to protect her? Susan pressed her palms together. They, too, were sweaty.

"You've been awfully quiet," Jake said just as the cab pulled up in front of Le Jardin. "Tired?"

"A little."

"It was a long flight and the time change always takes getting used to," he said sympathetically, as their driver came around to open the passenger door.

Susan hid a yawn behind her hand. "If you don't mind, I think I'll go directly up to my room and lie down for a while."

"That's fine. Only wait long enough for me to ask the desk clerk a few questions, will you?"

Susan tried not to let her fears show in her expression. She remembered that she'd had several conversations with the desk clerk about things she'd seen in Paris. He'd been very proud of his city and more than willing to lecture her on its glories as well as its pitfalls. She even remembered his name, Yves. If anyone at the hotel was likely to recognize her, it would be Yves. Of course, by now he might have changed jobs. Maybe fortune would smile and there would be someone new signing in guests.

But no such luck. The moment they walked into the tiny lobby, Susan spotted Yves behind the desk. The ends of his small black mustache were just as pointed and his dark eyes just as sharp and curious as she recalled.

"Good afternoon, *madame, monsieur*. What can I do for you?" His gaze traveled between them expectantly.

"We have a reservation under the name of Caine, Jacob Caine."

Nervously, Susan watched Yves's quick fingers flip through the contents of a file folder.

"Caine. *Ah, oui, certainement*. Two single rooms. Can that be correct?" Again, his bright eyes surveyed them. Was that recognition she saw flickering between his lashes, or merely gallic curiosity? Susan wanted to hide.

"Two separate rooms, that's quite correct." With only the faint lift of his well-cut mouth to indicate his amusement, Jake signed the register and accepted two keys. "Before we go up to our rooms, I wonder if you'd mind answering a question or two?"

"But, of course. Anything I can do to make *monsieur* and *mademoiselle*'s time in Paris a pleasant one."

"We are looking for a young lady who stayed here a year ago last June. Her name was Lynn Rice. Perhaps you might remember her?" Jake took out a photograph of Lynn Rice that showed her face still scarred and her un-lightened hair worn in a shapeless and unflattering shoulder-length style.

Yves studied the picture. "*Ah, oui,* I remember her well. A very charming young lady. So sad about her face, but still the personality, it was *charmante.*" Yves looked directly at Susan. "Do I detect a family resemblance? She is your sister, perhaps?"

CHAPTER EIGHT

"YOU HAVE A KEEN EYE," Jake interjected smoothly. "Miss Bonner is this young lady's cousin." He tapped the edge of the photograph, which Yves still held. "It's been months since anyone in the family has heard from Lynn, so naturally Miss Bonner's concerned. Isn't that right, Susan?"

Susan, who'd been standing frozen, jerked a nod. "Yes, I'm concerned about my cousin."

Yves pursed his lips. "*Mon dieu,* I fear there's little I can tell you. The *mademoiselle* only stayed a few days and that was over a year ago. But I will question the staff. Perhaps they will remember something, no?"

He gave Susan a sympathetic smile. "It's hard to lose a member of one's family. My own brother, Pierre, he disappeared for five years. For five years, nothing. Day and night I worry. Then, *pouf,* he walked in my door. Do you know where he'd been?" Yves shook his head and rolled his shoe-button eyes. "All those years he'd been working at a Caribbean resort, teaching waterskiing." Again, Yves shook his head. "And he never invited me to join him. Now all my worry has turned to anger."

"I doubt that Lynn Rice is teaching waterskiing," Jake murmured a few minutes later as he and Susan followed the bellboy.

"I'm certain that she isn't," Susan agreed wryly. Because her mouth was still dry from nerves over her narrow escape at the desk, she stumbled over her words.

Jake shot her a concerned look. "Are you okay?"

"Oh, yes—just still disoriented by the flight."

After the bellboy had shown her to her room, she shut the door behind him and then dropped down on the bed. She trembled from head to foot. Her stomach felt like an active beehive. When Yves had asked if Lynn Rice were her sister, she'd wanted to faint.

Firm knuckles thudded on her door and Susan's heart seemed to leap into her throat.

"Yes?"

"It's Jake."

"Just a minute." She walked across the room with legs that felt like noodles. "What is it?"

"Mind if I come in and talk a minute?" When she nodded, Jake pushed the door she'd opened a crack and walked past her. "My room is just across the hall," he commented. "It's exactly like this, only I don't believe the view is quite as good." He threw open the doors leading onto a tiny wrought-iron balcony and stepped outside.

Susan, who hadn't stirred, inhaled the scents and sounds of Paris and gazed after him mutely. He'd left his suit jacket in his room and stood with his back to her, his hands on his lean hips and his shoulder blades flexed so that she could see their sharp outline beneath the fabric of his blue-and-white striped shirt. Outside it was still overcast and the fine mist that hung in the air gave a sheen to the short strands of Jake's hair. For a brief moment Susan imagined the feel of it against her palm. The pad of her thumb tingled as she pictured herself running it along the border of tanned skin above his crisp white collar.

Susan's gaze wandered lower. How well his slacks hung on his trim buttocks and long legs. Jake's business wardrobe might be unvaried, but his suits were all made of the finest materials and so immaculately tailored that he invariably looked good. Even now, after their transatlantic flight, Jake appeared unwrinkled and ready to take on the world. She, on the other hand, felt shaky, rumpled and badly in need of a hot shower.

"It's a piece of luck that the desk clerk imagined a family resemblance between you and Lynn Rice," Jake said, turning and coming back inside.

"Yes, wasn't it?" Susan repressed a spurt of hysterical laughter.

"That will give us a good excuse to interview the staff. Who knows, one of them may remember something helpful."

"And if they don't?"

"Don't be so pessimistic. It's worth a try, anyhow. And if they don't, we may get something out of Interpol."

"Interpol!"

"Why, yes. I've already been in contact with them. While you're resting this afternoon, I'll drop in on their headquarters and see what I can find out."

"Maybe I should go with you," Susan said hastily. Who knew what Jake might learn? For some crazy reason she couldn't bear the thought of him finding out about her in her absence—though it would be perfectly horrid for him to learn the truth while she was standing there beside him.

Smiling and shaking his head gently, Jake crossed the room and briefly laid a hand on her shoulder. "No way. Lady, you look beat. The only other time I've ever seen you so pale was after you'd spent the night in jail. I want you to get some rest."

"But—"

"No buts. I'm the boss, remember?" Jake chuckled ruefully. "Lord knows, I have a hard enough time remembering it when I'm around you." He sighed. "Oh Susan, you don't have any idea what just being near you does to me, do you?"

"Jake..."

"Don't say another word. Now I'm going to get out of here before I say any more dumb things."

After he'd gone, Susan sank back down on the bed. What was there to do? she wondered. Really, right now everything was out of her hands. Back home Garrity was trying to find out about Christopher Byrnside's accident, and if she could avoid detection for just a couple more weeks, maybe some of the Byrnside puzzle pieces would start fitting together. She just had to hope that she could come up with some answers before Jake and his detective did. Jake, oh Jake! Susan squeezed her eyes shut. What was happening to her? Had she fallen in love with him? Could this constant pain that had settled around her heart be what the poets and songwriters sang paeans of praise about?

With a sigh, Susan slipped off her shoes, stretched out on the bed and laid her weary head on the bolster. Beyond the balcony she could hear the steady whoosh of traffic punctuated by the distinctive, combative honk of Parisian horns. Every now and then snippets of French conversation from pedestrians drifted up to her. But it was all muted by the soft patter of the rain that fell over the city in a fine gray veil.

With another sigh, Susan let her body relax into the mattress. Despite all her troubles, or maybe because of them, a few minutes later she was sound asleep.

SHE SLEPT late into the afternoon. She was still unconscious when Jake finally returned to the hotel. After he showered and changed, he tapped on her door.

"Hmm, hmm," he heard her mumble.

He smiled to himself. "Susan, wake up. It's Jake."

"Umm, Jake?" Her voice was still thick with sleep.

Jake tried the door. It was unlocked. "Mind if I come in?"

"Umm, okay I guess."

He poked his head in and grinned. She was sitting up, blinking. With her hair mussed into a buttery aureole and her face flushed, she looked like a confused child who'd just been awakened out of an overlong nap. To Jake she was utterly adorable. But everything about Susan had seemed utterly adorable to him for quite some time now. "Hey, sleepyhead, you've napped through the day. It's almost dinnertime."

"Dinnertime?" Experimentally, Susan touched the flat of her hand to her stomach. She nodded. "Yes, I guess it is. I do feel kind of empty in there." She peered at him. "What did you find out at Interpol?"

"You need to get out and start experiencing Paris. I'll tell you about my afternoon over a decent meal. There's a café in the Place du Tertre that you might enjoy."

She pulled her rumpled skirt down over her knees. "I'm a mess."

"A very charming mess. But there's no rush. Take your time." He withdrew his head and started to close the door. "I'll be down in the lobby when you're ready."

Doubtless interviewing chambermaids, Susan thought sourly. Fear shot through her, and she sprang off the bed. Obviously, Jake hadn't found anything out yet. So far she'd been lucky. But what if someone else on the hotel's staff had an even sharper eye and more retentive memory than did Yves?

Susan opened up her suitcase, withdrew a garment and rushed into the bathroom. A half hour later, showered and freshly made up, she'd donned an outfit she'd decided to splurge on. It was a pale blue wool sweater-coat over a matching ribbed skirt and collarless cream silk blouse. Her panty hose and low-heeled pumps were the same shade of blue. Her only jewelry was the pair of pearl buttons gracing her ears.

Downstairs Jake saw Susan come out of the elevator and rose to his feet. As she crossed the foyer coming toward him, his gaze never left her and his gray-green eyes were suddenly the misty color of a river at dawn. His deep voice, however, remained calm and controlled. "You certainly look fully recovered."

"I'm fine." She began to slip on the raincoat she carried over her arm and Jake hurried to help her. "Do you think I'll need an umbrella?"

"No. It's still overcast, but it's stopped raining. Ready for a night on the town?"

"I don't know. I didn't recognize that place you mentioned."

"The Place du Tertre? It's an old square in Montmartre, the old artists' area. You know, I never did ask if you'd been in Paris before. Have you?"

"No," Susan responded quickly, and then hated herself for having lied. It was horrible, the way she was always having to deceive Jake. It was even becoming a habit, she realized. In this case it might really have been better if she'd told the truth. After all, most people with the sort of background she was pretending to have traveled in Europe by the time they were her age.

"Really? This is your first time here? Well then, we can spend tomorrow seeing all the sights." He took her arm and led her through the tiled lobby and out the door to the street.

"I thought we were here on business," Susan protested.

"We are. But I've already interviewed the staff and gotten nowhere. There's not much more we can do until I hear from Interpol."

As they climbed into the taxi Jake had hailed, Susan gave a small inward sigh of relief. "No one remembered Lynn Rice?" she asked when Jake finished giving instructions to the driver.

"Oh, some remembered her, even after all these months. That scar on her face made her stand out in a crowd. But no one had anything useful to say about her. She was very quiet and polite. Didn't make trouble. That sort of thing."

"And what about your visit to Interpol this afternoon? You came up dry there, too?" Susan tried to keep the hopeful note out of her voice.

"Oh, it's not quite as bad at that. They said they were working on something and might have information for me in a day or two. So we'll just sit tight here and wait to see what develops." Jake gave her a smile. "I think that translates into, 'as long as we're here anyway, why not try and enjoy ourselves?'"

Why not, Susan asked herself, drinking in the admiration she saw glowing in his eyes. Of course, what he'd said about Interpol worried her. When she'd traveled through Europe under her own name she hadn't tried to cover her tracks; there'd been no reason to. In these days of computerization, all kinds of information could easily be retrieved.

But as she had reason to know, police departments were not always as efficient as the public liked to imagine. A lot slipped through the cracks. Interpol might come up empty, or take much longer than a couple of days to trace her. It was a gamble, but there wasn't much she could do about it. So why not try to enjoy these precious last days with Jake? Why not?

"Paris," Susan breathed a few minutes later after they'd left the taxi to stroll down a cobbled street that looked as if it were straight from the set of *An American in Paris*. Her gaze darted around, drinking in the buildings of brick and stone with their aged patina, the café tables under vivid awnings and umbrellas, the sidewalk vendors and artists with their easels.

The rain had washed everything clean and the cool air smelled of dampness and of something else indefinable but uniquely, seductively Parisian.

"There's no place else like it," Jake commented. "Even in winter it's beautiful. Whenever I come here I still find the same magic."

"I don't think I've ever heard you use the word 'magic' before."

"That's because back in Boston it's probably not in my vocabulary." Jake chuckled ruefully. "Here in Paris, I'm not the same dull, prosaic fellow I am back home."

"Now, why do you call yourself dull and prosaic? That's not the way I think of you at all."

He slowed his steps to search her face. "It isn't? Then how *do* you think of me?"

Susan studied him through her lashes, deliciously aware that for almost the first time since they'd known each other they were flirting. It felt wonderful, exhilarating.

"I think of you as the boss, of course—masterful and authoritative, a lordly lion stalking through the legal jungles of New England."

Jake laughed sharply. "Lion! More like a frightened monkey getting lost in the trees."

"Oh, no, that's not you at all. I've never met a more self-confident, more self-assured man."

"You surprise me." Jake stopped again. "Where you're concerned, confident and assured are the last words I'd use to describe myself."

"Where I'm concerned?"

"You know what I mean, Susan. From the first we've been dancing around each other. It's been a case of immovable object and irresistible force. Only you weren't having any trouble resisting my force."

Susan laughed. "Maybe Paris is affecting me, too," she said demurely.

Jake's eyes gleamed roguishly. "That's what I'm hoping for." He stopped to purchase a bunch of violets from a pretty little cart. With a gallant gesture, he handed them to Susan. "They suit you."

"Why, thank you, kind sir!" She buried her nose in their lush purple sweetness and mused with a shade of sadness, *For the rest of my life, whenever I remember Paris, I'll think of violets and the gallant way Jake presented them to me.*

The café he selected for their dinner was called La Bohème.

"After the café in the opera?" Susan questioned.

"I don't know, but it certainly looks right," Jake observed.

After they were seated, Susan looked around and agreed. The interior, dark and smoky, echoed with the rapid-fire chatter of vehement French voices. The cane chairs were painted orange and yellow. A candle in a wine bottle lit the center of each scarred wooden table.

"I feel as if I should be wearing an artist's smock," Susan joked.

"Why not settle for artist's model? The costume is so much simpler."

"Artist's models don't wear anything at all."

"That's the idea."

Susan stuck her tongue out at him and Jake laughed. "You don't have to worry, Susan. You're perfect just the way you are. When we followed the waiter to our seats just now, you turned heads at every table. It would have been funny if I hadn't been so jealous."

At that, Susan's eyebrows rose. *Jake, jealous?* "You're imagining things," she told him.

"No," he retorted, suddenly serious, "it's you who's not quite living in this world. Sometimes I get the impression that you have no idea how attractive you are or the effect you have on men. At first I couldn't believe that. I thought it must be some kind of act."

"Act!" She scowled.

Jake merely shrugged and went on. "Most women can calculate their impact on the opposite sex by the time they're twelve. But you really seem to be the exception to the rule. Don't you ever look in the mirror, Susan?"

"No, not very often." Even now, more than a year after her surgery, mirrors were disturbing. She still couldn't believe that the person looking back was really her.

"How can you resist?" Jake asked, "when what you see is so delicious?"

Susan's golden-brown gaze slid away from his laughing gray one. "Thanks for the compliment. But maybe when I was twelve I didn't look much the way I do now."

"Oh?" Jake leaned forward, very interested. His eyes studied her intently. "With that creamy, flawless skin, I can't picture you with acne, but a lot of kids suffer from it. And I suppose in later years it affects their self-image. Is that what you mean?"

"Not exactly."

"You're so slim, I can't picture you overweight, either. Was baby fat the problem?"

Susan didn't want to tell Jake any more lies. "No not that, either." Unconsciously, she began to wring her hands. Why had she allowed the whole painful subject to come up in the first place? "I just wasn't a particularly pretty adolescent."

"Tomboyish?"

"Yes," she agreed, which was true. To survive at all, she'd had to be as tough as the toughest kids around her. And she'd been exactly that, though it hadn't always come easily.

Jake opened his mouth to ask more questions, but just then the waiter provided a welcome break by arriving to take their order. Since the menu was in French and the waiter appeared to speak nothing else, Jake handled the whole transaction.

"Why don't we start with something light? What would you say to a *potage germiny*?"

"I'd say, what's that?"

"Cream of sorrel soup."

Susan took a sip of the white wine the waiter had already decanted. For a girl who'd grown up thinking of cheeseburgers as gourmet fare, she certainly had come up in the world, she thought. "Sounds delicious."

Amused, Susan spent the next few minutes debating her main course with Jake. Finally she settled on a fillet of sole with spinach and mornay sauce.

"Filets de sole à la florentine," he told the waiter and then went on to order *Bar braisé aux aromates* for himself.

Though Susan had never had the opportunity to learn French, to her ears Jake's accent sounded impeccable, a word that from the first had applied to his whole manner and bearing. Back in Boston he was impressive, a man who obviously knew his way around in a cosmopolitan setting. But here in Paris his self-assurance and easy grace were even more striking. When Susan had stayed in Paris alone, she'd felt distinctly intimidated. How different it was to be back in this sophisticated city with a man like Jake.

"You speak French like a native."

"Hardly, but it was an undergraduate minor and since I do a lot of traveling abroad I've had a good chance to keep in practice."

Susan studied the pale, straw-colored wine in the glass she held between her fingers. "Did you come here often with your wife?"

"Several times. Janet loved Paris. Does that bother you, Susan?"

"No, why should it?"

"Janet loved Boston, too."

"Then we have a lot in common. I like both places, myself. Did the two of you go to this restaurant together?"

"No, I discovered this place on one of my recent business trips." He reached across and touched Susan's wrist. "We've already talked about Janet, but let me say it one more time. I loved my wife. For four years I've mourned her. There was a time when that's all I thought I'd ever be able to do. But I don't think that anymore. I can't go on marking time like a lost soul. I want a future, Susan."

The expression in his eyes said what he didn't put into words. It said that he wanted, expected her to be part of that future. Susan blinked in shock. Oh, if only things were different. If only she hadn't deceived Jake, and if only he weren't about to uncover her deceit. Suddenly Susan knew that she must tell Jake the truth. She should tell it to him this very minute. She opened her mouth, but nothing came out, only a ragged sigh.

Jake gave her wrist a light squeeze and then sat back and smiled wryly. "I know, I know, this is something you don't want to talk about—yet. But there are things you want to do here in Paris. And we have twenty-four hours, so let's just enjoy them."

The waiter appeared bearing bowls of soup. "Yes," Susan murmured weakly as he set one down before her and lifted its cover with a flourish, "sounds good to me."

After Susan and Jake finished their leisurely and quite delicious meal with cups of strong French coffee, they decided to walk back to their hotel.

He didn't take Susan's arm, but as he strolled next to her, she felt the nearness of his tall, lean body almost like a physical embrace. Wrapped in the shield of its warmth, she looked around her, drinking in the sights and sounds.

Instead of going to sleep at night, Paris came even more vividly alive. Under the street lamps old ladies bearing huge loaves of bread in string shopping bags hurried down the street. Smartly dressed men bent on adventure crossed the avenue with a purposeful stride and a gleam in their eye. Couples strolled arm in arm, their laughing voices and flushed faces speaking of life and love. Their youth and vitality were a counterpoint to the patina of age that softened the streets and buildings. Other voices from other times seemed to echo silently within the ancient stones of Paris. But somehow their ghostly presence only underlined the *joie de vivre* of the here and now.

As Jake and Susan ambled along, they paused here and there to glance into shop windows. "What beautiful cut-glass bottles!" Susan exclaimed, stopping in front of an attractively lit *parfumerie*.

"Do you like perfume?" Jake asked. "I don't think I've ever smelled any on you."

"I like it, but the cheap stuff doesn't appeal to me. And good French perfume is so expensive."

"While you're here you should get some."

Susan shook her head. "I've read that a woman should pick out a fragrance that suits her and then stick with it, so it becomes her signature. But I can never make up my mind."

"They'll custom-blend a scent for you in this place. Maybe we should come back tomorrow and have it done."

"Oh, but..."

"My treat," Jake said, a twinkle appearing in his eyes. "An early Secretary's Day gift, if that's the only way you'll accept it."

Susan's gaze dropped from his and her thoughts swirled. Things between her and Jake had been changing like quicksilver these past couple of weeks. But since they'd arrived in Paris all the rules that had governed their relationship were dissolving entirely.

Just being alone like this with him, strolling at his side along this romantic foreign street was having the most intoxicating effect on her. She felt excited and warm all over. Her nerve endings seemed to tingle with awareness of Jake. Whenever she stole a glance his way, everything about him delighted her, his smile, the deep timbre of his cultivated voice, the tall, lean manliness of him. Every now and then she had to overcome a crazy urge to reach out and stroke his shoulder or touch his hand. And this was a man who would probably despise her when he learned the truth, which could happen very soon now. Very soon. Maybe she didn't need to tell him the truth tonight, but by tomorrow . . . yes, by tomorrow she had to come out with it.

"I wonder what a perfume made especially for me would be like," Susan murmured, looking for a way to distract her scurrying thoughts.

Jake's smile warmed. "That's easy. It would be spicy with an underlying sweetness. And once experienced, it would be unforgettable."

Susan felt herself go even warmer. She touched the violets pinned to her shoulder. "Am I spicy?"

"At times. At times you can be downright lemony."

"Lemony?"

"Tart and to the point. But lemons are refreshing."

"You make me sound like oven cleaner."

"Do I? Well, lady, you can clean my oven any time you like." Jake took her elbow and guided her away from the window.

Susan laughed and swatted at him lightly, but didn't pull away. After a few steps, she even leaned into him slightly. As they ambled along, it occurred to her that anyone seeing them might think they were lovers. Next to her, Jake had the same thought. But neither of them put the notion into words. They merely walked side by side, reveling in each other's closeness and the unnamed but powerful currents flowing between them.

BACK AT LE JARDIN, an inconspicuously clad figure prowled the corridor. The figure stopped in front of Susan's door, glanced both ways to make sure the hall was empty, and then took out a set of hooked instruments that made short work of the lock.

Inside the room, the intruder cast narrowed eyes around the darkened chamber, flicked on a small flashlight and then crossed to the suitcase that sat open on a chair next to the bed. It had been only partially unpacked. Clothing had been removed and hung in the closet, but loose items, underwear, vitamin pills and the like littered the container's silk-lined bottom.

With quick efficiency the intruder investigated the lining's pockets. An instant later deft fingers withdrew a small folder. Eyes lit with grim pleasure when the passport it contained was revealed in the flashlight's glow. It was even more satisfying to read the name on the passport and examine the identification photo.

"Lynn Rice," the intruder whispered. "We meet again."

A man and woman's voice filtered through the closed door. After a quick look in that direction, the interloper replaced the passport and headed for the window.

"TIRED?"

"Uh, yes. I guess so."

Jake nodded. "It's been a long day." He shot a glance at his closed door and then at Susan's. "We should both turn in early so we can get a good night's sleep and make the best of tomorrow. There's so much of Paris that I want to show you."

Yet neither of them made a move to go into their rooms. Instead, they lingered in the hall, looking at each other. Powerful yearnings welled up inside Susan and her throat constricted.

"Dinner was lovely. That was a terrific place to eat in, very Parisian," she managed to say.

"Yes, but there are hundreds of wonderful places to dine in this city. Tomorrow we'll try a spot I know that looks over the Seine. You'll like that."

"I'm sure I will. How could I not?"

Jake's head inclined toward hers. "Susan, dinner was wonderful for me, too. But it wasn't the food, it was being with you, looking across the table at you. I know I promised not to molest you, and I won't. But I can't walk away without doing at least this."

Quickly, Jake bent and pressed his mouth to hers. It was a swift, soft, gentle kiss. And it was over before Susan could react. "Good night," he said as he straightened. And only his roughened voice gave away the fact that the kiss had affected him in any way at all. "See you in the morning."

Inside her room, Susan touched the violets on her shoulder and leaned against the door with tightly closed eyes. "Jake, oh Jake," she whispered into the empty darkness. "I've fallen in love with you. What am I going to do?"

CHAPTER NINE

"DID I WAKE YOU?" Jake asked.

"No, I was just lying here in bed watching the morning light stream in from the balcony."

There was a brief silence. As Jake and Susan listened to the other breathing on the telephone line, each wondered what it would be like if Jake were watching the morning light alongside her.

Susan moved against the pillows and then clutched the phone more tightly to her ear. "You know, light looks different in Paris, more pearly somehow."

Jake chuckled. "Everything looks different in Paris. That's what I'm counting on. Listen, I know it's early, but we should get an early start. Can you meet me downstairs for breakfast in half an hour?"

"That sounds lovely. Make it forty-five minutes and you've got a deal."

When Jake hung up, Susan lay in bed for a moment, her fingers still curled around the receiver, which seemed warm from his voice. She replaced it and, smiling broadly, got up and headed to the closet.

For her day of playing tourist Susan selected a houndstooth wool blazer with a relaxed cut and wore it over jeans and a taupe cotton-knit T-shirt. She flicked back her hair from her forehead and held it in place with a small antique-design barrette. A bit of mauve shadow, a touch of blusher and some light pink lip gloss completed her toilet.

"Sleep well last night?" Jake asked when they'd settled down at a table near a tall window overlooking the hotel's courtyard garden. Susan didn't answer until after the waiter had served them milky coffee and croissants. Jake, too, she noticed, was casually dressed for a change. Could he have taken her remark about his three-piece suits seriously? He looked handsome in khaki pants, a chambray shirt and a corduroy sport coat.

"I slept all right—a little restless, maybe," Susan conceded when they were alone. "Strange bed, you know."

The corners of Jake's finely cut mouth dented. "I was more than a little restless, and it had nothing to do with the bed being strange." He took a travel book out of his pocket. "I've mapped out an itinerary for us. How does this sound—the Eiffel Tower, then the Place de la Concorde and the Place Vendôme? We have a look at the Arc de Triomphe and stop for lunch at one of the cafés on the Champs-Elysées. Then on to Notre Dame, Sacré-Coeur and The Louvre. We can finish up with dinner and a boat ride on the Seine."

"Goodness, that sounds very ambitious. Did you stay up late last night working all that out?"

With a sudden grin, Jake put the book away. "Ye little old tour director, that's me."

"Really?"

He stirred his coffee. "It gave me something to do. I was frustrated, you see. And when I'm frustrated, I make lists. I organize things, anything. My sister says I was born trying to set the world in order. Sometimes it helps, sometimes it doesn't. Last night it didn't."

"Oh?"

"Yes, my sweet Susan, oh. Helpless dreamer that I am, I kept right on picturing you, just three tantalizing steps across the hall, stretched out in a black lace nightgown. Do you wear black lace nightgowns?''

"No, pastel cotton shifts.''

"Hmm, we'll have to do something about that, because when this dream becomes a reality I want all the details to be right.''

"Jake—''

But he was not to be deterred. "Susan, I ache for you. With every day that goes by, I ache for you more. If you've got some idea of me as a playboy just out to carve notches in his bedpost, that's all wrong. It's not a casual thing I feel for you, you must understand that by now. It's not exactly a sudden thing, either. We've known each other for over a year.''

"That's true,'' Susan countered quickly, "but for most of that time it's been purely as business associates. In most ways we really don't know each other well at all.''

"Then let's rectify that. Ask me anything, and I promise I'll do my best to tell the truth and nothing but. I want you to understand me better. And—'' his voice deepened slightly "—I want to know you.''

As Susan stared across the table at Jake, taking in his earnest passion, the sincerity in his eyes, a cold knot tied itself somewhere deep in her stomach. Oh, if only they could talk, if only they could be perfectly honest!

"All right, counselor,'' she said weakly. "Until recently I couldn't picture you in anything but gray flannel. I still can't picture you as a kid. What were you like? Were you conducting cross-examinations by the time you were four?''

"Earlier.'' Jake laughed. "Actually, I was crazy about tennis. I dreamed of being a tennis pro and haunted the courts.''

"What happened?''

Jake shrugged. "Life, I guess. I won a few junior tournaments and played on the team in college. But then came marriage and law school and I didn't have the time for games, at least not the kind that involve nets and rackets."

Breakfast lasted longer than either of them had planned. While Jake described his youthful tennis matches, his battles with his older sister and the terrifying yearly visits of his formidable Great-aunt Beatrice, Susan nibbled her croissant, sipped her coffee and listened enthralled.

Jake's reminiscences about the goings-on at his prosperous family home described a milieu so utterly different from the one in which Susan had grown up. Yet it was strangely familiar. For it was not unlike the world of the rich she'd seen in the movies and on television—or so it seemed to her. Yet, that fact no longer made her feel resentful. For all his clean-cut looks and privileged background, Jake was a warm man, with carefully controlled but real vulnerabilities. *In the end we're all linked by the fact that we're merely human,* she mused.

After breakfast, they set off on their pilgrimage to see the sights of Paris. Susan found it wasn't difficult to play first-time tourist for Jake's benefit. Seeing things with him was like seeing them afresh.

At the top of the Eiffel Tower he rested a hand on her shoulder and together they stared out at the city. The great avenues swept out to all points of the compass, spires and monuments glistening in the sunlight. The angular, multi-leveled slate rooftops were pewter and lavender, colors that epitomized the ancient city. And even from this height the wind seemed to carry the damp winter fragrance of Paris with it.

A Métro trip took them to the Champs-Elysées where Jake insisted on buying the custom-blended perfume they'd discussed the night before. Jake teased Susan into smelling a multitude of little bottles filled with essential oils with exotic names. They debated the virtues of jasmine, honeysuckle, tuberose, and the controversial lemon.

"Honeysuckle is too sweet."

"Not for you."

"But mixed with lemon?"

"Just a hint. It'll be perfect, you'll see."

When the final selection was concocted and bottled in a handsome crystal container, Jake sniffed it appreciatively, then dabbed a bit behind Susan's ears and sniffed again. "Intoxicating," he whispered against the soft flesh of her earlobe. "Tart and sweet and tantalizing all at the same time."

Laughing a protest, Susan shot an embarrassed look at the smiling saleslady. But inside her practical walking shoes, Susan's toes curled with pleasure.

After a light lunch at a café they checked their maps and sauntered toward the Seine. It was a beautiful day. Bright sunshine showed off the architecture of the leafless chestnuts arched against a robin's-egg-blue sky. They visited the Louvre and the Musée du Jeu de Paume to see the Mona Lisa and the great Impressionists. But they didn't stay in either place for long. Susan wanted to be outside enjoying the crisp, clear beauty of the city.

They wandered back down to the river, browsing in the bookstalls and drinking in the special atmosphere. Then they inspected the stained-glass windows and gargoyles at Notre Dame. "It's just about dinner time," Jake finally pointed out.

"We haven't done half the things you had on your list."

"I know, and I don't think we're going to, either."

Susan laughed. "It would have taken three days to do all you planned."

Jake threw up his palms. "So I'm a little over-eager, so sue me. Hungry?"

"Just a little."

"Then let's head back across the Pont Neuf."

He took her to a restaurant with a view of Notre Dame's floodlit spires. Settling in a shadowy corner, they ordered the special of the day, a lobster soufflé. While they waited for their meal, they sipped their Chablis and talked.

"Maybe we didn't accomplish it all, but what we did do was wonderful. It's been a beautiful day," Susan said wistfully.

"Yes, a nice break. Tomorrow, I expect to hear from Interpol, which means we'll have to get back to business chasing down the third Byrnside orphan. But there'll be other trips to Paris and other beautiful days for us, Susan. At least, I hope there will." He set down his wine glass, folded his hands on the table and searched her face. "I've tried to answer all your questions about myself. I've told you how I survived measles, won a spelling bee in fifth grade and lost my dog when my dad took me hunting in Maine. But there's only one way a man and woman can really learn about each other."

"By living together," Susan said hesitantly.

Wry little brackets formed around Jake's lips. "You've got part of it. By living together, sleeping together, and loving together. All day I've talked about me because you said that's what you wanted to hear. But you haven't said much about you, Susan. Really, you're still a bit of a mystery lady. Is there anything you want me to know?"

Tongue-tied, she sat thinking about all the things she'd kept hidden from him, all the ways in which she'd deceived him. Now was the time to tell the truth, surely. But when she did that, what would be his reaction?

Jake, so handsome that the sight of him made her heart ache, was looking at her with the eyes of a man in love. Oh yes, her woman's instincts recognized that look—though she'd never seen it on any man's face before and had never expected to see it, never in her wildest fantasies dreamed she'd see it in the eyes of a man like Jake. How could she risk losing something so wonderful when there was so little time to savor the experience?

Susan reached across the table and laid her hand on Jake's tightly folded ones. She could feel his tension in the taut sinews and long, stiffly laced fingers. "Jake," she said softly, "would you like to sleep in my room tonight?"

His fingers uncurled and enfolded hers. "Yes," he said, breaking into a smile, "I most definitely would! But I'd better warn you now—" he gave her a meaningful look "—there isn't going to be much sleeping!"

AFTER DINNER they hailed a cab and rode back to their hotel. The atmosphere between them hummed with excitement. In front of her door, Susan paused, fumbling for her key.

"Nervous?" Jake asked her.

Susan lowered her eyes. "Yes. Very."

Jake laid a strong hand over hers. "I'm a lawyer, so I'm supposed to be a shrewd negotiator. I know I should press my advantage, not give you a chance to back out. But this is just too important for that, Susan. Do you want to say good-night to me right here?"

She shook her head. "No, I don't want to say good-night to you at all. But," she added more lightly, "as they say in the movies, I do want to slip into something more comfortable."

Gladness and relief shone in Jake's eyes. "Then why don't you go in and do that? I'll join you in a few minutes."

Susan watched him disappear into his own room. Then she unlocked her door and stood leaning against it, gazing at the smoothly made up double bed. What should she do? Should she strip and pose naked on it? The notion made her giggle nervously.

Before, when Jake had kissed her senseless in her apartment, the passion had flared up between them spontaneously. But this was going to be premeditated, a decision they had both made. It was a little daunting.

She went into the bathroom and looked at herself in the oval mirror. Then she began taking off her clothes. Beneath them she wore a black lace underwire bra and a matching pair of high-cut bikini pants. She'd purchased both expensive wisps of lace especially to wear in Paris—guessing that this might happen? Perhaps.

Leaving the sexy underwear in place, she opened the bottle of perfume Jake had purchased for her and began dabbing it about in strategic spots. She so wanted this to be a special night, a night she could remember when everything else fell apart.

When the perfume was in place, filling the small bathroom with its tart sweetness, she put on a flowered silk wrap, looped the tie around her narrow waist and then went to the fragile wooden chair opposite the French doors and sat down to wait.

Jake was taking longer than she'd expected. Was something wrong? Had he had second thoughts himself? When he finally knocked on the door, she was startled. Apparently she'd fallen into some kind of trance.

"Come in."

He'd taken off his jacket, but otherwise hadn't changed his clothes. He carried a tray with a bottle of champagne and two glasses.

"This is a special occasion," he said after he'd shut the door behind him and set the tray down next to the bed. "Very special," he added, straightening while his eyes drank her in.

Her knee-length wrap had fallen open so that the lamplight bathed her thighs and calves, making them look like pale pink alabaster. The V of the robe's neckline had fallen open across her breasts, too, revealing the upper half of her bra and the soft white swellings it cupped.

"You look so beautiful sitting there, Susan." He swallowed and suddenly she realized that he was nervous. Jake, nervous? What a startling notion! But, as the realization sank in it inspired Susan with a newfound confidence.

"Would you like the champagne now?" he asked.

"No, later." She rose and crossed to him. Maybe she was inexperienced, but that didn't mean she had to be unimaginative and she wanted this to be a night to remember—for both of them. She stood directly in front of Jake, looking into his eyes, and then began unbuttoning his shirt. The dark hairs on his chest that sprang forth as she slid each small white button out of its hole tickled her fingers.

"With the exception of my mother when I was a little kid, I've never been undressed by a woman before," Jake said huskily.

"Never?" She tugged his shirt out of his waistband and then studied the buckle on his belt.

"Never."

"Are you enjoying it? Am I doing it right?"

"Yes to both, but now it's my turn." He took her hands away from his belt and untied her robe. It fell open, revealing her breasts in the skimpy bra, her flat belly and the scrap of black lace panty.

"You were lovely before, but now you're breath-taking."

And, indeed, as Jake spoke his breath seemed to be catching in his throat. He shrugged out of his shirt and stepped from his shoes. Then he slipped the robe from Susan's shoulders. It slid down her body and puddled on the floor around her feet.

"Let me look at you. Oh, Susan."

"I'm just your average executive assistant in black underwear," she tried to say lightly. But her voice caught, just as his had a moment earlier.

"There's nothing ordinary about you, and there never has been." He pulled her to him and buried his face in the softness of her breasts. "I'd hoped you'd wear the perfume for me," he murmured as he inhaled its sweet fragrance. "There's a line of poetry about a drunken bee in a spring meadow drowning in nectar. I know exactly how the little guy felt."

"You're the bee and I'm the meadow?" she asked huskily.

"Right now, yes, though you don't need to be anything but you to intoxicate the hell out of me."

While Susan smiled uncertainly, he drew her to him again and kissed her eyes, and throat, then her mouth. Under his increasingly feverish caresses her lips grew warm and beneath his fingers her nipples hardened. With a passionate sigh, she arched her back and threw back her head, inviting him to explore the sensitive column of her throat.

"You like that, don't you?" he whispered.

"Yes."

"So do I."

She knew Jake as such a carefully controlled man. But he didn't seem controlled now. As his lips sought the tender hollow where her pulse throbbed, a hard flush lay along his cheekbones, and the skin of his broad chest and shoulders felt as if it were burning. Susan suspected that her skin must feel just as overheated. Then when his mouth crushed hers again, her knees weakened and she sagged against him, unable to think about anything but the riot of sensations he was sending scorching through her.

Jake made a rough sound at the back of his throat and led her to the bed, where they both sank down on the soft mattress. Jake snapped off his belt and kicked off his slacks. Then he unhooked Susan's bra, and once he'd freed her breasts, again took a moment to luxuriate in their rounded beauty.

While she thrilled with passionate response, he kissed one and then the other, sucking on each pink nipple until it rose into a tight knob of pleasure. The tips of her breasts seemed connected by hot wires that were singing to other pleasure centers she'd hardly known existed. At last Jake ran his hands down the slim length of her body, hooked his thumbs into the waistband of her panties and, after one quick, questioning look into her half-closed eyes to gauge her assent, slid them off.

"Susan," he muttered again, "Susan."

"Jake," she whispered back and clung to him as they swayed on the bed and then lay bound together by their burning limbs.

Jake began to weave a mesh of kisses over Susan's breasts, down the slope of her rib cage and past her coiled navel where the skin was increasingly sensitive and tightened with each kiss. He moved lower and her body convulsed with the intensity of the sensation.

"Jake!" Her hands caressed him frantically and he slid up and drew her close. Little rills of perspiration flowed between Susan's breasts and, as their limbs quivered together, she tasted the salts of Jake's body, the sweet pressure and motion of his mouth.

When he parted her legs and settled his body over hers, she lifted her hips and opened herself to him. He was not the first. When she'd been a runaway adolescent on the streets Susan had a few brief encounters with a boy she'd met there. But that was long, long ago and so utterly different. This was the first time she had truly given herself to a man.

He began to move inside her and she was shaken into a scarlet blindness. The mounting sensations grew into a crescendo and then ended in a sudden silence. When it was over, they seemed to flutter down together from a far height. For long exquisite moments they lay together bathed in the passionate dew of each other's bodies.

Finally Jake raised himself a little and, gently now, began to place little kisses along Susan's thighs, the curve of her hips, over her breasts and throat, and then on her lips and fluttering lashes.

"You're lying so still, like a beautiful marble statue," he whispered against her cheek. "Aren't you going to say anything?"

"No, I'm afraid to."

"Why?"

"Because I'm afraid if I say something it will break the spell, and I don't want this, this closeness to end," she whispered back.

"It won't," he told her, tightening his own arms around her and laying his hard cheek against the top of her head. "After what we've just shared, how could it?"

How indeed? A little dart of pain seemed to strike Susan's chest. But she pressed her eyes shut and refused to think about tomorrow and what it might bring. For now, the night stretched ahead of her and Jake, a magical night that had only just begun.

Bathed by the silver moon and the twinkling lights of Paris, they drank their champagne. "To you, beautiful lady, and what we've found here together in this room. May we find it many more times over in many more rooms," Jake teased, clinking his glass with Susan's. After a sip, she put her glass down and kissed his cheek. But that tender little caress soon turned into something far more passionate and before long they were making love again.

At last, sated, they lay twined in each other's arms, murmuring endearments, stroking and petting.

"Want to make some plans?" Jake finally said as his fingers traced a lazy series of curlicues on Susan's rib cage.

"What kind of plans?" Susan asked drowsily. "You mean about the Byrnside quest?"

"No, I don't mean that at all. I'm talking about you-and-me plans, plans for our future together."

Against him he felt her go still. Then she stretched elaborately. "It's late, and we're both sleepy," she said with a yawn. "Who knows what tomorrow will bring? Let's talk about it in the morning, okay?"

"Okay."

Jake watched as Susan closed her eyes and settled back against the pillow. Gradually her body relaxed, her breathing evened out, slowed, and he knew she was asleep. It was disappointing in a sense, because part of her had gone away from him. Yet it also gave him an opportunity just to look at her, to feast his eyes.

How lovely she was with the moonlight bathing her face and slender body. It turned her hair to silver and frosted her lashes so that she looked like some fairy creature and not the warm, flesh-and-blood woman he now knew her to be. Jake wanted to touch her, kiss her, mold her flesh with his hands. But he shouldn't wake her up. She needed her sleep because in the morning they'd probably have to get back to work.

Indeed, it would be sensible if he tried to get some sleep himself. But he couldn't. He was too stirred, too excited, too thrilled by the wonder he'd discovered. *No more loneliness,* Jake thought, *no more wandering the earth like some lost soul.* With Susan tonight he'd found a new life, a new future.

His eyes traced the line of her hip, and again, despite his better judgment, he was tempted to wake her up and shower more kisses on her. He was disappointed she hadn't wanted to talk about their future together tonight. But she was right—it could wait until the morning. But he didn't want it to wait. He was like a frustrated kid panting to make the packages under the Christmas tree all his. He wanted everything between him and this woman signed, sealed and delivered right now.

Restlessly, Jake got up and opened the French doors so that a light breeze blew in. Then, with a tender, slightly regretful smile, he covered Susan's body with a blanket so she wouldn't get cold. After slipping on his fallen slacks, he walked over to a chair lost in the shadows in the corner and sat down. He wasn't ready to go to sleep yet. He wanted to sit and think.

An hour crept past, and Jake sat nodding. Suddenly something jerked him awake and he blinked at the darkness. He must have fallen asleep in this damned uncomfortable chair, he thought as he shifted his weight against the restricted wooden framework and felt a spasm stab through his back. How stupid! I'll probably be crippled come morning, if I'm not crippled already.

Painfully, because he really had cramped a muscle in his back, he positioned himself to get up and make his way back to bed when something, a barely detectable noise, made his head turn toward the balcony where the doors stood open, allowing the night to flow in. His muscles tensed. There it was again, a faint scraping.

Now, what in the world . . . a cat?

But cats didn't cast shadows that large. A shape moved stealthily out of the darkness and slipped noiselessly into the room. Just inside the French doors it paused. Then, with creeping menace, it began to move toward the bed.

Susan! Jake's heart lurched and, cramp or no cramp, he shot out of the chair and launched himself at the intruder. As he leaped forward, his foot hooked a leg of the wooden chair and it crashed back. The shadow whirled. A long-barreled gun with a silencer snicked and Jake felt a hot streak whip past his ear.

"Susan!" he cried as the threw himself at his attacker. His arms only caught air, for the intruder was already back through the doors. Picking himself up, Jake ran out to the balcony, but, agile as a cat, the intruder had already let himself down into the courtyard. As lights began to flick on in some of the hotel's other rooms, the figure disappeared through an open gate into the alley beyond.

"WELL, NOW EVERYONE in the hotel knows we spent last night together," Susan said the next morning at breakfast. Glumly, she nibbled at her croissant.

"This is Paris. Take my word for it, they would think it odd if we *didn't* spend the night together."

As Jake studied Susan, a worried frown creased his brow. He couldn't quite fathom her reaction to last night's misadventure. They'd reported the intruder and the shot to the apologetic staff at the hotel and notified the police, so the dust had settled somewhat. Still, why was Susan so quiet? Why wasn't she talking about what had happened, speculating about it? To Jake's mind, ever since the incident she'd behaved strangely.

Jake finished the last of his coffee. "I just can't figure it," he muttered. "Why would someone sneak into your room with a gun?"

"Maybe because the doors were open and the balcony's on the second floor and easy to climb to."

Jake shook his head. "It still doesn't make sense. What was he hoping to find?"

"Money. We're tourists, after all." Susan's eyes didn't meet Jake's and he knew this was a discussion she didn't want to have with him. But why not?

"Susan, I watched him move toward you with that gun. It was you he wanted to hurt."

"I was lying there naked. Maybe he just wanted to get a better look."

"Maybe." But Jake didn't think that was it. "Susan, is there any reason you can think of why someone would deliberately want to attack you?"

"Of course not. What reason could there possibly be?" She laughed nervously.

"I don't know. All I know is that one of us could have been killed last night."

"Well, we weren't. And a minute ago you told me we'd be checking out and leaving the city today." At last Susan lifted her head. Her golden eyes, huge in her pale face, had a look of resignation in them. "You've heard from Interpol, haven't you?"

"Yes, and just before I came down I got a call from my detective as well. The news is interesting. They've traced Lynn Rice's movements. Last year she went from Paris to Switzerland—to Lausanne."

If anything, Susan went a shade whiter. "Is that where we'll be going?"

"Yes. As soon as we can get packed and book tickets, we'll be on our way."

Again, Jake was nonplussed by Susan's reaction. He'd expected surprise, elation that at last after all these weeks of frustration they'd finally be hot on a real trail. And this time they'd be working together as a real team, not just as boss and assistant but as lovers. Instead, she looked as if she felt ill. Perhaps the incident last night had affected her more than he realized.

After breakfast they parted to do their packing. But as Jake went up to his room he felt weighed down by a load of questions, worries, half-formed fears. An intruder with a gun sneaking into Susan's room, her peculiar reaction to the fact, her equally peculiar lack of interest in the news about Lynn Rice and Switzerland. Something was wrong, very wrong. But what? Inside his room he was just slipping the last of his ties into his garment bag when the phone rang. Boston seemed like another world, so the sound of Frederica's voice came as a shock to Jake.

"Freddie, what in the world . . . is something wrong?"

"Well, I hope not, but I thought I'd better call and let you know."

"Let me know what?"

Freddie's voice had a self-righteous tone. "Are you there with that assistant of yours, that Miss Bonner?"

"Yes, Susan's here. Don't talk about her as if she were a stranger. You met her."

"I certainly did. And I remember how you said she'd claimed she'd graduated from Radcliffe. Well, Molly just found her yearbook and made a few calls. It's as I thought. Your Miss Bonner is lying to you, Jake. She never set foot in Radcliffe."

CHAPTER TEN

SUSAN PEERED OUT the window at the green and orderly undulations of the Burgundy landscape, which seemed to be rolling past the tracks.

She was glad she and Jake had decided to take a train instead of flying. As he'd pointed out, it was not only a lot more scenic, it made sense. Switzerland was the railway junction of western and central Europe. In Paris they'd been able to step right onto a train with a stop in Lausanne, whereas finding a flight would have involved more time, long taxi rides, extra connections.

But the real reason Susan was glad to be gliding along through the French countryside instead of zooming through the sky was that it gave her a chance to think, to try to adapt to the circumstances which had changed so dramatically in the last twenty-four hours.

With a shiver, she remembered how it had been to wake up to the snick of a silencer bullet aimed at Jake and to realize that because of her he had nearly been killed. For, of course, she knew perfectly well that the intruder had come for her. Despite what she'd said to Jake at breakfast, she knew it had been no chance robber sneaking into her room. Somehow, her cover had been blown. Whoever had tried to kill her in Switzerland a year earlier had seen through her masquerade and had tracked her down in Paris to make good on his unfinished business.

Susan shot a glance at Jake who had his aristocratic nose buried in a Swiss guidebook. It seemed as if he'd been reading either that or a newspaper all afternoon. In fact, since leaving Paris he'd been awfully quiet, she suddenly realized. Of course, she hadn't exactly had much to say herself.

Susan's eyes traced the line of Jake's brow, his straight nose with its sculpted nostrils, the clean, slightly ascetic mouth and squarish jaw. She loved this man, she acknowledged with a pang which shot clear through her. After the joys of their lovemaking, after the way he'd stripped off his mask of cool control and shown her such wild yet tender passion, the thought of losing him made her want to curl up and die inside. And she could have lost him forever. If that assassin's bullet had been closer by an inch . . .

Stifling a gasp, Susan clasped her hands together so tightly her knuckles whitened. She should tell Jake the truth, and she should do it now.

"Jake—"

"Um." He looked up from his book and Susan found herself wondering with a disturbing little shock if this could really be the same man who'd made such unreserved love to her only the night before.

His gaze as he studied her was cool and distant, as if she were a stranger he wasn't sure he wanted to meet. In fact, it was the way she'd seen him look at clients he didn't trust. Perhaps she'd imagined last night, she thought a little wildly. Perhaps right now she was just in the middle of a bad dream. .

"We should be pulling into Lausanne around midnight," he said. "I know that's late, but we can grab a taxi directly to the hotel. I've made reservations at the Carleton, the same place where Lynn Rice was registered."

"Oh." A chill ran up Susan's spine. That was where she and the assassin had first encountered each other. His attempt to kill her was all tied up with the Byrnside quest. That, by now, she knew. But even after a year of effort she was little closer to discovering his identity or motive. And now they were headed back to the scene of the crime. What if he attacked her there again?

Suddenly the train entered a tunnel. As it rushed through the close blackness, Susan choked back a panicked scream. That's what her life had become, she thought. She was locked into a dark tunnel from which there was no escape, and she was about to shoot out the other side into a terrifying unknown.

THE TRAIN WHIRRED through the darkness on its steel tracks, and Jake sat staring straight ahead. Next to him he could hear Susan breathing, feel her tension. He could tell she was upset and he longed to reach out to her, take her hand. But his fingers remained clamped around the book in his lap, the book he'd been using as a pretext for not talking to her.

Last night he'd thought he knew the woman lying in his arms. Last night he'd thought he loved her, and that if she could only be brought to agree, he wanted to try to build a new future with her. He'd even pictured what their children might be like—blond, with his gray eyes, brown-haired with her golden-brown eyes, quick and efficient, slightly shy yet eager, like both of them. Oh, he'd allowed himself to build a whole card castle of pretty fantasies.

But now, now after Freddie's call and the doubts Susan's strange behavior had raised, Jake didn't know what to think. Did he really know this woman sitting so close to him he could smell the sweet, clean scent of her hair, feel the warmth of her skin, this woman he'd made love to and woven such foolish dreams around? Or was she a cold and calculating stranger, silently laughing at his naive infatuation?

FOUR ROWS DOWN the train's aisle a cold and calculating stranger sat gazing at the backs of Jake's and Susan's heads. What charmed lives these Byrnside orphans had! Never before had the killer felt so frustrated. And now it was too late. After being informed of last night's fiasco, the killer's employer had announced that their contract was about to be terminated.

"Follow them, see where they go and report back," the killer's employer had said. "But don't make any further contact. It's too late for Plan One now. I'll just have to see what develops and think of some other way to deal with this damnable situation."

SUSAN AND JAKE arrived at the Carleton very late and very exhausted. Nevertheless, as they approached the registration desk Susan was suddenly on pins and needles. Had Jake booked one room or two?

He'd been so withdrawn all day. At first, taken up with her many fears and worries, she hadn't noticed. But gradually the change in him had penetrated her consciousness. It wasn't anything dramatic, just a slight coolness in his expression, a reserve in his voice when he spoke to her, on the rare occasions he did speak. Probably it was just the stress of all that had happened since last night, she told herself. Jake had a lot on his mind, and after all, she didn't feel much like talking, either.

Still, the change in him was beginning to worry her. Was there any chance that Jake knew more about Lynn Rice than he'd told her?

"Ah yes, Miss Bonner and Mr. Caine. Welcome to Switzerland. I have your reservations right here," the man at the desk said in his faintly accented English. "Oh, and I have a message for you, Mr. Caine. It arrived late this afternoon." He handed Jake a small sealed envelope, which Jake, after nodding his thanks, tucked into his breast pocket without opening.

The man took out two keys. "Miss Bonner will be in room 402 and Mr. Caine, you will be in 406. And I hope you will have a most pleasant stay."

With smooth efficiency, the desk clerk directed the bellboy to collect their bags and take them up to their rooms. While they followed behind, Susan's mind whirled. So Jake had booked them separate rooms. After last night, oughtn't he at least to have asked her if she wanted to stay with him? And what was in the message Jake had received that he hadn't read in front of her? Again she wondered if he knew something about Lynn Rice that he was keeping to himself, something that was changing his attitude toward Susan Bonner.

Still, when the bellboy left and she had finally closed the door of her room behind her, she had to admit that she was glad to be alone. Perhaps Jake had arranged for them to spend the night separately out of simple consideration. As she'd learned, he was a very thoughtful man. Perhaps he'd known how tired and disoriented she would feel after such a quick departure from Paris—though he couldn't have known all the reasons for her emotional fatigue.

Susan walked to the window and looked out. The Carleton was situated between the city center and Ouchy. This was not the actual room where she'd stayed during her surgery, but it looked out on the same quiet residential street. A sense of déjà vu assailed Susan so strongly that she turned and stared into the mirror over the bureau on the adjacent wall. Despite her pallor, the woman who looked back at her was pretty—small, delicate, blond and pretty.

It was in this hotel that Susan had seen her Cinderella transformation for the first time. It was here that the set of unflawed features that gazed back at her now had emerged from beneath the plastic surgeon's bandages. And she still hadn't come to terms with that reflection. She still couldn't truly believe that it was really her. Yet it was this image that Jake knew and wanted to make love with. So their whole relationship was based on a lie, she thought in sudden sharp despair. And it was a lie that was about to blow up in both their faces. She had to tell Jake the truth! Tomorrow, first thing, she'd make herself do it, no matter what.

STILL FULLY DRESSED, Jake leaned back against the headboard in his darkened room. He'd just put down the phone and was thinking about the new information he'd received from his detective. At last the man was earning his keep.

After another moment's thought, Jake straightened, retrieved the receiver on the bedside table and asked the hotel operator to put him through to the States. It would be very early in New England. But, as he recalled, Owen Byrnside almost always woke up at the crack of dawn and it was time he reported to the old man. This particular bulletin should interest him.

"It's about time, Caine," Owen exclaimed, sounding surprisingly close, considering that he was on the other side of the Atlantic. "I've been wondering what you were up to."

"I didn't wake you, did I?"

"I may be old and feeble," Owen shot back, "but I'm not a mummy—yet. Unlike the rest of the slugabeds in this house, I still wake up with the birds. But if you have information on my third orphan you can call me anytime, day or night. Haven't I already made that plain?''

''Well, I do have information. And it's fairly intriguing.''

The old man's voice sounded suddenly intent. ''What? Tell me, Caine.''

''In Paris I learned from Interpol that Lynn Rice went on to Switzerland, to Lausanne, in fact.''

''Lausanne. Now let me see. That's one of those medieval mountain resort towns stacked up around a lake, isn't it?''

''Yes, it's two-thirds of the way along the north shore of Lake Geneva, a major metropolis but very charming and picturesque. Up in the foothills overlooking the lake there are some old castles and estates that have been turned into chic resorts and health spas.''

''I'm not interested in a travelogue, Caine. As you may recall, I'm not exactly in shape to go mountain climbing these days.''

The corners of Jake's mouth twitched slightly. ''I had a reason for mentioning those health spas, Owen.''

''Why? Is that where Lynn Rice has been hiding out all this time? At a Swiss health spa?''

''Not exactly. But, according to my information, a year ago she was heading for one of them. Or, rather, not to a spa but to a private clinic called Château de Grâce.''

Jake heard Owen expel a sharp breath. ''Why would she go to a damn-fool place like that?'' he demanded. ''Was she sick?''

''Not to my knowledge. The clinic in question is very private and very exclusive. It caters to wealthy women and specializes in plastic surgery.''

"Plastic surgery!" Owen's astonishment rang down the line.

"Owen, all this time we've been searching for a woman with a badly scarred face. But maybe that was a mistake. Maybe Lynn Rice lost those scars when she came out here."

"Or why else would she have gone at all," Owen added. "But that raises another question. Didn't I hear you say that this Swiss place of yours with the la-di-da name caters to rich women?"

"You did. Private clinics with world-renowned surgeons on the staff don't come cheap."

"But that third girl of mine was a cop with a salary that could hardly fit under a microscope. Where would she have gotten that kind of money?"

Jake shifted his weight. "Good question, Owen. And one I've been asking myself. The plot thickens, doesn't it?"

"Thickens! It's turning into pea soup! My God, but I wish I were a younger man with a decent ticker," Owen muttered. "Like a shot I'd be on the first plane out there to look into this business with you."

"You can count on me to do your legwork, Owen. First thing tomorrow morning I intend to pay the Château de Grâce a visit."

"You keep me informed, you hear?"

"I'll do that."

"How's that Miss Bonner of yours doing?"

Jake's dark brows drew together slightly and he cast a glance at his closed door. "She's not my Miss Bonner, Owen."

"Well, she works for you, doesn't she? What's wrong? You two have a spat?"

"No, everything's going smoothly," Jake fibbed. No point bringing up his fresh doubts or the business about the intruder—not until he knew more.

"Well, I took a shine to that girl, so you take good care of her."

"I will, Owen."

"And call just as soon as you find out anything because I'll be waiting around on pins and needles."

"Will do." A-okay, roger and out, Jake added mentally just as soon as he'd replaced the receiver.

He pushed himself off the edge of the bed and began to pace in front of it. He thought about his plans for the morning and about Susan. Again, he glanced at the door. What was she doing now, he wondered. Sleeping? He pictured her lying in bed, her slim body swathed in a white nightgown, the moon frosting her hair and silvering her lashes. A painful shudder rippled through Jake and he stopped short, raised a weary hand and began to massage his temple.

Normally he would have planned to tell Susan about the clinic while they breakfasted together and then taken her with him when he went out to investigate the place. But now things were different. Now perhaps that wasn't what he should do at all.

SUSAN WAS SURPRISED when she opened her eyes and read the time on her wristwatch. Eight a.m. She'd slept longer than she'd expected, but she'd also expected that Jake would have called to wake her by now. She sat up against the pillows, ran a hand through her tousled hair and gazed at the puddle of sunlight that spilled across the foot of her bed. Usually Jake was so eager to get an early start. What was different about this morning?

Susan got up, went to the bathroom and listened for the phone while she dressed herself in a casual skirt, blouse and matching cardigan. When her phone didn't ring she picked it up and asked the operator for Jake's room. But no one answered there. Had Jake assumed she'd meet him for breakfast at eight? Was he down there now waiting for her?

A few minutes later Susan crossed the lobby and peered into the hotel's dining room. Prosperous-looking businessmen sat huddled over silver coffeepots. Smiling family groups passed platters of pancakes and baskets of glazed rolls back and forth while they planned their day's outing. But Jake was nowhere to be seen.

As Susan looked around she got a panicky feeling in the pit of her stomach. Something was wrong; she knew it. Uneasily, she retreated and approached the desk clerk.

"Ah, yes," he told her. "Mr. Caine left the hotel very early this morning. But he did stop and drop off a message for you. Here you are, *mademoiselle*."

Susan opened the folded square of note paper and felt her heart drop. "I have a million things to do this morning," it read, "but there's no reason why you should have to tag along. Take the morning off to get some rest or see the sights. Meet me at the Beau-Rivage at one o'clock for lunch. Jake."

She reread it, and then read it again. The third time through, her stomach settled somewhat. Maybe she was overreacting and it meant just exactly what it said. Why imagine something sinister just because Jake had decided to spend the morning working without her? He knew she was tired and that she'd had a bad experience in Paris. Maybe this was just another instance of his thoughtfulness. Still, as Susan folded the note and stuck it in her pocket, her uneasiness didn't go away.

After a light breakfast of coffee and cereal, she decided to spend the morning in the old *cité* clustered around Notre Dame and the castle of St. Maire, a fine example of carefully restored Burgundian Gothic. After visiting the cathedral and a few other of the medieval buildings recommended by her guidebook, she wandered to the marketplace. There, the French character of Lausanne was strong. Everywhere local citizens bustled about with string bags, carefully selecting the ingredients for tonight's exquisite dinner.

As Susan wandered among the stalls admiring the colorful displays of fresh fruit and vegetables, she wished she felt like the carefree tourist she was impersonating. But that was impossible. She kept thinking about the killer who'd attacked her and wondered if he were circulating somewhere in the crowd near her. What's more, try as she might, she couldn't stop worrying about Jake. Where was he now, she fretted, and what was he doing? More to the point, what was he finding out?

JAKE STEPPED OUT of the taxi, paid the driver, and then peered up at the discreetly lettered sign next to the closed wrought-iron gates. Château de Grâce. He rang a bell and waited until a porter materialized from a gatehouse and asked in French about the purpose of his visit.

"My name is Jacob Caine," Jake replied in the same language. "I called early this morning and was given an appointment with your director, Monsieur DuVerlis."

"Ah, yes. Just one moment, please."

The little man disappeared to make a call, then reemerged a moment later to press an electric button that opened the gate. Jake strolled through and up the brick-paved avenue that led to the main building, still hidden by evergreens at the top of the hill. As he walked, he glanced around at the clinic's carefully maintained grounds and enjoyed the sparkling clarity of the air and the stunning view of a wind-ruffled Lake Geneva that stretched out in sapphire splendor below the road.

When he emerged from between a dense row of pines he got his first unobstructed view of Château de Grâce. It had been appropriately named. The sprawling mansion with its deep eaves, red-tiled roof and soft gray stucco walls and outbuildings was beautifully preserved. Everything about it exuded a decorous prosperity. Obviously, the plastic surgery business was a profitable one.

Inside the Château, this conclusion was underlined by the polished black-oak floors topped by Oriental rugs, the perfectly maintained antiques, and the air of quiet elegance worn by the multilingual receptionist who greeted Jake and bade him take a seat in the large, airy waiting room.

"The director will see you now," she said a few minutes later and led him into a large office that enjoyed a sweeping view of the gardens and lake.

Monsieur DuVerlis was a portly, balding man with a tiny mustache and observant brown eyes behind round, gold-framed spectacles. "Ah, Mr. Caine. I hope you had no trouble finding us."

"None at all."

"*Bon.* We are a bit out of the way here and I must confess we like it that way, as we enjoy our privacy. Please sit down. Now, how is it that I may serve you?"

Jake cleared his throat, arched his hands over his knees and began an edited version of his employer's search for Lynn Rice. "Our latest information indicates she came to the Château, possibly for plastic surgery," he concluded. "I'm hoping, naturally, that you may have some record."

As he'd listened, Monsieur DuVerlis had tented his own small, carefully tended hands over the handsome leather blotter on his desk. Now he stood, went to his files and withdrew a folder which he opened with a brisk snap and set in front of Jake. "Was this the young lady you seek?"

Jake studied the pictures of Lynn Rice, which were much better than any he'd yet seen of the woman. Before him lay a series of mercilessly lit photographs showing her full face and both profiles. As he studied the images, a knot began to grow in his stomach. There was something in them he hadn't seen before, something distressingly familiar.

"Yes," he said tightly. "This is the person."

The director nodded. "Ah, then perhaps I can be of some small assistance. You see, I remember this particular patient very well because of the many unusual circumstances surrounding her stay with us."

"Unusual circumstances?"

"Indeed." Monsieur DuVerlis gathered up the photographs and documents. "You see, first of all Mademoiselle Rice's surgery to have her burn scar removed was arranged and paid for by an anonymous donor. That alone is unusual enough."

"It certainly is," Jake exclaimed, his mind reeling. "An anonymous donor, you say?"

"Yes, but what is even stranger is that after Mademoiselle Rice's surgery was complete, on the day when her bandages were to have been removed in fact, she vanished—which is, to say the least, a most unusual occurrence, even unheard-of, as for most of our patients this is a long-awaited occasion of some importance."

Once again Jake's square jaw slackened. "You mean she never showed up to inspect the results of her operation?"

Monsieur DuVerlis's lips pursed into a moue of disapproval. "Naturally, she could not walk around in bandages indefinitely, so it is likely that she unveiled those results in private. But she did not keep her appointment to allow us to scrutinize them, which is most irregular and distressing. And when we tried to contact her at her hotel, we were told that she had checked out and left no forwarding address.''

Deep in thought over this new development, Jake scowled and rubbed his chin. ''That would mean you have no record of Lynn Rice's altered appearance.''

''Normally we would keep before-and-after photographs,'' Monsieur DuVerlis agreed. ''But as you can see, in this case it was impossible. However, we are not entirely at a loss,'' he added with a touch of pride.

''Oh?''

''Before such delicate surgery is undertaken at Château de Grâce, our technical staff develops a computer image of what the patient can expect the final result to be. Unless I am greatly in error, it would still be possible for us to call that image up onto our screens. Would you care to inspect it?''

''Yes, I would.'' Jake rose up out of his chair. ''As soon as possible.''

''Then come with me to the technician's area, and we will see what can be accomplished.''

Jake followed the director from his office and down a short corridor to a room where several computer screens glowed. After Monsieur DuVerlis issued some rapid-fire instructions to the woman in charge there, the two men stood waiting behind her while she manipulated a keyboard.

During the long seconds while names and serial numbers flashed on the screen, Jake felt himself go into a cold sweat. This whole scene was beginning to feel like a nightmare. He had to be wrong, he told himself. He had to be!

But when the image the director had boasted of finally materialized and was spat out by the dot-matrix printer, Jake knew that his suspicions, incredible as they seemed, were right. He accepted the sheet of paper the technician tore off and, trying to master his reactions, studied it. The hair was different—darker, longer, a much less flattering style. And the features weren't quite exact. But he recognized the face and knew the woman who now wore it. It was Susan. Lynn Rice and Susan Bonner were the same person.

CHAPTER ELEVEN

THE BEAU-RIVAGE was justly famed as one of the great hotels of Europe. It stood in its own gardens facing the lake at Chemin du Beau-Rivage. As Susan wandered through those gardens, she tried to relax and enjoy the wonderful scenery surrounding her and the crystalline beauty of the perfect day.

With a nervous little sigh, she checked her watch. It was almost one, time to meet Jake. At the entrance to the hotel's dining room the maître d' acknowledged Jake's reservation and led her to a table by the window. Since Jake hadn't arrived yet, she ordered a mineral water and settled back in her chair to wait.

Ten minutes later she spotted his tall, lean figure striding toward her. At the sight of him, her heart fluttered and, automatically, the corners of her mouth lifted. He was such a strikingly well-put-together man. Even in this urbane assemblage of wealthy Europeans on holiday, admiring eyes, both male and female, followed after him.

But Susan's reaction was tempered somewhat when she saw the look on his face. He was wearing his "lawyer" expression—cool, controlled and shuttered.

"Sorry to keep you waiting. My taxi ran into a traffic snarl."

"I haven't been waiting long, Jake."

"Beautiful day." He sat down and shook out a napkin. "Have you ordered a drink?"

"Just mineral water. I don't want anything stronger."

"Well, I do." He asked the waiter who had materialized at his shoulder for a martini, dry and up.

"I don't believe I've ever heard you order a martini before."

"There are certain occasions for which their acerbic quality and numbing alcoholic content seem suited."

Susan blinked. "Oh? Is this one of them?"

"Yes, I'm afraid it is." He folded his hands on the table in front of him and gazed at her so long and so searchingly that she felt as if she were in the glare of a spotlight. "I'm afraid it is," he repeated softly, "Lynn."

The name hung in the air between them, vibrating in the taut silence like a struck bell. Lynn could think of nothing to say. No response seemed appropriate. Her mouth had gone dry as cotton batting and her tongue felt glued in place behind her clenched teeth.

She was given a brief moment to gather her wits by the waiter who came with Jake's drink and set it down in front of him with an obsequious little flourish. She watched as Jake took a long, careful sip. All the while his flinty eyes never left hers.

"When did you find out?" she asked, unable to control the quiver in her voice or the nausea creeping through her stomach.

"This morning, though I began to suspect the truth our last day in Paris after I got a call from Freddie. She'd checked out Molly's yearbook and discovered that Susan Bonner hadn't gone anywhere near Radcliffe."

Good old Freddie, the working girl's friend, Lynn thought. But what did it matter if Freddie had suspected her? She'd known it was only a matter of hours before the truth finally came out. Oh, why hadn't she had the courage to tell Jake herself! She took a deep breath. "What happened this morning?"

Jake finished his drink, grimaced and then gave her a clipped account of his visit to the Château de Grâce. Lynn listened carefully, images of the place rolling before her mind's eye as she remembered all the details of her stay there. It all seemed like something someone else had done. That had been another life, another person.

"I'd forgotten about that computer thing," she muttered.

"Would *monsieur* or *madame* like to order now?"

Jake glanced at the smiling waiter. "I think not, though I'll have another martini. *Mademoiselle* and I have something to discuss." When the waiter went away again, Jake looked at Lynn. "That's right, isn't it? Or are you very hungry?"

Lynn gazed at him in dumb misery. "I couldn't eat lunch now, Jake."

"Really? That's a shame. This place is rather famous. I was lucky to get a reservation. Should I have waited until we ordered before I used your correct name?"

"No."

"Oh, but maybe I should have. My little discovery appears to have cast rather a pall on our luncheon."

"Oh, Jake, please..."

Suddenly Jake's cool mask dropped away, and she caught a glimpse of the icy anger beneath. "Don't say 'please' to me, Susan—no, Lynn. That's your name— Lynn. There really is no such person as Susan Bonner at all, is there?"

"No." Her voice was a choked whisper.

"You just made her up?"

"I just made her up."

"Well, you did a damn good job of it." His gaze raked her. "You certainly had me fooled. I bought the whole act—the efficiency, the slightly mysterious reserve, the private-school education, the Alice-in-Wonderland air. It never even occurred to me that it was all a lie."

Lynn opened her mouth and then shut it again. What could she say that would make any difference now? He was right. Susan Bonner had been a lie. She *had* deceived him.

"Lady, you are quite an actress. The person you really are isn't anything like Susan Bonner, is she?"

"No I suppose she's not, not in the obvious ways."

"What's that supposed to mean?"

"Only that in outward things she's a vast improvement. You've seen my picture and read that report on me. You know that I was scarred, and not just by the fire that burned me when I was a baby. I grew up in some pretty tough circumstances, experiencing things that you don't even know about—that nobody knows about. But Susan Bonner—she didn't have that kind of background. Not only was she far better-looking than poor, ugly, little Lynn Rice, she was far better educated and a lot more respectable."

"And you liked being her, didn't you?"

Lynn fiddled with the white linen napkin in front of her. "Yes," she admitted.

"I just bet you did!" Jake spat out.

She was stung. "Do you blame me so much? All my life I'd envied girls like Susan, girls who seemed to have it all, who looked right, talked right, had the right kind of background. It was exhilarating to slip into Susan's skin and to find that I could actually do it, addictive almost."

"Addictive?"

"Yes." As Lynn made the admission she realized just how true it really was. She hadn't acknowledged the fact to herself before, but being Susan Bonner *had* been addictive. Maybe that was why, despite her better judgment, she'd carried the masquerade on for so long.

It hadn't been solely because she'd wanted to find out who was stalking the Byrnside orphans—though that's how she'd justified it to herself. There'd been the thrill, the narcotic satisfaction of becoming someone else, the type of someone she'd always fantasized being. She hadn't wanted to give that up. Even now, she still didn't want to. *In some ways,* she thought, *I've begun to feel that Susan is more me than Lynn ever was. I've even, despite all my doubts, begun to accept that glamorous new image in the mirror.*

Jake had started in on his second martini. "Your résumé was a total fraud, but you're probably the most knowledgeable executive assistant I've ever had. How did you manage to pull it off?"

"I did a lot of paperwork as a police officer."

He shot her a derisive look. "I wasn't referring to the fact that you can file letters. I was referring to your polish. You have the vocabulary, the mannerisms, the attitude of someone who's well-bred."

Her head lifted slightly. "I know I'm not what you would consider well-bred or well-educated, but I am well-read and you can learn a lot from between the covers of a book. Ever since I was a kid I've always had my nose in one. Actually," she added with a touch of bitterness, "I didn't have much choice since, with my looks, none of the other kids wanted me around. I have a good memory, and I'm a quick study. In Police Academy I was at the top of my class."

"Congratulations." Jake's hard gaze roved over her, coming to rest on her hair. "It's hard to tell from those black-and-white pictures. What color was your hair originally?''

''Mousy brown.''

''The blond is an improvement, I'd say. Is that why you changed it, or did you just want a disguise?''

''Both. Though I have all the normal female vanity, I'd never attempted to do anything with my appearance before. It seemed . . . useless. The argument that I needed a disguise gave me an excuse to do what I'd wanted to do for a long time and never had the nerve to. I bought a new wardrobe, went to an exclusive salon and had my hair styled and lightened.'' *I'm babbling,* she thought, and cut herself short. ''They do say that blondes have more fun.''

Jake was not amused. His mouth twisted. ''Is that what it's been all this time, fun? Were you having fun with me, Lynn?''

The bitterness in his voice ate at her. ''Oh, no! It was never like that. Jake, please believe me!''

''Believe you? That's a laugh!'' Though he didn't show it, Jake was beginning to be affected by the two martinis he'd just downed cold. He'd thought he had his resentment well under control. But now it spewed forth like acid under pressure. ''How can I ever believe anything you say again? You've done nothing but con me. From beginning to end, it's all been one big scam. And I've been the dumb fool who swallowed it whole.''

Though it hardly seemed possible, Lynn's face turned even whiter. Her throat worked, yet she seemed unable to speak. Suddenly she grabbed her purse and stood, almost knocking her chair over backward in her haste. ''I'm sorry,'' she threw out. ''What more can I say? I'm just sorry!'' And then she was gone, rushing headlong between the rows of tables until she disappeared beyond the restaurant doors.

JAKE'S WEREN'T the only pair of eyes that followed Lynn's progress. A nattily dressed individual lunching alone behind a potted ficus had been closely observing the tense interchange between Lynn and Jake. When it terminated so abruptly, the luncher threw down some money and walked out into the lobby behind her. After seeing Lynn ride off in a taxi, the observer went to the phone near the elevator and punched out a number.

"Caine knows who she is," the observer said when the right voice answered on the other end of the line.

There was a pause and then a sigh of resignation. "What was his reaction?"

"They appear to be somewhat irritated with each other."

"Not enough so that he could be blamed for murdering her, I suppose."

"No, I don't think that would wash."

"Just a random thought. Well, we'll have to think of some other way of dealing with this, won't we?"

"I thought you were firing me."

"I spoke too hastily. Perhaps there's another way. I'll have to give it some thought. And I know how inventive you are, so you do the same."

The luncher's mouth twisted into a thin smile. "I'll do that. And you're right. When the occasion calls for it I can be quite creative. Some might even describe me as being an artist in my particular line of work."

JAKE SAT STARING at the carpeted route Lynn had taken out of the dining room. Slowly, his eyes moved to the empty chair across from him, to her half-drunk glass of mineral water, the napkin which she had unconsciously twisted into a point.

"Would *Monsieur* like another drink, or would *Monsieur* care to order now?"

Jake glanced up at the waiter and down to the second empty martini glass. That was a damn fool thing to have done! What was wrong with him? Was he losing his grip altogether? "Neither," he said to the waiter. "I won't be having lunch here, after all."

Outside he grabbed a taxi and directed it to the Carleton. He couldn't be sure that Lynn had headed back to the hotel. But where else would she have gone? And he had to catch up with her because there was too damn much left unsettled between them!

LYNN HURRIED into her room and stopped dead. Disoriented, she stared around her. *Of course,* she thought with grim humor, *when I left here this morning I was Susan. Now I'm coming back as Lynn. It's like having a split personality.*

But the next instant her whimsy faded. There was nothing funny about this situation, not when you happened to be the split personality in question.

She raised her hand to her mouth and stifled the sob that had been aching at the back of her throat all during the cab ride. *Oh, God,* she thought. *I've made such a mess!* Her eyes burned with pent-up tears. They flooded out and gushed down her cheeks in such a torrent that they wet her chin and the sensitive skin between her fingers. Jake's image as he had been at the restaurant rose up before her and once again she saw the distaste for her that had been etched on his face. *He'll never trust me again,* she thought despairingly. *From now on he'll always think of me as the woman who played him for a fool.*

Actually, she reflected, when she'd said to Jake "what more can I say?" before she'd run out of the restaurant, she hadn't been right. There *was* plenty more she could say to him, there were more ways she could try to explain her masquerade. But at that moment she'd been so over-wrought she hadn't been able to think of them. All she'd known was that she had to get out of there. She couldn't bear him looking at her like that. But what did it matter? For a man like Jake, the single fact that she'd duped and deceived him would change his attitude toward her forever.

Lynn gave a small gasp and then dropped down on the edge of the bed and covered her face with her hands. For several minutes she sat breathing quietly, trying desperately to get her brain to start working again. What now? Was there any point in hanging around here now that the search for Lynn Rice was so obviously over? The sooner she headed back to Boston, the better. And what was the point in traveling together with Jake? If she could get out to the airport and arrange to board the next flight headed west, all the better.

Lynn had dragged out her suitcase and was filling it with underwear when a sharp rap rattled her door. She knew it was Jake, just as though she could see through the wood. And the last thing she wanted now was another confrontation. She stood undecided, a wispy lace bra dangling from her hand.

"I know you're in there Susan—Lynn." He sounded even more irritated by his mistake. "I want to talk to you." When she didn't answer, he turned the knob, which in her distress she'd left unlocked, and walked in.

For a long moment he stood surveying her and Lynn was suddenly conscious of her red eyes and swollen, tear-streaked face and of the undergarment she held. Only two nights ago Jake had tenderly unclasped it and taken it off her body before they made love, but now it seemed as if all that happened in another life. Suddenly Jake's glance moved toward the bra in her hand and she knew he was thinking the same thing—and remembering. She pitched it into her luggage. *Damn him,* she suddenly thought defensively. What right did he have to make her feel as if she were a criminal? What right did any man have?

"What are you doing?"

"Isn't it obvious? I'm packing."

"So I see. Were you planning to skip out on me?"

"Why do you call it skipping out? There's nothing left to do here, is there? You've managed to track down Lynn Rice."

"Hardly." Jake crossed the room toward her, his jaw clamped. Only the muscle that ticked in his forehead gave away his agitation. "There's still a lot I don't understand about that lady and what's happened."

"Then we have something in common, after all. There's a lot I don't understand, too." She looked up at him through wet lashes, her golden eyes as defiant as a cornered cat's. Since it was over between them, at least she could preserve her dignity, she told herself. No more groveling and apologizing. She'd done what she'd felt she had to, and that was it.

Lightning seemed to flash in Jake's gaze and he reached out and gripped Lynn's wrist. "I'm curious. Are you referring to the reasons for your deception or my reaction to it?"

Lynn tried to pull her hand from his, but she might as well have been wearing a tempered-steel handcuff. "Oh, there's nothing mysterious about your reaction," she cried bitterly. "Don't forget, when I was a cop in Boston I worked with a pack of men. I know what guys are like when their male pride is threatened by a woman. Hell hath no fury!"

He grabbed her shoulders, yanked her close and glared down at her. "Is that all you think this is? Male pride?"

Jake's gaze had been caustic before, but now it seemed to burn through her like dry ice. "Yes," she hissed. Her nerves felt scraped raw. She was wounded and hurting, but she was not going to back down with him looking at her like that. Adrenaline pumped through her veins. Her heart pounded. Inside her, emotions clashed and split apart into wild fragments.

"Then you know even less about men than I thought!" Jake cried. "I was falling in love with you, lady! God help me, I was turning myself inside out for a woman who never even existed. But the other night I was sure I was making love to a real person. Oh, you had me fooled, all right! And I'm no naive schoolboy." He jerked her closer, his gaze suddenly homing in on her lips. "But I must be wrong about that, because when I kissed you I thought I'd found heaven. I never dreamed it was nothing but lies, nothing but a big con. The thought never even entered my head."

Lynn was breathing hard, confused by Jake's closeness, the challenge in his voice, the emotions roiling inside her. Her pulses throbbed, and the heat of her body seemed to rush out to swirl with the simmering currents inside him. Her lips parted to issue a fiery protest, but the words never formed.

Jake's hands tightened, his head dipped, and his mouth came down hard on hers. She stiffened in surprise. Then she gasped and tried to rear away. But Jake's arm whipped around to manacle her waist and he hauled her so close that her breasts were flattened against his chest and their hips came into compelling contact. Lynn realized that Jake was aroused and she felt her own body tighten. Maybe it wasn't all over between them, she thought with a fierce surge of hope and a hot rush of excitement that more than matched his. With that, their embrace changed from an assault into something quite different. The temperature flared and burned higher and the kiss became mutual. Lynn's arms went up and tightened around Jake's neck, and she kissed him back with all her strength.

"I want—" Jake muttered, as his mouth finally slid from her lips to her chin and then her upturned throat.

"I know, I know." With her hips pressed to his, Lynn had arched back. Her eyes were closed and a deep flush suffused her face and throat. This was inappropriate. Some sensible part of her passion-drugged brain knew that. But it didn't seem to matter. Maybe this shouldn't be happening. But it was!

Jake's response mirrored that of the woman in his arms. For two days now he'd been strapped to a lunatic emotional roller coaster, torn apart by doubts, angered and hurt, sunk to depths of disappointment he hadn't even imagined. Now it all came together into something new and too powerful to draw back from.

His mouth went from Lynn's throat to the V between her breasts. At his touch, she felt her nipples stiffen and ache. A hot thread wound tight, deep in her belly.

"My God, Lynn," he muttered thickly. "My God!"

As the exclamation tore from his throat, he swept her into his arms and carried her to the bed. With one arm he knocked the suitcase away. It crashed to the floor, spewing its contents helter-skelter. But neither Jake nor Lynn paid the slightest heed.

They were both on the bed, their lips once again locked. Their tongues dueled, entwined. Then Jake reared up and shrugged out of his jacket. While Lynn reached blindly for his belt, he all but tore the buttons open on his shirt. Her blouse, skirt and underwear followed, and a moment later hot flesh met hungry flesh. Groaning, they rolled together, devouring each other with their mouths and hands, stroking and writhing to assuage the craving running a riotous course through both of them.

Soon there was no holding back, and they came together completely. While Lynn clung to Jake's lean waist, they both drove for the release their bodies demanded. It came quickly and explosively. When the sharp spasms died away they fell against each other and lay for several minutes breathing hard. Both their naked bodies were damp from the struggles of their frantic lovemaking, and the animal musk of passion.

At last the silence between them grew too heavy to ignore. Jake groaned and rolled to one side. He flung his left arm up over his creased forehead. "I'm sorry."

Now that Jake's body no longer covered hers, Lynn was cold. Feeling terribly exposed, she looked around for the sheet, but in their urgency she and Jake had fallen down on top of the bedspread. She dragged a pillow out from under the spread and clutched it over her breasts. "For what?"

"For treating you like that, for taking you like that."

"I wasn't exactly uncooperative." *Far from it,* she thought as she stared up at the ceiling. She didn't regret what had happened between her and Jake just now. How could she when she'd needed it, and it had been like rain after a thunderstorm, uncontrollable?

Jake raised himself up on his elbow, stared at her profile a moment and then swung his long legs over the edge of the bed and reached for his trousers. "Lynn—it's still hard for me to call you that. This is crazy. We have to talk."

"I know."

He stepped into his pants, zipped them and then found a blanket in the closet and dropped it so that it covered her.

She repressed a bleak smile. A moment ago she'd wanted to hide under the sheet. Now that Jake had made the gesture for her, she resented it. She didn't want him to be sorry they'd made love. She only wanted him to be sorry for the things he'd said at the Beau-Rivage.

"Believe me," Jake said, "when I met you at the Beau-Rivage I meant to handle this situation like the well-trained professional I supposedly am." He laughed humorlessly. "I intended to be cool, collected, discreet. You weren't supposed to know how angry I was, or how torn up. It didn't happen that way, did it?"

"The two martinis probably didn't help."

"No, drinking myself silly that way was stupid. Everything I've done this afternoon was stupid. I should never have come back here and attacked you like some sort of sex-starved animal, not with so much left unresolved. I should never—"

He groaned faintly and rubbed his forehead. "But where you're concerned, my brains were never in the driver's seat, were they?"

"I don't know, Jake. I don't really know how you feel about me."

"Well, let me try and clarify, for myself as much as for you. I'd built Susan Bonner into such a fantasy. After Janet died I was so alone, so empty. Life seemed like a long, gray endless tunnel. But Susan was going to change all that. I'd pinned a whole Christmas tree of wishes on her." He sat back down on the bed, his broad shoulders drooping.

At last Lynn moved. Shooting an anguished glance at Jake's back, she pushed herself up and reached for her clothing. "Jake, even if Susan Bonner had been a real person and all the things she'd claimed, she probably couldn't have lived up to that fantasy you'd built around her. Probably no woman could." Lynn sighed. "Maybe, in a way, we aren't so different. We were both looking to change our lives and hoping that some fairy godmother would come along and wave a magic wand for us."

Jake's head swiveled and he stared at her, frowning. "But you must have had other reasons for what you did. Otherwise it doesn't make sense. The mystery with the plastic surgery, the whole elaborate Susan Bonner charade. Why would you want to avoid being identified as a possible heiress when most people would jump at the opportunity?"

Carefully, Lynn began to explain. She described the letter that had come offering to pay her way at the Château de Grâce and then the attack at the hotel and her decision to flee.

As Jake listened, his frown deepened. "So you were just trying to protect yourself."

"That was partly it, but not all of it," Lynn acknowledged. Avoiding looking directly at Jake, she buttoned her blouse. "After my surgery I was at a jumping-off point in my life. I no longer knew myself when I looked in the mirror, and I felt disoriented and, I don't know, as if I couldn't and shouldn't go back to anything I'd known before. Assuming a disguise to hide from my attacker gave me the excuse I was looking for. And then when I found out about the Byrnside quest, I really had a rationale for changing my identity. And I grabbed at it, Jake. It was just your bad luck and mine—" awkwardly, she stood and fastened the waistband on her skirt "—that we became so attracted to each other when the infatuation was built on sand."

"I think the infatuation has something to do with chemistry as well," Jake muttered, his eyes following all her movements intently. "I think we just demonstrated that." Abruptly, he walked to the window and stood there looking out. "There's something else I need to ask you, Lynn." Jake put his hands on his lean hips.

"What's that?" She sat back down on the bed, stuck her feet into her shoes and fumbled at their ties. Her fingers felt like clumsy sausages, and she was trembling. What had she expected, she asked herself—that Jake would declare it didn't matter that both her face and her name had been manufactured? That he wouldn't care she'd never seen the inside of Radcliffe, or any college for that matter and that she'd practically been brought up on the streets? To a man with a background like Jake's, how could all that not matter?

"You've explained the reasons for your masquerade, and I understand them, though I can't completely sympathize. But it's made me think again about our intruder in Paris. He wasn't trying to steal from you, was he?"

"No." Lynn's voice was low.

Jake turned to face her. "He broke into your room to kill you, didn't he?"

"That's the logical explanation. Apparently you're not the only one who's figured out who I really am. And it's all tied up with this Byrnside thing. First Maggie, and now me again."

"It was sheer luck I was in your room. You could have been killed."

Sheer lust was more like it, she thought sourly. Aloud, she said, "Yes, I know."

"So why couldn't you have told me then? Why did you persist in keeping the truth about your identity hidden when you knew it had to come out?"

"I couldn't be sure who was behind that attempt to murder me or what was really going on. I just thought it was smarter to investigate the situation on my own for as long as I could." What was the point of telling Jake how much she'd dreaded his reaction when he knew the truth?

"I suppose that means you were suspicious of me."

"Of you?" Lynn was too flabbergasted to answer instantly. Though there'd been a time when she'd been dubious about everyone connected with Byrnside, including Jake, she certainly didn't suspect him now.

Jake's eyes had already hardened. "Well, if it weren't for that attempt on your life in Paris, I'd be more than a little suspicious of you, Lynn Rice. You have as strong a motive as anyone for wanting the other two orphans out of the way, and I've seen you use a gun."

CHAPTER TWELVE

OUTSIDE THE CAR WINDOWS the road spun out between winding bands of pine-studded green. Inside Jake's Mercedes a flute concerto whispering on the CD player only seemed to punctuate the muted silence. When Lynn recrossed her legs, the silken rustle of her panty hose beneath her suit skirt was audible despite the music.

Next to her Jake sat concentrating on his driving, his expression strained. That was how it had been ever since they'd left Lausanne, Jake tense and making sure that he was too busy to talk and Lynn restless and uncertain. But now that they were approaching Taleman Hall for the first meeting with Owen Byrnside as one of his prospective granddaughters, Lynn's restlessness had reached a fever pitch.

"Relax," Jake suddenly said, as if he'd read her mind. "The old man's not going to eat you."

"No, but he's not going to be too pleased with me, either, not when he's spent a fortune looking for Lynn Rice and all this time she's been under his nose."

Jake's mouth tightened. "How perceptive of you."

Lynn shot him a quick little glance and then averted her eyes. It was hopeless, she thought. After Lausanne, she and Jake would never be truly comfortable with each other again. That much was obvious from the sharp little remarks he couldn't seem to resist jabbing her with whenever she let down her guard. Not that she blamed him—not really. If only she'd been honest with him earlier! At the thought, a cold spring of fresh misery flooded through her.

Jake cleared his throat. "Sorry about that. There's not much point in our needling each other, is there?"

"No, not really."

He massaged the deep crease between his dark eyebrows and then, as he paused at a stop sign, closed his eyes as if his lids were suddenly too heavy for him. Lynn took advantage of the moment to study his face. He looked tired, she thought, and drawn. There were shadows under his eyes and the creases in his forehead and around his mouth seemed deeper. *He's suffering,* she thought suddenly, *just as much as I am and maybe more. It can't be easy to have to be with me, deal with me, when he feels I'm some sort of changeling Mata Hari.*

"Remember Rona Chastain?" Jake said, looking both ways and then proceeding through the intersection.

"The contract killer who almost got Maggie? Of course I remember."

"Well now that my detective isn't searching for Lynn Rice anymore, I've put him back on Rona's trail."

"Because you think she might be the intruder we ran into in Paris?"

"I suspect there's a very good possibility of that, yes."

Lynn nodded. Earlier, she'd come to the same conclusion.

"That night I assumed your attacker was a man. But I never saw him clearly, and there's still quite a bit of doubt about Rona's true gender. Anyhow, it's a lead and if we can track it down it might take us to whoever is behind all this trouble."

Lynn nodded again.

"There's another thing. I intend to find out who wrote you that letter and paid for your plastic surgery."

"How?"

"It was paid for with a check drawn on a bank, and banks keep records. With the proper authority, I can have those records searched and I intend to do exactly that. It's one mystery I can have cleared up within a few days."

"I appreciate your trying to protect me."

"No need for thanks. That's my job. Among other things, it's what Owen Byrnside is paying me to do."

Was that all that counted with Jake now? Lynn wondered forlornly. She thought of the violence of his love-making that day in Lausanne and couldn't believe such strong emotion had fizzled to nothing. Even though she wasn't what he'd thought, he *must* still care for her. Surely it was just a matter of time before he recognized that fact.

At that instant the Mercedes swung past the wrought iron gates of Taleman Hall. The moment for Lynn's first real meeting with Owen Byrnside was at hand and as she contemplated the fact her heart began to beat double time.

The Mercedes purred up the winding road and swung around the circular driveway in front of the mansion. When it stopped, Jake and Lynn stared up at the turreted, castlelike structure looming over them.

"Well here we are at Owen Byrnside's rose-covered cottage," Jake remarked.

Lynn gazed up at the stone facade of Taleman Hall and said nothing.

"Do you feel as if you're coming home?"

"I feel as if I'm being dragged before the Lord High Executioner." Lynn watched as Jake got out and came around to open the passenger door. Suddenly she remembered Wendell Wrigley, Owen Byrnside's chauffeur, and made a mental note to try to have a private word with Wendell before she left the estate.

Loretta Greene flung open Taleman Hall's massive oak door. Framed by it, she looked particularly dramatic in a sleek black wool suit that tapered from broad padded shoulders to a knee-hugging skirt. Her hair slicked back from her face had the sheen of patent leather and her lips were a vivid slash of scarlet.

Loretta's gaze fastened on Lynn, who was just walking up the steps. "Well, well, well, at last the prodigal arrives." The private secretary's mouth drew up in a smile, but there wasn't any humor in her eyes, Lynn noted. "Owen has been in a snit all day. He wanted to press a button and bring you both back from Europe in ten minutes flat."

"Someday that may be possible," Jake murmured as he took Lynn's arm and guided her over the threshold. "But not yet."

"He's waiting for you in the library," Loretta said. "I'll take you."

"No need." Jake steered Lynn past Loretta and through the foyer. "I think by now we know the way."

The minute Lynn and Jake walked into the library, Owen pinned them with his sharp gaze. "At last! Well, young lady, what do you have to say for yourself?"

A fire crackled in the paneled room's handsome marble fireplace. It cast a glow over the leather-bound books lining the walls, walls that reached up fourteen feet before they met a ceiling.

Owen Byrnside sat in his wheelchair to one side of the stone hearth. As usual, a plaid blanket swathed his knees. Above it he sported a vintage green velvet jacket. It was the first time Lynn had seen him in anything so dressy. Despite his frailty, he looked rather dapper, she thought. She could imagine that as a younger man he'd been quite attractive. In fact, even now he still was.

"I—I don't have anything to say for myself," Lynn stammered.

"I think you'll find she has a great deal," Jake countered. "In fact the tale she has to tell would rival an Italian opera."

Owen's thin mouth turned down. "I never could stomach those damn-fool operas. Just a lot of nonsense, if you ask me. Couldn't sit through one of 'em to save my soul."

"I can guarantee you'll want to sit through Lynn's aria." Jake stuck his hands in his pockets. "Owen, would you like me to stay for this, or would you rather I made myself scarce?"

The old man cocked his head. "Skedaddle, Caine. Go admire the hollies in the east garden. I'd like to have a word with Miss Rice in private."

Jake nodded, glanced briefly at Lynn, who was staring at him resentfully, and then strode out of the room. As the sound of his footsteps died away down the hall, Lynn returned her gaze to Owen Byrnside's hawklike visage, though part of her mind was still on Jake. What had that crack about Italian opera been for? Had he decided that everything about her was a fraud?

"Well, young lady, you still haven't properly answered my question. What have you got to say for yourself? Why have you been playing this game of hide-and-seek for so many months? We're not children here, you know."

"I know that, sir."

"Then don't waste any more of my time. Pull up a seat and spill it."

Lynn dragged a wing chair close to the fire. When she had lowered herself into it, she folded her hands in her lap. "I'm not sure where to start."

"Start by telling me a thing or two about yourself. Where'd you grow up, and more important, how?"

Lynn looked down at her fingers, which she'd unconsciously woven into a tight mesh. "I grew up mostly in foster homes," she began, and then described as best she could what her childhood had been like. She tried to be brief and dispassionate about the mistreatment she'd received from her last foster father.

Nevertheless, Owen's scowl deepened. "If only I'd known," he burst out at one point. "I would have had that damn scar taken off your face before you hit nursery school. So much misery over a mark left by a fire. It's a shame."

Lynn's gaze went to the flames which danced in the hearth. "Surgical techniques were a lot less sophisticated twenty years ago. You might not have been able to get it removed."

"Mebbe, but you'd be surprised what money can buy in the way of medical talent, or any other kind of talent. Happiness may not be for sale, but just about everything else is."

Lynn laughed at his cynicism, but she suspected he was right. When she told the old man about the letter that had sent her to Switzerland and changed her life, his grizzled eyebrows rose sharply. Owen sat through the rest of the tale in taut silence.

"So, you see," Lynn finished up, "that's why I didn't reveal my identity even though I knew you were looking for me. I was sure your orphans were in danger and before I identified myself as one of them, I wanted to find out who was behind that danger." She sighed. "Unfortunately, I didn't succeed."

A ruminative look had come over Owen Byrnside's craggy features. "I have to give what you've told me some thought. It may be that I can come up with an idea or two that might shed some light. In the meantime, let's get back to talking about you."

"I've done nothing but talk about me for the past—" Lynn smiled and checked her watch "—for the past hour." She'd relaxed a bit. Owen Byrnside hadn't lectured or threatened or shouted. But the interview wasn't over, and she still felt nervous about where it might lead.

"Yes," he said, "but I haven't begun to ask questions yet, have I? Well, now's my turn. First off, I want to tell you something. Happens I wasn't all that surprised when I got Jake's message about your real name. I always did have a feeling in my gut about you."

"You did?" Lynn gazed at the elderly millionaire warily.

"I liked your looks. Always did have a soft spot for blondes with turned-up noses. Is that cute little nose yours, by the way?"

Lynn shrugged and laughed. "Not quite. When the surgeon removed the scar he did a few other things. Originally my nose had a slight bump on the bridge. The bump got taken off."

"I see. Your doctor was one of those artistes, huh? Couldn't stop until he'd achieved perfection. Believe me, I know the type. Well, the fella did a good job."

"Thank you."

"But that's not what I'm talking about. From the first time I laid eyes on you I said to myself, now that's a young woman with an agenda. She's up to something, and she's strong-minded enough to carry it off, whatever it may be."

"You mean you were suspicious of me?"

"No, just intrigued. Being a simpleminded fella' where women are concerned, I thought maybe your plan was to nail Jake. I was all for it. Every man needs a good woman and Jake's been a loner too long. That's why I made him take you along with him to Paris."

"You were matchmaking?" Lynn was shocked. Owen Byrnside was the last person she'd imagine playing Cupid.

Owen shrugged. "I figured if you wanted him, I'd do my good deed for the decade and help you to it."

The old man looked at her expectantly, but Lynn didn't care to discuss her feelings for Jake, not the way things stood between them now. "You were mistaken," she said flatly. "Where Jake was concerned, I had no agenda."

"No? Pity, because if I have eyes in my head he's stuck on you."

Lynn shook her head emphatically. "You're wrong again. He's very angry with me. Can't you tell?"

"I can tell he's got his New England nose out of joint." Owen gave a raspy chuckle. "Doesn't like it that you were fooling him all this time, eh?"

"No, of course he doesn't. He thinks I'm dishonest, a fraud."

"Well, he's a Bostonian born and bred, you know, and they can be rigid as picket fences and just about as much fun. If you're really worried about Jake, don't be. He's got way too much pride, but he's also got more than his share of sense. In the end that'll come to his rescue. Now me, I like a tricksy woman. Give me a lady who can lie without blinking and I'll give you an interesting afternoon."

To Lynn's astonishment, Owen winked at her—a flirtatious wink. "It wouldn't surprise me if a granddaughter of mine had the stuff to survive the kind of childhood you say you've been dished out. And it would tickle me if she were smart enough to fool a tough customer like Jake Caine, to boot. You'd come by it honestly, you know. I didn't get to be a rich man by wearing a halo and Chris, my boy—and one of you girls' father I hope—he was no angel, either.''

As he mentioned his dead son's name, a subtle change came over the old man's features. Lynn caught it and felt sympathy well up inside her. ''I'm sorry about Christopher. That must have been awful for you. What was he like?'' she asked softly.

Owen kneaded the edge of the blanket at his waist. ''Willful, stubborn, spoiled, foolish. He was weak, I'd guess you'd say. But I don't blame him for that. Maybe he'd have been different if he'd had a different kind of father. It was no easy thing to be my only son.'' Owen cocked his head and regarded Lynn with suddenly brightened eyes. ''You know, you're the first one of the girls who's really seemed interested in Chris. Would you like to see his room?''

''Yes, I would.''

''Then come with me. We'll take the elevator.'' The old man pressed a button and his motorized wheelchair began to hum. As it glided forward over the Oriental rug, Lynn hastily stood and followed. They took an elevator in a hall off the library up to the second floor.

''I'd like to see a floor plan of this house sometime,'' Lynn murmured. ''I don't know how you find your way around.''

''It's a rabbit warren, all right,'' Owen agreed. ''I wanted to build a castle for my Alice because she was the queen of my heart. Guess I went a little overboard.'' He stopped his chair in front of a door, took a set of keys from the pocket of his velvet jacket and inserted one. ''Don't go in here much,'' he muttered. ''Truth to tell, the room hasn't been used since poor Chris made a cinder of himself. Alice wanted it left exactly as it was, and I wanted no part of it at all. Maid comes in here to dust occasionally.

That's about it." He pushed the door open, maneuvered his chair to one side and motioned Lynn past him.

As she stepped over the threshold, she paused and stared around at English antiques against a handsome maroon-and-white striped wallpaper. Though Christopher's room had a deserted, haunted feeling, it was beautiful.

Next to the four-poster a carved Hepplewhite desk was laden with silver-framed photographs. Gingerly, Lynn approached it. A glamorous picture of Gloria Dean in a white leather minidress caught her eye and she picked it up.

"Think that might be your mom?" Owen's chair whirred behind her.

"No. Why would I want to have a mother who abandoned me? Anyhow, we look nothing alike and I'm not musical. Oh, and as I've already told Jake, I don't have the locket she's supposed to have left around her baby's neck. Since nobody else does either, that appears to have been a red herring. I'd say of your three orphans, Kate's the musical one, and she's even a redhead."

"True, but Kate's a softhearted angel. She's nothing like the cold, grasping, self-destructive bitch Gloria Dean was."

When Lynn shot a startled look over her shoulder, Owen grimaced. "No, at my age I'm not one to mince words. She's at least partly responsible for what happened to Chris. The young fool went gaga over her. And once she got her hooks into him, the harpy could make him dance to her tune. I wonder if he would ever have gotten so deep into drugs if it hadn't been for her and the crowd she ran with."

"If you hated her so much, why are you anxious to take in her child?"

"Because if that child was Chris's, then she's mine, too and the only thing I've got," he spat out with abrupt ferocity. "You're too young to understand what it's like to lean over the grave knowing you're not leaving anything behind you."

Lynn couldn't help but raise her eyebrows. She glanced around at the room's rich furnishings and then outside at the lush grounds of Owen Byrnside's palatial abode.

The old man instantly realized what she was thinking. "Oh, things, things!" he exclaimed. "I'll leave plenty of things behind, and a bank vault stuffed with money to ice the cake. But all that's not worth spit. You realize the truth of that when you're looking death in the eye. I realized it when I lost Alice. If you've no flesh and blood to leave behind you, your life has been a failure."

"I don't agree," Lynn declared. "If that were true, some of the most important and valuable people in history would be failures, men like Leonardo and Michelangelo, women like Queen Elizabeth and Joan of Arc. Surely a person's deeds count for something. And you've done a lot of things, created a lot of things you can be very proud of."

"Oh? Name some, then," Owen said belligerently.

"Your companies. Think of the people they employ all over the world, the goods and services and creative endeavors they support. I think you can be very proud of what you've built, and of what you'll leave behind you for others to enjoy and build on top of. What does it matter that those people aren't related to you by blood? We're all related to each other in the long run."

"Disputatious little thing, aren't you?" Owen huffed.

Lynn felt very strongly about what she'd said. But she wasn't inclined to argue the point further, not when Owen's emotions on the subject obviously ran so high.

She turned back to the desk, set the photo of Gloria Dean down and scanned the other pictures. They were snaps of friends and family taken at picnics, parties and sporting events. They were filled with happy, smiling faces. Several were of Christopher laughing into the camera. He'd been a handsome young man, Lynn thought. Knowing the way his life had ended made her heart twist. How much more painful must Christopher's tragedy be for his father?

Her gaze fell on a snapshot showing Christopher in a rowboat with another young man. Something familiar about Christopher's companion made her pick up the picture and study it more closely. "This is Winston Deeping!" she exclaimed.

"Yes, he and Chris used to be pals."

Wrigley had already told her that, yet somehow seeing the photograph made the relationship much more real.

"Deeping liked pop music," Owen went on. "That's how he came to be part of Gloria's crowd, but he wasn't like the rest of them. He had a sensible head on his shoulders. After Chris died he came and told me how he tried to keep my boy off drugs, showed me letters he'd written urging him to drop Gloria. He didn't succeed with my son, but I was grateful that he tried."

"Is that why you hired Deeping to run your recording division?"

Owen shook his head. "Before his accident Chris had recommended Winston to me and I'd taken him on as a talent scout, more as a favor to my son than anything else. Winston justified Chris's praise. He signed up some people who sold records for us, which was a godsend. At the time the recording branch of my company hadn't been doing too well. I knew what I liked, but apparently it wasn't what the public wanted."

Owen rolled his chair to a baby grand piano next to the window. He ran a gnarled finger along its out-of-tune keyboard and then looked back at Lynn. "When I decided to shake up management and moved Deeping into the top spot, he turned losses into gains. Over the years I haven't agreed with all his decisions, but I have to admit that he's been right more often than not. Nowadays the recording division of Byrnside Enterprises is consistently one of the top performers."

Lynn listened to all this with great interest. "Did you know that after Christopher's accident and probably just after Gloria Dean abandoned her baby, Winston Deeping signed her to a lucrative contract with your company?"

Owen's jaw dropped. "He did? Are you sure?"

"There's a copy of the papers in our files."

The old man shook his head. "Now I wonder why Winston would have done a damn fool thing like that. He knew I hated the woman."

"Maybe he thought she was very talented."

"Wouldn't matter if she'd been the reincarnation of Jenny Lind with a little of Maria Callas on the side, I wouldn't have wanted her on my payroll. Course, Winston's fond of going his own way, making his own decisions. Lately we've been at daggers drawn over some of those decisions. But usually he's enough of a diplomat not to want to offend me deliberately." Owen rubbed his chin. "That's strange, very strange. I guess she died before I got wind of it."

Lynn gazed across the room at the aged millionaire, her fine brows slightly puckered. "Mr. Byrnside, is there anything about your finding a living granddaughter that might threaten Winston Deeping?"

"There's something about my finding a living granddaughter that might threaten all my top executives, and there are an even dozen of them. Truth to tell, lately I've been wondering about that—though I certainly wouldn't peg any of them as murderers.''

"What do you mean?''

Owen laced his hands together over his thin belly. "After Alice died I lost interest in running the company and in life, I guess. But I was smart enough to know that I couldn't just let my hirelings take charge without giving them a stake that would make them into decent caretakers. It's not generally known, but I drew up an agreement stating that if I died without issue they each stood to inherit a controlling share of the stock in their particular bailiwick.''

"And if you left a legitimate heir?''

Owen's eyes narrowed. "Well, at my age that wasn't likely. But I had my lawyers write in a provision that if I had legitimate issue then the deal was off. Because that would make it a whole new ball game, wouldn't it?''

"I HAD NO IDEA you were this interested in herb gardens.'' As Loretta Greene strolled toward Jake an amused smile curved her red mouth.

"I'm not, but it gives me something to do while Owen's having his interview with Lynn.''

"Ah yes, the mysterious third orphan.'' Loretta glanced back at the house. "Quite the clever little minx, isn't she?''

Though he'd been thinking of Lynn in similar terms, Jake felt unaccountably irritated. "I don't know that I would describe her as a minx.''

"That's the trouble with you, Jake, you're too nice.''

Jake laughed. "Nice? That's not what a lot of people I know would call me.'' Lately he hadn't been feeling the least bit nice.

"Then you haven't been paying proper attention to the women in your life.'' Loretta bent down to pluck away a dead onion head left over from the fall. "Janet worshipped the ground you walked on."

Jake felt his smile die. "I adored her, too."

"Everyone knows how much you've suffered over her loss."

"Is it that obvious?"

"Oh, you never say anything. You've always been the stiff-upper-lip, suffer-in-silence type. But anyone with eyes can see that you've been like a lost soul these past four years." Loretta shook her head. "It was such a senseless, tragic shame, her drowning like that. In so many ways you two were the perfect couple. You had the same sort of backgrounds, the same sort of education. Janet was so slim and elegant, you even looked alike."

Jake eyed the brunette woman curiously. What was she getting at? he wondered. And what was so great about being your mate's mirror image? That could lead to complacency, boredom. It would be much more challenging to love someone who was very different and who forced you to rethink some of your attitudes. A woman like Lynn would make a man with a tendency to get into a rut rethink a lot of things.

Loretta sighed, a hardness coming into her dark eyes. "So many people make foolish mistakes when they fall in love, especially when they fall in love young. But you and Janet were ideal together. She was such a lady, for one thing. Not like that little sneak in there." Once again Loretta glanced sharply back at the house.

Jake's curiosity as well as his irritation deepened. "Are you talking about Lynn Rice? You certainly do seem to have taken a dislike to her."

"I can't abide liars and sneaks, never could. When I think that she's been creeping around here like a snake, acting as if butter wouldn't melt in her mouth when all the time she was just spying out the territory hoping to get her hands on Owen's money, it makes my blood boil!''

At that, Jake balked. ''Aren't you being a little harsh? I don't think she was fooling us because of Owen's money. It was something else.''

''Oh, I know what you mean,'' Loretta countered. ''I can't live here and not hear things. It's this business about the girls being threatened by some mysterious assassin. Well, if you want my opinion, it's one of them.''

''You think one of the orphans is trying to kill the other two?'' It was a thought that had already occurred to Jake but, despite what he'd said to Lynn, he didn't really take it seriously.

''Yes. Well, it makes sense, doesn't it? They're the ones who stand to gain the most. And it isn't as if any one of them has had the kind of upbringing likely to instill strong moral values. Obviously Lynn Rice is a practiced deceiver who was raised on the streets and who doesn't think twice about passing herself off as something she isn't. What I saw of Maggie Murphy didn't impress me, either. She was brought up helter-skelter by a postman with a herd of other orphans.''

''Maggie is a nurse, a very dedicated one.''

''And who better than a nurse would know how to go about killing someone and be hardened enough by the sight of death not to mind doing it?''

''Oh, come now, Loretta!''

''Just think about it, Jake. And then there's Kate Humphrey. Look at the life she's led, performing in sleazy nightclubs since she was a teenager. You can't tell me she wouldn't kill to get her hands on Owen's fortune. Oh, they're quite a bunch, those three girls. I can't wait until next week.''

''Next week?''

Loretta pursed her mouth. "Hasn't Owen told you yet? He's already had me go ahead and make the arrangements. On this day next week he plans to assemble his orphans here and have the tests performed."

"No, Owen hasn't told me that yet." Jake stuck his hands in his pockets and gazed out over the gardens. "So," he murmured, "in a week's time we'll know the answer to the mystery and Owen Byrnside's heiress will be named."

"Yes." Loretta laughed shortly. "That is, we'll know if the three haven't found a way to strangle each other before then."

CHAPTER THIRTEEN

FROM THE TERRACE at the back of Taleman Hall Lynn watched Jake and Loretta Greene. What were they talking about? she wondered.

She glanced at her watch. Almost four. After she and Owen had left Christopher's room, he'd directed his wheelchair toward his own bedroom and asked Lynn to ring for his nurse.

"I'm pooped. Time for my afternoon snooze." His eyes had probed hers. "I won't forget what we've talked about today. And you won't let it slip your mind that next week at this time you'll be coming back to meet with my other two chickadees and take those tests, now will you?"

"Of course not. How could I forget a thing like that?"

"Tell Jake for me."

"All right."

"Give the two of you something to talk about. Can't spend all your time dancing around each other like suspicious cats. Or cats in heat." He'd cackled then and seesawed his head with weary glee. "Oh, life is grand, I can tell you. Who would ever have guessed that with all ten toes practically in the grave I'd have such entertaining things happening around me. Now, scoot and give Jake the message."

But now that Lynn had finally located Jake, she'd seen from her spot on the back porch that he was otherwise occupied. And she didn't feel like breaking into his and Loretta's private little tête-à-tête. Maybe this was her chance to have another word with Wendell, Lynn suddenly thought.

Glancing around, she decided to explore a brick path that led to a complex of outbuildings on the left side of the gardens. It directed her through a grove of fruit trees. On the other end of the grove she came upon a large brick carriage house with open double doors. Inside, Wendell, dressed in coveralls, was whistling under his breath and polishing up the fenders on a 1948 four-door Packard convertible.

"Oh, what a gorgeous car!" Lynn exclaimed as she strolled up. "I didn't know Mr. Byrnside owned this model. It was one of the last four-door convertibles made, wasn't it?"

Wendell stopped whistling. Behind his glasses he shot her the gratified look of a proud parent who'd just had his baby complimented. Then he pushed himself up on one knee and began wiping his hands with a rag. "Good afternoon, miss. You're right about Lady Matilda, here— that's what I call her." He patted the hood affectionately. "She's the last of a classic breed. As you can see, Mr. Byrnside has eight cars." He gestured around at the collection of vehicles that were parked in the barnlike structure. "But in the old days, before Mr. Byrnside's son died and before Mr. Byrnside lost his wife and became bedridden, there used to be a lot more." Wendell shook his head sadly. "Matilda's the only antique I could persuade him not to sell, and that's only because his wife liked to take Sunday drives in her. All Christopher's cars went to auction."

Lynn was pleased that Wendell had opened up one of the subjects she wanted to discuss. "Yes, Christopher liked sports cars, didn't he?"

"Loved 'em." A reminiscent smile lifted the corners of Wendell's thin lips. "He used to have a half dozen, mostly British, though his father didn't approve of buying anything but American. After the accident, Mr. Byrnside got rid of the sports models. But they were beauts. It was quite a job with all those cars to see to, but I took good care of them. Whenever young Chris wanted a spin, they were oiled and purring like jungle cats, not a speck of dust on 'em."

"I'll bet they were something else." Sympathetically, Lynn studied the man. "You really were very fond of Christopher, weren't you?"

"Well, I knew him since he was a towheaded little tyke. He was wild, got into some bad trouble and made some bad friends, I guess. But there was a lot of good in him, too, and he could be a charmer. It was a shame what happened, a real tragedy."

Lynn nodded. "Wendell, you must remember that conversation we had on Newberry Street."

A guarded look came into the chauffeur's pale eyes. "Sure I do. But that was a while back. Something I can do for you now, miss?" His voice was cautious.

Lynn didn't miss the change in his tone, the withdrawal. Something had happened to make him wary of her. She phrased her next words carefully. "We talked then about Miss Greene and Winston Deeping, and you told me some surprising things about their relationship."

"I shouldn't have been shooting my mouth off," Wendell interjected. "Fact is, it's probably a mistake for me to be standing here jawin' with you right now. Miss Greene came out of that shop on Newberry like a buzz saw just after you left. She'd seen me talking to you and she was mad as a wet hen. Said she'd have me fired if she caught me at it again."

"Fired? Really? But you've been with Mr. Byrnside far longer than Loretta has. You don't really think he'd let her fire you just for talking to me, do you?"

Wendall snapped his rag. "Who knows what he'd let that woman do. She's really taken over around here. He lets her get away with murder."

"That's only because he's old and tired, Wendell, and doesn't know some of the things that happen. But I'd like to change that."

Wendell studied her. "Miss Greene wouldn't have been so heated up about me talking to you if she hadn't been afraid of you some way or other."

Lynn decided to go out on a limb. "Maybe if I find out what I need to know, she *should* be frightened of me. I can't be sure of that. But I'm certain Mr. Byrnside wouldn't allow her to fire you. Why, you're really all he's got left of his family."

"That's true enough." Wendell's mouth tightened. "You mean that about needing the right information to change things around here?"

"Yes, yes I do."

"I know you might be the old man's granddaughter. Don't look so surprised. It's no use trying to keep a secret from the help. We get to hear about everything." Wiping his hands on the rag again, he walked to the door and peered outside, carefully looking both ways.

"Miss Greene's in the garden on the other side of the house talking to Mr. Caine. She can't possibly hear us," Lynn assured him.

"You never know with that woman." Wendell pivoted. "She's got ears and eyes in the back of her head." He hurried back inside, his brow creased with resentment. "But you're right about Mr. Byrnside not firing me. I can't believe the old man would let her do it. Cause if she tried it, there's a thing or two I could tell him that she wouldn't care for him to know."

Lynn pressed her fingertips together. "You mean the fact that she and Winston Deeping once had a relationship?"

Wendell gave a sharp laugh. "Relationship's a fancy word for it. And I don't think it's all over between them, either. After that big charity affair in Boston and after that fancy wife of his took herself and her mink coats back to England, he was around here talking to the old man and buttering Loretta up. Oh, when it comes to women, that Deeping is mighty fancy pickin's. He can lie out of both sides of his mouth, and he doesn't mind going after another man's property while he's doing it."

"But Loretta's not another man's property, is she?"

"It wasn't her I was talkin' about."

Sensing that Wendell was in the mood to reveal something even more interesting, Lynn strained forward. "Then who? Who did you mean?"

"I don't know much about what Deeping's been up to since Chris died, but I know what he was up to before. I was talking about Gloria Dean, miss."

"Gloria Dean!" Lynn felt a sudden coldness at the top of her head.

"Yes," Wendell hissed, then lowered his voice confidentially. "I'm one to mind my own business, so I never told this to anyone, not even Mr. Byrnside. But if there's a chance you might change things— Just before Chris got killed, I heard him and Deeping arguing, arguing right here in this carriage house."

"About what?"

"Beggin' your pardon, miss, Chris had found out Deeping was having Gloria on the side. It was Deeping who supplied Chris with his drugs. Oh yes, I even seen him do it once. And Chris returned the favor, if you can call it that, by getting Deeping hired on with the Byrnside company. I know the story on that. Well, Deeping wouldn't be where he is now if Chris hadn't driven off the road that very night."

"You mean Chris would have had him fired?"

"That's exactly what I mean."

"Did Loretta know about Winston Deeping and Gloria Dean?" Lynn asked tensely. A terrible picture was beginning to take shape in her imagination.

"Now that I can't say." Shrugging, Wendell rubbed an imaginary speck of dust off the Packard's gleaming fender. "There's a lot that people don't know about Mr. Winston Deeping."

"Yes," Lynn agreed thoughtfully. "I think you're right. And I think it's time that some of those little mysteries were uncovered. Thanks, Wendell."

As JAKE GUIDED his car back to Boston, he listened in silence while Lynn described her encounter with Owen Byrnside and the conversation with his chauffeur that had followed. "Whether you trust me or not, Jake," she finished up, "you must see what all this means."

He slanted a speculative glance at her. "I see that you've taken a dislike to Owen's top recording executive. You're suggesting he might be involved in these attacks on the Byrnside orphans, aren't you?"

"Well, now we know he had both motive and opportunity."

"That goes for a lot of other people, including Owen's other kingpins, all of whom are well-respected men. I must say it annoys me that I didn't know about this private agreement he drew up with them. Foster, Brighton and Caine is his company's law firm. When he brought his business to us we should have been informed of anything as far-reaching as this."

Half turning so that she could study the shifts of expression on Jake's profile, Lynn said, "I don't think Owen was deliberately keeping it a secret. I think he was just ashamed of the agreement and didn't want to think about it or talk about it." With a stab of almost painful affection, she pictured the fiercely proud old man who might be her grandfather. "He probably sees delegating authority like that as a sign of weakness."

"It *is* a sign of weakness. But it sounds as if Owen did it at a time when he was feeling pretty overwhelmed by personal losses."

Lynn nodded. She thought of what Owen had said about not having anything important to leave behind him. Maybe his strong and, to her mind, irrational feelings about that were just a reaction to his personal tragedy, too. It was a safe bet that before Christopher's death Owen had been a workaholic and neglected his family in favor of building his business empire. Now, with his family blown away like dust, he probably blamed himself. Perhaps signing over his company to underlings had been a way of doing penance.

"Don't you think there's a possibility Winston Deeping could be behind some of our problems?" Lynn asked.

Several seconds went by before Jake answered and Lynn reflected that she wasn't learning much from his expression. What a wonderful poker player the guy must be. His clean profile might have been etched in stone. "Winston is a successful man in an established position and he has a very wealthy wife. Why would he risk all that?"

"Why, if his wife is so wonderful, would he take up with Loretta Greene again? I think there's a lot we don't know about the man. Maybe his financial position isn't as secure as you think. And what about that business with

Gloria Dean?'' Lynn pressed. ''According to Wendell, Deeping and Christopher argued about her just before Christopher was killed. Owen Byrnside's son might have had Deeping fired if he hadn't had that accident first.''

Jake shot her a hard glance. ''You were a tough little cop, weren't you? You're even thinking that Deeping might have been involved somehow in Christopher's death?''

''Well, that would make more sense out of what's happening now. And you're right, I was a tough cop. I had to be.'' She sighed. ''Jake, we're allies in this. Believe me, we both want the same thing—to uncover the truth and see Owen Byrnside well served. Consider that contract of Gloria Dean's. What if she knew Deeping had had something to do with Christopher's accident and was blackmailing him? That's the only logical reason why Deeping would have signed her to a contract like that. Otherwise why would he have risked offending Owen?''

''Maybe he was in love with Gloria. A man will do crazy things when he's in love.''

Lynn's mouth turned down. Jake was talking about them as well as Winston Deeping and Gloria Dean. Well, two could play at that. ''So often what men call love is something much shallower, something that will blow away like smoke at the first hint of a storm cloud. Anyhow, I don't think a man like Winston Deeping is capable of truly loving a woman. From what I've seen, he plays women like chess pieces, uses them for what he can get and then loses them. Besides, according to what everyone says, Gloria was a manipulative bitch herself. I can't believe a man like Deeping was about to make any unnecessary sacrifices for her.''

Jake cast another quick glance at the woman beside him, a woman who, despite his lingering confusion and resentment, still stirred his senses and awakened something deeply protective in him. Was she right in implying that what he'd felt for her was shallow, something that had fallen apart at the first shock of reality? But what *was* the reality of their relationship? There'd been so much deception, so many illusions—where did the truth begin?

With a will of their own, his eyes sought her profile again. God, she was lovely, he thought. What did it matter that her beauty had come from a surgeon's knife? It was beauty that went more than skin deep, for she had a strength, a gutsiness and a persistence he had to admire. "It might be your mother you're talking about, you know," he said softly.

Lynn took a deep breath. "That's another thing."

"What now?"

"Why would Gloria abandon a child who could give her access to an enormous fortune? Even if she didn't want the baby—and I guess she wasn't the motherly type—from a purely practical standpoint, it doesn't make sense."

Jake's brows shot together. "What are you suggesting now?"

Lynn gripped her purse. "That Gloria may have known the baby wasn't Christopher's, that it didn't have Christopher's blood type and so it wasn't any good to her. That's why she was willing to dump it off in front of an orphanage as if it were garbage."

"Then whose baby do you think it was?"

Lynn took a deep, ragged breath. "God, it hurts me to say this because what if that baby really was me? And it would be just my luck! But I guess I have to come out with it. We know that Gloria was having an affair with Winston Deeping, don't we? There may have been others, but I guess he has to be a possibility."

Jake's voice was harsh. "If there's anything to that, then the whole Byrnside quest, a whole year of searching half the globe, has been an exercise in futility. You know what finding that out would do to Owen, don't you?''

"I—" Lynn's voice caught. Again she pictured the old man who'd looked at her with such delight and who was so pathetically eager to have a granddaughter. "He would be very disappointed."

"It would kill him! I think—no, I know—that believing he has a granddaughter is the only thing that's kept him going. Maybe he's not the picture of health now, but you should have seen him before this thing started. He was just lying in his bed waiting to die. As he's found you one by one, he's fallen in love with all three of you. I can't imagine anything crueler than the possibility you've just suggested. Owen can't learn it from a lab technician. He has to be warned!"

"But it's just a theory and maybe it's all wrong." Lynn's voice was anguished. She knew that what Jake said was horribly true.

After that, silence returned to the car, an oppressive silence that weighed heavily on both of them. Jake drove like an automaton and Lynn, lost in thought, gazed blankly through the windshield. It wasn't until Jake had pulled up in front of the ferry to Hull, where she'd asked him to drop her off, that he finally spoke again.

"You've already told me you're planning to visit your friend Maudie for a couple of days. Will you be coming back to the office this week?"

"Why? The masquerade is over, isn't it? There's no point in my being Susan Bonner anymore."

"Your name may be spelled differently now, but you still have to give me some notice if you want to quit your job," Jake retorted harshly. In a more conciliatory tone, he added, "And, frankly, I wish you'd stay on at least while I'm out of town."

"You're going out of town?"

"After what you've told me, I think I have to. Before I tell Owen any of what we've discussed, there are some pieces of this puzzle I must put in place for myself, and I have less than a week to do it in." A cloud of gulls screamed close to the dock and an incoming boat tooted its foghorn. "That's your ferry," Jake observed.

"What will you do, and where will you go?" Lynn asked, her mind still on Jake's plans and the possibility that he might be putting himself in danger.

"I'm not exactly sure of my agenda, but London will be one of my stops."

Lynn's golden eyes clouded with worry. "You're planning on having it out with Winston, aren't you?"

"I'm planning to see him, yes, but not until I'm more certain of the hand I'll be playing."

"Oh, Jake, I . . ." Lynn's voice died away. She wasn't sure what she wanted to say. Just the sight of Jake sitting so close to her wrung her heart. She wanted to reach out and touch his hand, stroke his cheek. But she didn't dare. She knew he was still angry with her, still resentful.

"Lynn, before you board that ferry coming in, before we say goodbye, I have to be honest with you."

"Yes?" Her heart seemed to leap. Was he going to tell her that he still loved her? Or that there was no chance they could ever mean anything to each other now?

"Right now I don't care what your name is, or who sired you. All I want is to take you in my arms and kiss you until we both forget everything that happened in Lausanne. But I can't do that. It isn't fair to you, it isn't fair to either of us, not when we haven't resolved anything." For the first time since he'd started speaking, he shot her a direct look. "That's right, isn't it?"

Lynn swallowed. The temptation to cry *no*, to throw herself at him and cling was overpowering. In the short time that they'd been lovers, she'd become addicted to his kisses, to the protection of his arms around her, and now when she was feeling so confused and vulnerable she craved that protection desperately. But it would be a mistake to accept it again under anything but the right conditions.

Lynn opened the door and stepped onto the concrete siding. Then she bent so that her gaze met Jake's squarely. "About the office—when I get back from Hull I'll try to keep an eye on things for you. About us—I think right now there are too many feelings running too high. We both need time, Jake."

AN HOUR LATER as Lynn walked up the slightly weedy path that led to Maudie's front door, she gazed at the lights shining out of the living-room windows as if they were beacons of hope and safety. Tears misted Lynn's eyes, tears that she'd been struggling not to shed since her unsatisfactory parting with Jake.

The front door was flung open and Maudie, wrapped in one of her ancient sweaters, came hurrying out. "Lynnie, you're here at last," she cried. Maudie clattered down the wooden steps and Lynn, her overnight bag bumping against her legs, broke into a trot. An instant later they were in each other's arms, Lynn shedding her suppressed tears at last and Maudie giving her silky blond hair motherly pats and hugging her.

"Oh, honey, honey, I'm so glad to see you! When you called last night, you sounded so unhappy. I've been worried about you."

"I've been worried about me, too."

"What's happened? Are you okay?"

"I don't know," Lynn said with a sniff.

Maudie searched Lynn's tear-streaked face. "I'll fix us a nice pot of coffee and you'll tell me everything." She threw an arm around Lynn's shoulders and guided her up to the porch. "You've got quite a homecoming to look forward to here. When the girls heard you were coming, they decided to fix another one of their not-so-gourmet banquets. For tonight they chose Italian. I think it's lasagna."

Lynn gave a watery giggle. Then her expression shifted. "I should have asked about Pasty before. How is she?"

"All three girls are doing fine. Patsy's a little shakier than the rest, maybe. That was a pretty bad experience she had with Bucky. But she's back on track now, and very grateful to you."

Maudie opened the door and pushed Lynn inside. From upstairs came the sound of high-pitched giggles and a rock tape.

"Well, I guess they're not in the kitchen," Lynn commented. She set her bag down and unbuttoned her jacket.

"No, they just shoved the lasagna in to bake, and with that music turned on loud enough to drown out a herd of freight trains they can't hear us, which gives us a few minutes to ourselves," Maudie commented. "Let's go see about that coffee."

More than ready to enjoy the sensation of someone else taking charge, Lynn followed the other woman back to the old, high-ceilinged kitchen. Pleasant aromas were already beginning to emanate from the interior of its chipped enamel stove. While Maudie got the percolator going, Lynn, who'd dropped down on a stainless-steel-and-plastic chair, described what had happened in Paris and then Lausanne.

"My goodness, you've had quite a time of it," Maudie exclaimed as she carried mugs of coffee to the table. "No wonder you're upset after being caught out that way by your fancy lawyer. But I'm glad this charade of yours is over and I don't have to worry about calling you by the wrong name in front of the wrong person anymore. You'll always be my Lynnie to me, you know."

Lynn lowered her eyes and sipped gratefully at the rich, milky brew Maudie had placed before her. As she drank in the unconditional love and acceptance radiating from the older woman's voice, she couldn't help thinking of Jake and the way he'd rejected her when he'd learned the truth. At the dock that afternoon he'd said he still wanted her. Yet what did that mean, really?

They'd already learned that the chemistry between them was still explosive. Okay, so maybe he still wanted her physically. But she needed more from him. What if, with her lie between them and their differences out in the open, he just couldn't give it? And what if it turned out that she was the Byrnside heiress after all? If Jake was willing to accept her then after rejecting her now, how would she ever be able to believe that his acceptance was genuine? If he waited too long, it would be too late. Maybe it was already too late.

"There's more to the story," Lynn said. "I haven't told you yet about what happened when I went to see Owen Byrnside today."

"Well, you've got a captive audience who's all ears."

As Lynn began to speak again, the smile left the older woman's face and her expression grew troubled. "My Lord, but you've stepped into a hornet's nest," she finally broke out. "I don't like this. I don't like this one bit. And I especially don't like hearing that there's someone out there who might still want to hurt you."

"I don't think it's me in particular, now, who's in danger. I think it's all three of Owen Byrnside's orphans."

"That's not a threesome I care for you to be a part of."

Lynn downed the last of her coffee. "Not even if there's a possibility that I might come into a fortune?" she questioned lightly. "For years now I've wished I could repay you for the help you gave me when I was a scruffy, homeless brat. You know that if I ever came into money I'd see that you got some to fix this place up for your foster kids."

Maudie regarded her solemnly. "Well, I can't deny that money would come in handy. And I've never been too proud to accept it. But money isn't the most important thing here." Her brows were knitted as she ran a finger around the edge of her mug. "Lynnie, of all the kids I've taken in, you've been the dearest to my heart. I want things for you the same way I would if you were my own daughter. I'm proud of you and what you've accomplished, but I see that you're unhappy. It makes my heart ache because I know perfectly well money isn't going to fix that."

"Shucks, Maudie, don't ruin my day by telling me I can't buy happiness!"

"I think you've already had your day ruined, and not by me. It's that lawyer of yours, isn't it? More's gone on between you than you're admitting. Have you fallen for him?"

Lynn didn't answer because she couldn't. The tears she'd thought she'd finally conquered, suddenly gushed through her guard again. They ran from her eyes in hot streams and trickled in salty rivulets down her cheeks. Quickly, she covered her face. But she couldn't hide what was happening.

"Lynnie!" Maudie cried in a stricken voice. "Oh, honey!"

"I'm sorry, I'm sorry," Lynn sobbed through her tears. "I don't know why I'm doing this. It's just...I've had such a hard day. And oh, Maudie, you're right. I'm in love with Jake Caine and it's just not going to work out. It's just not going to!"

IF I HADN'T NEEDED CLEAN socks, I might just as well not have unpacked at all, Jake thought the next morning as he shoved his toilet kit back into his small suitcase and snapped it shut. He glanced at the clock on the bedside table. Seven-thirty, which gave him exactly an hour to get to the airport and grab the flight to London he'd booked the night before.

"Before this is over I'll have the most complicated case of jet lag on record," he muttered. Not that it mattered much when he hadn't been able to sleep at all. As the dark shadows under his eyes testified, Jake had spent most of the night pacing in front of his bedroom windows, thinking about the Byrnside imbroglio, thinking about Lynn and how much he wanted her in his arms that minute, whoever she was, wherever she came from, whoever she looked like!

"First things first," Jake said to himself as he picked up his case and checked his pocket for keys. Before he could do anything else, he had to get to the bottom of this business with Winston Deeping, which meant he had to confront the man in London.

Jake was halfway to the door when the phone rang. For a split second he hesitated, thinking that he didn't want to chance being late and the answering machine would take the call. But what if it were important?

With a sigh, Jake walked back and picked up the receiver on the fourth ring. The voice on the other end of the line was that of his detective. "I have something interesting for you," the man said. "You wanted to know who paid for Lynn Rice's surgery?"

"Yes?" Jake felt his heartbeat accelerate.

"Well, guess what? It was Loretta Greene."

LYNN WALKED UP the steps to her apartment building. Before she had a chance to unlock the front door, it was thrown open by Mrs. Crumper. "I saw you coming up the street and I got so excited. Oh dear, I'm so glad you're back! I've missed you!" Mrs. Crumper's white curls bobbed and her pink mouth was pursed into a tiny wrinkled rose. Teary-eyed, she threw her arms around Lynn and gave her a quivery hug.

Lynn was touched. Truthfully, since leaving Boston she hadn't given Mrs. Crumper a thought. There'd been too many other things to occupy her mind. "It's wonderful to see you again, too. How've you been?" she said with determined cheer.

The old lady drew back and folded her hands over her small, round stomach. "Not so good. My television broke down, and I haven't been able to get out to have it fixed. I've been lonely."

Mrs. Crumper without her soaps and game shows? It was unthinkable! "I'll drop your TV off at the fix-it shop first thing tomorrow morning on my way to work," Lynn promised. "How's that?"

Mrs. Crumper's lower lip began to tremble and her eyes glistened. "Would you, dear? Oh, that's so kind! I'm sorry you're going to work tomorrow, though. I can't tell you how isolated I've felt with you away, as if I'd lost the only friend I had in the world. But that's not so surprising, is it? Really, you are my only friend. All my other friends are dead."

Lynn gazed at the old lady in consternation. Usually Mrs. Crumper made such an effort to be upbeat. Was she really that lonely? How terrible for her if all her friends really were dead! Oh, how could this world be so crowded with people who were all lonely—like herself, like Jake, like Owen Byrnside?

As she thought of Owen, a crazy idea popped into Lynn's mind and she cocked her head. "Mrs. Crumper, what are you doing next weekend?"

"Next weekend? Why, nothing dear. I never go anywhere, you know that."

"How would you like a weekend at a beautiful country estate north of Boston? You can go as my chaperon."

"Your chaperon? Oh, but young girls these days don't want chaperons."

"This one does, and she thinks you'd be perfect. Will you come?"

"Certainly, if you really and truly want me to."

"I really and truly want you to. And besides," Lynn added with a lift of her mouth, "there's someone I want you to meet."

A few minutes later Lynn proceeded on up the stairs to her apartment, her mind once again occupied with her own problems. The weekend with Maudie and the girls had helped put her back on a steadier emotional track. And, momentarily, it had cheered her to think of asking Mrs. Crumper to go with her to Taleman Hall. But those were purely temporary breaks from problems that weren't going to go away, problems she had to solve for herself.

Frowning as she pondered her myriad difficulties, Lynn unlocked the door and walked inside. She'd taken only a few steps when something stopped her cold. She stiffened, her head came up and all her senses went on red alert. Something wasn't right.

She glanced around, noting the position of the furniture, rugs, magazine-filled Mexican wicker basket. Had something been disturbed in her absence? No, that wasn't what had her bothered.

A smell registered on her nostrils, a sweetish smell that—oh God!—she recognized. She started to whirl around, but already it was too late. A hand wrapped in a chloroform-soaked rag clamped down over her nose and mouth while an arm dragged her against a bony chest and locked her in an unyielding grip. She fought—biting, kicking. Once she managed to free herself. But her reactions, slowed by the drug, weren't quick enough and the hand hammered down again. A heavy darkness swamped her, and her struggles grew weaker. Then, with a choked sob, she slumped into unconsciousness.

CHAPTER FOURTEEN

A MAID NAMED NANCY opened Taleman Hall's big front door. She looked surprised to see Jake standing there. "Why, Mr. Caine! Are you here to see Mr. Byrnside? I'm afraid he's just settled down for his midmorning nap right now."

"It's not Owen I'm here for this time, Nancy. I'd like to speak to Loretta."

The maid's brow cleared. "I believe she's out in the greenhouses. Shall I call her for you?"

"No, I'll go out there myself, if you don't mind."

Relieved of the need to do anything but go on with her usual morning routine, Nancy smiled. "Of course I don't mind. I'm sure she'll be happy to see you, sir. You know the way?"

"I know the way." Instead of going through the central corridor inside the house, Jake took the brick path that led around to the back where the complex of greenhouses lay, screened behind a yew hedge on the other side of the solarium. Owen had originally built the greenhouses for his wife, who'd been an avid gardener. Now they provided cut flowers as well as many of the fresh fruits and herbs used in the house.

Though the day was warm for February, beautiful and cloudless, Jake walked along beside the fragrant boxwood plantings with his head down, his hands jammed in his pockets. He was glad he'd picked up that phone call

from his detective. After receiving his detective's new information about Loretta, he'd decided to put off his London flight until he'd talked to the woman. He'd spent the
weekend going through the Byrnside files at the office, and
he felt well prepared. Still, Jake was not looking forward
to the upcoming confrontation. Loretta Greene, Lynn's
anonymous patron? It was incredible!

After he opened the greenhouse door and stepped inside, he stood for a moment adjusting to the heat and hu-
midity. Though the place no longer held the masses of lush
greenery it had housed in Alice Byrnside's day, it still
smelled strongly of earth and plant life. In the distance
Jake caught the click-click of shears.

Jake walked through the first greenhouse, which held
fruit trees, and into the second, which was ablaze with flats
of flowers. At the end of the long glass-roofed shed Loretta Greene, her pink silk blouse and matching skirt
swathed in a long apron, stood snipping painted daisies for
a basket she held gracefully cradled in one arm. When she
heard Jake's footsteps, she turned and her large dark eyes
widened.

"Why Jake, I didn't know you were coming today."

"Neither did I." Jake stationed himself directly in front
of her. "How are you, Loretta?"

"Oh fine, fine."

"And Owen?"

"He's all right, too. Though his interview with Lynn
Rice yesterday tired him out." She made a little moue of
distaste. "I just hope that when all three girls come here
next week the excitement doesn't send him straight into a
decline."

"Even if Owen knew it were going to do exactly that, he
wouldn't give up on it. Having all three orphans under his

roof is something he's been looking forward to for many months.''

"Oh, I know, I know." Loretta threw up one hand. "I just hope it turns out for the best. And I hope it doesn't turn out that the Rice woman is the heiress." Again, Loretta made a face.

As Jake absorbed all this, his jaw hardened. "You know, Loretta, I find it strange that you've taken such a dislike to Lynn Rice because, in a way, she's your creation, isn't she?''

"What?" The heavy garden shears dropped from her hand and clattered to the cement floor. She stared up at Jake, her face suddenly bloodless. "Why, whatever do you mean?" She laughed nervously.

Jake bent and picked up the scissors. As he straightened, he tested their sharp points against the pad of his thumb. "I know you contacted Lynn Rice anonymously and arranged for her plastic surgery. I strongly suspect it was you who sent the anonymous letter to Owen telling him about his grandchild. What I can't understand is why.'' Jake shook his head. "Why on earth would you be the one to set this whole orphan search in motion?''

Loretta jerked around so that her back was to Jake. Her head bent, revealing a web of creases in the white skin beneath the black hair coiled on her nape. And for the first time, Jake saw the woman was vulnerable—and not getting any younger, either. When she spoke, her voice quivered. "How—how did you find out?''

"I have a detective who knows his way around bank records.''

She swallowed. "I was afraid of something like that. I've been living in fear all this time, actually.''

"Why, Loretta? And how? How did you know about the orphans, and about Lynn?''

When the woman didn't answer, Jake stepped closer to her. "Maybe I've already put some of the pieces together," he said harshly. "It's something to do with Winston Deeping, isn't it? In the old days, before Christopher Byrnside was killed, you and Winston were lovers, weren't you?"

A tear glistened in Loretta's black-mascaraed lashes, and she bit her lip. She and Jake stood for several seconds in taut silence.

"Weren't you?" he repeated, hating to have to do this, but determined to get beyond their impasse.

"Yes," Loretta whispered. "But it was all so long ago."

"This whole situation we're dealing with got its start a long time ago. You haven't answered my other questions. How did you know about the orphans?"

When Loretta's mouth compressed in stubborn silence, Jake cleared his throat. "Let me guess, then. You probably knew that Winston cheated on you with Gloria Dean. Later, when he lost interest in the woman and you forgave him, he probably told you that she'd blackmailed him into giving her a contract he didn't want your employer to find out about. Somehow you also learned that she'd been carrying a child that she abandoned, and you also made it your business to find out what happened to that child."

"It might have been Winston's," Loretta burst out. "If things had been different, it might have been mine!" She threw down her basket and covered her face with her hands. "I couldn't believe he wasn't interested in the baby. Oh, men are so cold! But women aren't and I had to know. Gloria was a heartless monster. She just threw that baby away!"

Jake gazed down at Loretta, his thoughts snapping together like plastic building blocks. "But that doesn't explain why you wanted to stir this whole thing up again by telling Owen about the orphans, and then, on top of everything else, why you wanted to pay for Lynn's plastic surgery." His eyes narrowed. "Or does it? That letter to Lynn must have gone out almost two years ago. As I recall, that was not too long after Winston's nuptials to Tabissa."

Loretta's head jerked. "That silly, silly woman!"

"Could you have been carrying a torch for Winston all that time?"

"Torch! You call it a torch?" She stamped her foot, grinding one of the flowers scattered from the fallen basket beneath her heel. "For more than twenty-five years that man strung me along. For all that time he pretended that he loved me and that some day he'd marry me. And I, gullible fool that I was, let him sweet-talk me into settling for such crumbs."

"I gather, then, it came as a surprise when Winston announced his engagement to Tabissa."

Loretta's white face froze into a mask of hatred. "He told me it was just money, that he'd made some bad investments and needed her money. But he had no right, no right! How dare he!"

Jake nodded. "So that was it. You wanted to get back at Winston. You knew that if you stirred Owen Byrnside up about a granddaughter, eventually some of Winston's doings would come to light and embarrass him. But what about Lynn's surgery? That still baffles me."

Loretta had begun to look exhausted, as if talking were draining away all her strength. "Over the years I'd kept track of those abandoned babies. Of the three, Lynn was the one who'd been really hurt by that fire. I'd never laid eyes on her, but I'd always sympathized with her particularly. I'd even felt guilty about Lynn, though I can't imagine why, since I had nothing to do with what happened to her. Maybe it was because when I was younger I wanted a baby desperately. Just before Winston decided to marry that . . . that woman, I had to have my ovaries out and I realized I was never going to have a child of my own.''

Jake regarded Loretta with more sympathy. So Winston had deserted her at just the time when she'd needed him most. No wonder she'd gone into an emotional tailspin.

"Owen has always been generous with me, and all my investments have been good, though not good enough for Winston," she went on. "I know that Owen has left me money in his will, so I feel financially secure. I don't know, it just seemed . . . appropriate . . . to do something for one of those orphans. Of course," she added acerbically, "that was before I'd met any of them."

And when she'd met them, Jake mused, she'd taken an instant dislike to all of them. That, too, made sense on some elemental level, he supposed. Before they'd walked in the door of Taleman Hall, they'd been fantasy creatures—Lynn most of all. Suddenly, seeing them as flesh-and-blood young women who had agendas of their own had probably been like a shower of icy water for Loretta.

And in Lynn's case that had been doubly true, for all this time Lynn had been playing spy, trying to uncover the truth of the situation. Now that Jake thought about it, he could see where Loretta probably felt that as some sort of personal betrayal—almost the way he'd taken it, he mused, more than a little disturbed by the parallel. Why had he reacted so violently to the truth of Lynn's identity? he asked himself. Because, like Loretta, he'd been idealizing Lynn and she'd betrayed that fantasy image he'd been cherishing.

Mechanically, Jake bent and began to pick up the scattered flowers and replace them in the fallen basket. When he straightened, he handed the basket to Loretta. She accepted it, her dark eyes wary, her lips trembling slightly. "What—what are you going to do now?" she whispered.

"Loretta, I think there's more to this than you've told me. I think Winston may have been involved with Christopher's death and all these years you've suspected it and kept your suspicions to yourself. That would explain the guilty feeling you mentioned, now wouldn't it?"

Loretta began to shake her head. Her painted lips formed the word "no" but no sound came out.

"Obviously," Jake continued relentlessly, "I've got to have it out with Winston. I meant to do that today, actually, and with a lot less to go on than you've just given me. Now it will have to wait until I can book another flight to London." He cast another look over Loretta, a look that held both sympathy and regret. "I'm sorry for you," he said. "I'm sorry for Owen Byrnside's whole family— whatever may be left of it. I'm sorry for this whole damn situation. Goodbye, Loretta."

LORETTA WATCHED Jake stride from the greenhouse. When he was gone, she slumped against the edge of the aluminum table tray that held the planting boxes. Her heart thumped and her breath came in short, spasmodic jerks. "Oh, what have I done?" she moaned. "What have I done?"

She pressed a palm to her forehead and then jerked it away and rubbed her cold hands together as if she were trying to wash them clean. "Winston, Winston," she gasped, "Oh, God!"

Suddenly Loretta pushed herself upright. Ignoring the flowers she'd cut, she hurried outside. Instead of taking the path to the front of the house as Jake had done, however, she flitted through the hedge and across the shaded patch of rear garden into one of Taleman Hall's side doors. Breathing like a winded runner, she skittered up a flight of winding steps that had an entry on the second floor adjacent to her suite.

Decorated in a complicated pattern of lush yellow and red roses that was repeated in wallpaper, draperies, slipcovers and carpeting, Loretta's private rooms were spacious and sunny. She rushed into her sitting room, locked the door carefully behind her and then hurried to a yellow silk antique loveseat. Picking up the phone on the small inlaid table next to it, she began to dial an overseas number.

ON THE OTHER SIDE of the Atlantic, Winston Deeping sat on the terrace of his posh town house. With an elaborately worked silver spoon, he chipped at the thin shell of a coddled egg and eyed the headlines of the London *Times* at his side.

Opposite him, dressed in a voluminous pink silk robe with wide satin lapels, his wife sipped coffee from a thin china cup and perused the latest article about herself in the society pages. "This is a positively dreadful picture of me," she commented.

"What's so dreadful about it?"

"Really, I look like a skinny old hag. I do believe it's time for a bit of a collagen touch-up."

For the first time, Winston lifted his eyes from the paper. As they studied his wife they were cold. "You're not planning to go off to that French clinic again, are you?"

"Why yes, I do believe I am. Any objections?" Tabissa looked amused.

"Many. The last time you went it bankrupted me. I'm still grappling with the monstrous bills."

"Really, dear, you must get over being such a nasty little money-grubber. I know it's a matter of class, your Yorkshire origins being what they were, and you really can't help yourself. But it's such a dead giveaway that we're utterly mismatched in every imaginable regard. Do try to put your mind on a higher level."

Winston gazed at his wife with something close to hatred. When he'd married her he'd thought she would solve his financial problems and bring him the social status he craved. Instead, once they were legally tied he found she'd misrepresented her fortune, which was really no longer in existence. She and her blue-blood forebears had frittered it away and somehow still managed to go their merry way for generations, living on credit and fancy house parties.

Instead of plumping up his bank account, Tabissa had drilled into it and sucked it dry. And now, unless he could somehow retrieve the situation, there wasn't anything left for her to take.

Tabissa pushed her wrought-iron chair back across the paving stones. "Oh, by the way, I ordered a frightfully smart new desk for you. I know you'll adore it."

"A new desk? I don't need a new desk."

"Oh, yes you do, darling. The tooled leather on your old one is scratched. Well, I think I'll go off for my bath. Do try and look a little less grisly, won't you? Nasty expressions like the one you're wearing now will make you old before your time."

As Tabissa, balancing her cup in one delicately upraised palm, glided through the French doors trailing pink silk and insults, her husband regarded her regal backside with murderously slitted eyes.

Women, he thought venomously. There wasn't one of them in his life who hadn't brought him a packet of trouble. Even Loretta, that poor stupid little dupe, had almost ruined everything by writing Owen Byrnside and telling him about his grandchild. Winston had been furious when Loretta had admitted to him what she'd done. But he'd gone out of his way to be nice to her on that last trip to the States just to be sure she wouldn't cause any more trouble. And in fact, he still worried that she might do something idiotic. Then there were those damnable orphans. Well, he would have dealt with them soon, very soon.

"There's a long distance call for you, Mr. Deeping. Will you take it in the study, or shall I bring the phone out here?"

Winston frowned at the maid who'd poked her frizzy head through the doorway. "I'll take it in the study."

A few minutes later he picked up a receiver and sat down in front of a wide mahogany desk. Idly, he scanned its green leather top. If there were any scratches on it, they were not visible to the naked eye. When he heard the voice on the other end of the line, he jerked to sharp attention.

"Loretta? I told you never to call me here."

"I know, Winston, but you wouldn't be in your office this early and I had to warn you. I just had to."

"Warn me about what?"

"Oh, Winston, despite everything I still love you. I know I wouldn't admit it before, but it's true. You're in my heart, my soul. You're in my blood."

Winston tapped impatient fingers on the leather. "Loretta, what's wrong? Why did you call?"

He heard a convulsive gulp. Then, when she started to speak again, he listened with his bones going icy cold. "And you told Jake Caine all this?" he hissed explosively. "Why, in God's name?"

"I couldn't help it, Winston. It just came spilling out. I was still angry with you, and part of me wanted to hurt you. But now I'm sorry. That's why I'm calling. I had to warn you."

"Thanks a lot," Winston snapped. "You put a noose around my neck and then you warn me. Well, it's too late, Loretta. You should have kept your damned mouth shut!"

Furiously, Winston slammed down the phone. Then he sat gnawing his knuckles while his mind whirled like a dervish. Damn Loretta! Now that Jake Caine knew so much of the truth, it was all over, he realized. All his dreams, all his efforts to pull things out of the fire. It was all over. He groaned and a bitter black bile seemed to run through him.

What was left? Well, he'd have to abandon all of this, he thought, glancing around the room his wife had furnished with her customary spendthrift luxury. He wasn't going to be around to see this new desk she'd bought, and he wasn't going to be around to pay for it, either.

Well, at least that was one saving grace. Every cloud had its silver lining. He wouldn't have to eat breakfast with Tabissa or listen to her stinging little insults anymore. But where would he go?

There were places in South America where a man could disappear forever, places of incomparable beauty where a relatively small amount of money would go a long way, and where with a large amount you could live like a king. And, if he was quick, he could still draw on the company funds. But first he had to make a phone call. No sense getting any deeper into hot water than he already found himself.

Winston picked up the phone and dialed a number in Boston. It rang four times before a whispery voice answered.

"Noel?"

"Yes, Winston."

"Did you pull off the job?"

"Yes. Right now she's tied up like a birthday present and locked in the closet."

"You haven't . . . you haven't done anything to her yet, have you?"

"Not yet, not until I take care of the other two and plant her fingerprints and a few other choice bits of evidence at the scene of the crime. As a matter of fact, I was just going out the door when the phone rang."

Winston rubbed the deep crease between his thin brows. Yes, that had been the plan. Kidnap Lynn Rice, murder Kate Conti and Maggie Marlowe and then make it look as if the Rice woman had been behind the killings. When the other two were permanently out of the way, he and Noel had planned to dispose of Lynn and make it look like a guilty suicide. "You can forget all that."

There was a second's stunned silence. "What do you mean, forget it? What are you talking about?"

"It's over, Noel. That silly bitch Loretta Greene just spilled ninety percent of the story to Jake Caine. He's probably arranging to have me arrested at this precise minute. It would be quite idiotic to go ahead with this plan now. Jake and the old man would know that I was behind it."

Winston heard a snort of fury. "Where does that leave me?"

"Out of a job and reading the want ads."

"The hell you say! You owe me money, Winston. A lot of money!"

"Tough luck. You can't get blood out of a stone, and this stone is about to sink out of sight."

"You're planning to skip town?"

"It's either that or wind up in jail, a prospect I do not find appealing."

"Where are you going to go?"

Impatiently, Winston shifted the receiver from his right to his left hand. "You don't really think I'm stupid enough to tell you, do you? I'm afraid it's *adios*, partner."

"Wait! I told you, I've the blonde tied up in the closet right now? What am I supposed to do with her?"

"Your call. I have a plane to catch."

"She's seen my face. She knows who I am."

"That's your problem."

The fury in Noel's voice hardened. "Oh, it is, is it? Well, let me give you a goodbye present, Winston. Wherever you're planning to go, and I don't care what kind of a rat-hole it is, I'll find you. Nobody treats me like this and gets away with it—nobody. So enjoy your little escape while you can. Because after I get on your trail, it's going to be very short."

An icy ripple shot up Winston's spine and he slammed down the receiver. Why had he let that weasel keep him on the phone so long? Time was too precious to waste. And wasn't it a lucky thing that he and Tabissa kept separate bedrooms? He'd be able to pack and get out of the house without her being any the wiser. Winston stood and hurried to the door. But before he opened it, he cast a last, haunted glance back at the desk where he'd just had two very disturbing long-distance conversations. What if Noel had meant that threat about finding him no matter where he hid? Having Noel on your trail was like being followed by a bloodhound, or a snake. Shivering once again, Winston hurried out.

IN AN UNTIDY APARTMENT in Boston, Noel glared at the phone. He slammed a tightly balled fist into his cupped palm. As he contemplated the frustrations of the last months in Winston Deeping's employ and now the man's double cross, he muttered a long string of curses. Then he turned his attention to the closed closet door off the kitchen. Behind it, Lynn Rice lay gagged and tied. Once he had killed Kate and Maggie and made it look like Lynn's doing, Noel had looked forward to the final pleasure of disposing of Lynn as well. But now, thanks to Winston, that plan was kaput, shot!

Why did I ever get hooked up with that little creep in the first place? Noel asked himself. I should have known he'd leave me holding the bag. This whole thing has been nothing but trouble. It's as if those girls have charmed lives. Noel, a slim young man with an androgynous face and reed-slim body, scowled. Today he was dressed in jeans and a plaid shirt and could easily pass for a teenager. Other times, as when he'd called himself Rona Chastain and stalked Maggie Murphy on Barbados, he had donned a wig and transformed himself into a woman.

A cunning look came into his slitted eyes. Maybe this wasn't a total loss, after all. It was just a matter of using some smarts. So okay, the three Byrnside orphans weren't valuable dead anymore. But they might be worth quite a bit alive—to the right person. Noel cast another look around the room, checked the contents of his pockets and then gathered a leather jacket resting on the back of a chair. Pretty redheaded Kate, he thought, whatever you're doing right now, enjoy it while you can. Because, babe, you ain't gonna be doing it much longer.

As Jake pulled into the outskirts of Boston, he debated his next move. He could go directly to the airport, or he could stop first at the office and put in some of the calls that now needed to be made. If he did that, he might see

Lynn. That was more than enough to convince him in favor of the office. They needed to talk, really talk. It was stupid to go on letting things stand as they were—idiotic when he now knew beyond a shadow of a doubt that he was still crazy about her, no matter what. He needed to tell her that.

But when Jake arrived at his destination Lynn wasn't there. "She never came in this morning," the receptionist informed him.

A TALL, SHAMBLING MAN in an ancient, threadbare sport coat badly in need of cleaning approached the brownstone building where Lynn Rice lived. He eyed the gold numbers on the beveled glass door, cocked his head at the names on the mailboxes and then buzzed the one reading "Susan Bonner". When no one answered he turned around, stuck his big hands in his pockets and studied the street. Then, with a little lift of his burly shoulders, he swiveled back and rang some of the other numbers on the boxes.

Garrity was about to give up when he heard a door open just inside the white tile foyer. Quick feet approached and he saw a tiny, white-haired little woman peer at him through the glass.

"What do you want?" she mouthed.

"I'm here to see the young woman who lives in 204," he replied.

"You mean Susan Bonner?"

"Yes."

"Are you a friend of hers?"

"I'm a very old friend of hers. Ancient, you might say."

The old lady pushed open the door and stood aside. "Come in, come in. My name is Crumper, Daisy Crumper. I live right here." She pointed at a door to the right.

"How do you do, Mrs. Crumper. Thanks for letting me in. Shall I just go on up and give the door up there a knock?"

"You can try, but I don't think it'll do you any good. I've been knocking all day, but no one answers. So, I guess she isn't home." The old woman's mouth puckered, and for an alarming moment she almost looked as if she were about to burst into tears over the fact. "The funny thing is I never heard her go out this morning, and she promised she'd come take my television set to be repaired before she went to work. I know I'm only a poor old woman, but it's not like Susan to forget a promise, you know. Oh, it's not like her at all."

Garrity's shaggy brows knit. "You're ever so right, it isn't. Not a bit of it. The girl I know is simply not the forgetful type." He lifted a sneakered foot and began to climb the steps to the second floor. For several seconds Mrs. Crumper stood watching. Then, like a miniature Yorkshire terrier in pursuit of a large sheepdog, she began following behind.

When Garrity reached Lynn's door, he gave it a sharp rap and then stood back, rocking on his large feet.

"Do you think she could be sick in there?" Mrs. Crumper asked anxiously when no one answered.

"Now, why would you imagine a thing like that? Did she look sick when you saw her last?"

"Oh, no, no! It's just so unlike her, forgetting a promise. And she knows how important my TV is to me."

Just then they heard the buzzer ring inside the apartment. "Now who could that be?" Mrs. Crumper exclaimed. "She doesn't normally have visitors at all." The old lady turned and scurried back down the steps to the front door. This time the man on the opposite side of the glass was Jake Caine.

"Goodness, what a coincidence," the old lady twittered when she opened it. "You're the second gentleman caller who's come to see Susan within the last ten minutes."

"Oh?" A guarded look came over Jake's face.

"Yes," Mrs. Crumper went on excitedly, "and her other visitor is upstairs knocking on her door now, though no one's answering. I don't believe she's home, you know."

Jake cast a look up the stairs. "If you don't mind, I'll just go up and see for myself."

"Of course I don't mind! Now, why should I mind?"

Jake, bounding up the steps two at a time, was too preoccupied to answer. When he reached the second floor and saw Garrity standing in the corridor, he stared at the rumpled policeman in surprise. "Are you a friend of Ly—Susan's?"

Garrity studied Jake with interest. "Unless I've got the address wrong, I'm a friend of the young lady who lives in there. Who are you?"

"She works for me. She didn't come into the office today, so I thought I'd stop by and check to see that she's okay."

"She didn't come to work?" Garrity's brow folded into deep pleats.

"Oh dear, oh dear," Mrs. Crumper exclaimed as she puffed back up the last step. "I'm really afraid that something's dreadfully wrong."

Garrity and Jake were still concentrating on each other. "Do you have any reason to think that our young lady might have run into some kind of trouble?" Garrity questioned.

Jake's face had gone rigid. "It's a possibility."

"Then, maybe we'd better have a look inside." Garrity turned to the old lady. "It so happens I'm a police officer, ma'am, and I also happen to be carrying a set of keys with me that will get me past just about any door. If you have no strong objection, I'd like to open this one up just to make sure everything's okay in there.''

Mrs. Crumper tiptoed up to him, her palms pressed prayerfully together in front of her. ''Oh, please do. Now I'm really, really worried. I won't rest until I know Susan isn't sick in there.''

Garrity drew a bunch of hooked instruments from his pocket. After experimenting with several, he found one that unlocked Lynn's door. When it swung open, he stepped inside and Jake and Mrs. Crumper followed. The first thing they saw was a rucked-up throw rug and an overturned hatrack.

Jake's face went pale. ''It looks as if there's been some kind of a struggle.''

With surprising lightness for a man of his size, Garrity walked around the area on the balls of his feet. Intently, he gazed about him. Then he knelt, picked up a bit of rag and sniffed. ''I don't like this.''

''What is it?'' Jake asked while Mrs. Crumper goggled.

''There's not much odor left, so it must be almost a day old. But I think I can still smell chloroform.''

CHAPTER FIFTEEN

A GRIMY SCARF throttled Lynn's groan. *"Ooohf,"* she moaned as she arched her neck back and then forward. Loose bricks seemed to be ramming around inside her head. Every cramped muscle in her body screamed. Ignoring the pain, she retested the cords binding her hands and feet. No use. The knots wouldn't budge.

How long had she been in this dark little closet? Lynn wondered. A day, two days? Since she'd been floating in and out of unconsciousness the whole time, it was impossible to tell. All she knew was that twice a shadowy figure had brought her sandwiches and untied her long enough so that she could eat them. He'd also left a bucket and informed her that it was all she could expect in the bathroom department.

Who was this Mr. Nice Guy, she wondered, and how long would he keep her here? And what did he ultimately intend to do with her? She shuddered as her imagination began to run wild and forced herself to clamp down on the gruesome thoughts springing up like hideous tropical growths. It would do her no good to be paralyzed with fear. The only thing that might help her now was to start thinking clearly so she could find a way of getting out of this mess.

But how? Well, judging from the lack of noise, her captor wasn't around now. So she had some time. The first order of business, obviously, was to figure out how to get herself untied.

Lynn was wriggling her fingers, trying to restore some circulation, when a noise outside the closet made her freeze. He was back. A shaft of pure terror ripped through her. What now? Had he returned to kill her? And, oh God, how would he do it?

Thump, thump, thump. Suddenly the door opened. Lynn blinked fearfully. Her eyes, so long deprived of light, could make out only a bulky figure. It wasn't until the figure bent down and placed a bulky shape on the floor beside her that she realized her jailer had been carrying something heavy and almost as large as himself.

"Have fun, you two," he said with a hyena laugh that intensified her chills. "Don't do anything I wouldn't do." With that, he slammed the door shut and Lynn was left with whatever he'd dumped to the floor. It was a person. It had to be. But was that person dead or alive?

Slowly, painfully, Lynn began to wriggle toward it. If her new roommate was alive, she wanted to know. And if not—well, she wanted to know that, too. Suddenly her leg encountered a texture that felt like denim. Whoever lay there had on jeans. And that person was breathing, she realized with deep relief as she heard a weak indrawn breath and then a moan.

Lynn gasped in excitement. The voice had been feminine. Thinking fast, Lynn turned so that she faced away from the other's prone body. Since her wrists were tied behind her back, that gave her fingers some room to feel. The first thing they encountered was a knee. Lynn squeezed to the right and touched a trim waistline. She moved another couple of feet and then leaned back to explore. Hair, curls and, yes, a gag just like her own tied over the person's mouth.

Lynn's fingers moved through the curls until they found where the scarf had been knotted. It wasn't easy to undo the knot, but at last she managed to loosen it enough so that it slipped from the woman's mouth.

"Ummmmm, ohhhh..."

Was that to be her only reward, Lynn thought impatiently, moans that weren't any more illuminating than the sounds she could make? *"Eleeeyuuuunaaa,"* was the best she could do. But, of course, it was useless. The only way she was going to learn this person's name was if she could get rid of her own gag.

Desperately, for Lynn suspected there wasn't much time for introductions, she worked her way back down the body until she found its hands and began picking at the knots that bound them.

Suddenly a voice said fuzzily, "What...what's going on? Where am I?"

"Oooofcooo!" Lynn retorted. All the while she continued to pick at the knots. Somehow she had to untie this woman and then persuade her to return the favor.

"Hey, what are you doing? Listen, my name is Kate Humphrey Conti. Who the hell are you?"

As JAKE STARED DOWN at the rag in Garrity's hand, he felt the blood drain from his head. "Chloroform," he muttered. His gaze swung back up to Garrity's face. "What do you think's happened?" It was an inane question, since he already knew the answer. But he had to ask it.

"Looks like our girl's been kidnapped."

"Kidnapped!"

Behind them, Mrs. Crumper let out a shriek. "Kidnapped!"

Ignoring the old woman's yelps, the two men continued to stare at each other. *Lynn!* an anguished voice deep inside Jake seemed to cry. When he actually spoke, he surprised himself with his controlled tone. "You say you're a friend of Lynn's. I don't know you, or how much you've been told about this situation."

"Precious little," Garrity answered, "but enough to figure that Lynn is in some deep trouble."

"Lynn, Lynn—who are you talking about?" Mrs. Crumper danced around the two men. "It's Susan who lives here! Don't you even know her name? I'm going to go down and call the police right this minute."

Garrity reached out and patted the old woman's shoulder and then, with his other hand, pulled out his identification. "I'm a policeman, ma'am, so take my word for it. Sometimes in a case like this it's better to talk things out a little before you start making any calls. Can you give this gentleman and me a minute or two to do that?"

Mrs. Crumper wrung her hands. Her eyes filled with tears. But, accustomed to trusting the authority of men, she finally nodded. "I'll wait downstairs," she whimpered. "But don't leave without telling me what I should do."

"We won't," Garrity promised and then showed his identification to Jake. When the old woman had left them, he said, "I worked with Lynn. She saved my skin a couple of times and I'll do the same for her any time I can. Like I said, she's told me some of what's been going on with her. In fact, that's why I'm here, to tell her I came up dry on Christopher Byrnside's accident. It just happened too long ago to uncover anything new from the files. But now I need to know more about the whole situation. Can you fill me in?"

Jake nodded, and quickly recapped all that had happened with the Byrnside quest. If things had been different, he might have felt jealous of Garrity's previous relationship with Lynn. Now, all that mattered was finding her.

When Jake finished, the big Irishman rubbed at his bristly chin. "There's only two reasons why someone would use chloroform on a woman. One, to get her out of her apartment without a struggle and take her someplace where he can dispose of the body easily."

"Is that what you think has happened?" Again the two men stared at each other. Jake's face was stricken. In his mind's eye he visualized Lynn's body in a ditch, her golden hair streaked with mud. An unbearable sickness and horror spread through him. He loved her, he acknowledged starkly. He loved her so damn much! It couldn't be true. He wouldn't allow it to be true!

"If that's what happened," Garrity answered grimly, "there's nothing we can do by now. So it's the other possibility we have to worry about."

"And what's that?"

"She's been kidnapped, and she's being held for ransom. If that's what's happened, Owen Byrnside is the logical one to pay up."

Like a drowning man, Jake seized on that and held fast. "I'll call now and see if he's heard anything." He strode into the kitchen and with cold but steady fingers dialed Taleman Hall. But when he ended his clipped conversation with Owen Byrnside, he returned to Garrity with misery in his gray eyes. "Owen's heard nothing so far."

Garrity paced in front of the couch. "It may be that it's too early. Or it may be that there's another reason for the delay."

Jake nodded. "That's occurred to me, too. There's a possibility that Lynn may be Owen's granddaughter, and I'm sure he would be willing to pay her ransom. But there are two other girls who might be his as well. If I were a kidnapper, I'd figure I held a much better hand if I had all three to dangle in front of Owen."

Garrity nodded. "Can you get in touch with the others?"

"Kate Conti lives with her husband in Virginia. But it's possible she may already be in Boston. I'll call her at her farm to find out."

Jake dialed Virginia and talked with a housekeeper who gave him the name of her hotel in Boston. When he dialed the hotel he reached Nick Conti. "I don't know where Kate is," he told Jake. "She went out this morning to spend the day shopping and she isn't back yet." Nick's voice grew sharp when Jake explained the reason for his call. "I'll check around a bit and get back to you," he said shortly.

Sixty agonizing minutes later, the phone in Lynn's apartment gave a sharp *brrr*. Jake seized it and Garrity came up behind him. After listening to what Kate's horse-trainer husband had to say, Jake turned to Garrity. "Nick combed the neighborhood where Kate intended to shop. A waiter in a restaurant where she had lunch said he saw a man carry her into a car and then drive off. He assumed it was some sort of love scene he was witnessing. Nick also found a man knocked out cold in a car a little way down the street. That was the guard I had watching over Kate."

"Then it looks as if our ransom theory may be the right one. What about the third orphan? Is she still in Barbados?"

Bleakly, Jake shook his head. "If I remember the schedule right, Maggie Marlowe and her husband, Fitch, were due to arrive in Boston this morning. They've probably checked into a hotel by now."

"Do you know which one?"

Jake raked a hand through his hair. "No, I don't. But Owen might." He dialed Taleman Hall, and after a brief conversation, dialed a second number. This time when he hung up the phone, his expression was grim. "Maggie's gone, too," he said.

"SHHHHH! He's back." It had taken hours, but Kate had just managed to free Lynn's hands when they heard a door open somewhere beyond the closet. The door closed and there was a muffled cursing as something was dragged across the floor.

Hastily Kate and Lynn pulled up their gags and leaned against the wall as if their hands were still tied behind them. No sooner had they settled into place when the closet door opened.

"How ya doin', girls? I've got a third little playmate for your fun house." Noel cackled as he pushed another trussed-up body into the dark little room. "'Fraid it's going to be a little crowded in there for a while, but I'm sure you can manage. I've been a busy fella today and my work isn't done yet. I have to go off and make a few calls. Now, be good and when I get back I'll bring you each a hamburger and fries. Not quite the gourmet fare you're used to, I know. But, hey, this is the real world, kids. You gotta take what you can get."

He slammed the door and locked it. In the darkness Kate and Lynn were silent while they listened to his movements in the outer room. Sounds of banging and shuffling penetrated the walls of their tiny prison. Finally they heard the outer door open and then slam shut.

After a moment of silence had passed, Kate pulled down her gag. "He's gone."

Lynn pulled down hers as well and then took her hands out from behind her back and began to massage her aching wrists. "Yes, thank God." She moved over to the body on the floor and touched it gingerly. She sighed with relief. "It's alive and it's a woman. It must be Maggie."

"Let's get her untied and find out for sure," Kate said.

They undid her gag first. But Maggie was still unconscious and only moaned faintly when they'd freed her mouth. Next they set to work on her other bonds.

"What do you guess that creep was talking about just now?" Kate said as she worked on Maggie's feet.

"I've been thinking about that," Lynn mused. "He said he was going out to make some calls. But there's a phone in the apartment. I know because I heard him use it once to have pizza delivered. The only reason he'd go out to make a call is if he didn't want to take a chance on having it traced." Her fingers hovered over Maggie's wrists.

"I know what you're thinking," Kate said. "Now that he's got all three of us, he's going to call Owen Byrnside and demand money."

"That's the only thing that makes any sense," Lynn agreed. "And I bet the bastard will ask for a bundle." Her fingers paused at their work again. "You're the first orphan Owen found, and you know him better than I do. Do you think he'll pay?"

Even though it was too dark in the closet to see, Kate nodded her head of red curls emphatically. "Yes—yes, I do."

"But then what? What do you think will happen once that jerk has the loot? Do you think he'll let us go?"

Kate's voice faltered. "I—I don't know."

"Well, I'll tell you what I think," Lynn said firmly. "This is not your average run-of-the-mill kidnapper. He's a killer, a man who's capable of impersonating a woman and befriending a woman he intends to murder. That's what he did to Maggie, here. I don't believe he'll let us go free. I think once he's got his hands on Owen's money we have about as much chance as turkeys at Thanksgiving.''

Kate groaned. "Don't try so hard to cheer me up. Maybe we'll be rescued. Nick must be frantic by now, and Fitch, too, probably.''

Lynn wondered if Jake would be frantic when he found out. She tried to imagine the expression on his face—horror, indignation, indifference? But she couldn't think about Jake and his feelings for her—whatever they might be—now. She had to rely on herself, on her own wits and guts. "We can't wait around hoping they'll do something,'' she declared.

"What do you suggest?'' Kate removed the last of the ropes around Maggie's ankles and began to chafe them in hopes of restoring the unconscious woman's circulation.

"I suggest we do our best to wake Maggie here up and then when our jolly little playmate comes back holding a bag of hamburgers, we jump him.''

"WELL, THAT'S IT,'' Jake said, returning from the kitchen in Lynn's apartment. His face looked gray. "Owen just got a call demanding ransom.''

Nick Conti, a wiry man with a handsome face which was now contorted by worry and rage, jumped up. "How much?''

"Ten million dollars.''

"Ten million!'' Tall, redheaded Fitch Marlowe began shredding the crumpled newspaper he held between his muscular hands. "If I liquidate all my holdings I might be able to raise half that.''

"Byrnside's willing to pay the whole amount,'' Jake said, "but I have to tell you that I'm not exactly certain the kidnapper will keep his word, even if he gets the money.

It's got to be the guy who dressed up as Rona Chastain, you know, and he's not exactly a man of his word."

Nick looked beside himself. "You're saying that my wife is in danger no matter what we or Byrnside do."

"And *my* wife!" Fitch threw in. "I can't lose Maggie," he declared explosively. "If only I could get my hands around this kidnapper's throat."

Jake looked at the two men. He felt just the way they did. It would kill him to lose Lynn. But he didn't have the right to say so, not after his stupid treatment of her in Switzerland. Oh God, what he wouldn't give to replay that scene in Lausanne! If only—but he couldn't go back, only forward. He just had to get her back safely somehow.

Jake's gaze turned to Garrity. The big policeman was slumped on the couch, apparently lost in thought. "We've got to find this creep's hideout," he muttered. Glancing up, he met Jake's gaze. "You told me that you and Lynn had figured out a man named Deeping might be behind some of this."

"I did," Jake agreed, "and there's a piece of news I haven't given you. Before I talked with Owen I was in touch with the London office of Byrnside Enterprises. They say Deeping didn't show up at the office today, and his wife doesn't know where he is, either."

All four men stared at one another. "I don't even know who this Deeping is," Fitch said gruffly. "But that sounds suspicious."

"Just before Lynn was kidnapped, she and I had figured out that Winston Deeping might be behind these attacks on the girls," Jake said. "My guess now is that Rona Chastain—alias whoever—was in Winston's pay. Somehow Winston got wind that we were on to him and took off, which might mean that the kidnapper is operating independently now. But this is all guesswork."

"Right now guesswork is the best we can do," Garrity retorted. "Any chance that Deeping is headed this way?"

Jake shook his head. "I doubt it. If I were him I'd be running in the opposite direction. But I've had an idea. Winston may have been too smart to place any traceable phone calls to his hired hatchet man. But on the off chance that he wasn't, I've asked the people in London to check the activity on his office and home phones."

The three other men pricked up their ears. "It's a long shot," Jake admitted, looking from one to the other, "but right now it's all we've got to go on."

Garrity pushed himself to his feet. "How long before we find out?"

"They said a couple of hours." Jake jammed his fists into his pants pockets and walked to the window. "We just have to wait."

While they cooled their heels the four men, none of whom had eaten any lunch, ordered out for beer and pizza. When the food arrived they talked in desultory fashion while they made an effort to eat it.

"Kate and I have been so happy these last months," Nick murmured gruffly. "Maybe nobody's meant to be that happy. Maybe it was just too good to be true."

"I feel the same way," Fitch allowed. "Since we found each other, Maggie and I have been living in a dream world."

Garrity swigged the last of his beer. "You two are certainly advertisements for marriage. Wish I could say the same. How about you, Jake?"

"I'm a widower," Jake muttered. The slice of pizza he held in his hand suddenly turned his stomach and he set it back down in the carton. He wasn't thinking of Janet, but of Lynn. Could he stand to lose another woman that he loved? No, he couldn't! He just couldn't! Where was Lynn now? What was happening to her? And, oh, God, why didn't that damn phone ring?

A few minutes later it cut through the silence and he rushed into the kitchen, the other three men at his heels. They watched anxiously as he listened to a voice on the other end of the line and then jotted down some numbers. When he hung up, there was a martial light in his steely gray eyes.

"Finally, we've lucked out. Early this morning Winston made a call to the States, to a number in Boston. Now it's just a matter of matching that number with an address."

"YOU'D THINK I'd be too scared to think about food," Kate murmured into the darkness of the closet, "but I keep visualizing those hamburgers Mr. Nice Guy promised and wanting to wolf them down."

"I could use a decent meal," Lynn agreed.

"Well, I couldn't," Maggie dropped into the conversation. "I still feel sick to my stomach."

Lynn shifted her position and then stood up and stretched. "It's the chloroform," she said as she touched her toes. "How'd he get you with it?"

"I'm not sure. I was just walking down the hall toward the elevator in our hotel when suddenly everything went black."

"I was out shopping," Kate said. "I stopped on the street to adjust some of my bags when everything went black. When I came to I was here. I'd just bought a neat new dress, too. I wonder what happened to it."

"If our kidnapper is who I think he is, he probably plans to wear it himself," Maggie muttered.

"Well, I hope it's too tight in the hips," Kate replied sharply. "Oh lord, if we could only get out of this closet."

"Well, we tried and we can't. That's no ordinary lock our friendly neighborhood kidnapper has got this place sealed up with. Lynn tried everything she knew to get past it and she's an ex-cop. So I guess we're not going anywhere until he comes back."

As Lynn listened, a strange feeling came over her. "You know, it's pretty peculiar that after all this time we should finally meet like this. You realize, don't you, that the last time all three of us were together was the night we were abandoned at the orphanage."

"We do seem to have a habit of meeting only in crisis situations," Maggie agreed. "Actually, I've really been looking forward to a reunion with you two, but not like this."

"Me, too," Kate chimed in. "Nick thought I was crazy, but I was really looking forward to this get-together at Taleman Hall, and not because I was anxious to learn the results of those tests, either. What I really wanted was to get to know you two. Don't laugh, but it's almost as if you're my sisters."

"I'd have to be crazy to laugh in a situation like this. But you're right, it is almost as if we're sisters," Lynn mused. "We certainly have a lot in common. I know I felt a sense of kinship when I met the two of you. It really hurt me that I couldn't identify myself."

"Why couldn't you?" Maggie asked.

As Kate and Maggie listened, Lynn explained the reasons for her long charade.

"Of the three of us, you've gotten the worst deal," Kate murmured sympathetically. "If we get out of here, I hope it turns out that you're the heiress."

"Same here," Maggie said. "I don't want the money. Fitch and I have everything we want at MarHeights now. I'm afraid that if I inherited a pile of money it would only spoil things. Yet I'd like Owen to go on being my grand-father. That part of this business I've really enjoyed. He's such a sweet old guy, even though he pretends to be so grumpy. I've really grown to love him."

"How could you not love him?" Kate stretched out her legs and touched her toes. "But I know what you mean about the money thing. It's worried me, too. Nick is so proud. How would it affect our relationship if I were sud-denly able to buy and sell him? Actually, I've even con-sidered refusing to take the tests and just telling Owen to give the money to one of you two."

"Not to me, for heaven's sake!" Maggie protested. "When it comes to male pride, Fitch is in a class by him-self!"

Lynn listened thoughtfully. Her feelings about the in-heritance were more ambivalent. There were things she could do with money, good things such as supporting the activities of people like Maudie. On the other hand, she'd already realized that if Jake suddenly declared his love af-ter she'd been named an heiress, she wouldn't be able to believe in it. If there were any chance at all that she and Jake could forget the past and come together without any shadows on their relationship she'd be glad to kiss off ten fortunes like Owen Byrnside's.

"Maybe we should all refuse to take the tests," she murmured.

Before Kate or Maggie could comment, the sound of a door opening electrified the atmosphere in the closet. "He's back," Kate whispered.

"Remember our scheme," Lynn hissed.

They'd rehearsed the plan they'd worked out so many times that they all quickly fell into position. Maggie stretched herself out in front of the doorway and wound a rope loosely around her ankles to make it look as if she were still tied. Kate did the same and then leaned against the wall with her hands behind her back. Lynn took up a stance to one side of the doorway. Between her hands she held one of the ropes Kate had removed from her ankles.

"God, I'm so scared," Maggie muttered.

"Shhhh!" the other two cautioned.

It was a while before their captor came to them, however. With nerves fluttering in their empty stomachs like frantic moths, they strained their ears as he banged around in the outer room.

"What's he doing?" Maggie whispered.

"Eating our hamburgers," Kate retorted.

Lynn was far too nervous to talk. She waited tensely, her fingers clasping and unclasping around the rope. Would luck be with them? Could she pull her part of this off? Their lives depended on it.

Finally they heard him approach the closet. All three young women held their breaths. The door knob twisted and they heard their jailer's jeering voice.

"And how are Flopsie, Mopsie and Cottontail doing this evening? Your rich old sugar daddy must love you bunny-rabbits. He's willing to pay more than three million a piece to save your cute little tails." Laughing at his own joke, he peered in, but not as far as Lynn wanted him to. She had hoped he'd take a step or two inside the closet before noticing that one of them was not lying bound and gagged on the floor. Instead, he was standing just outside the threshold.

"I brought you something to eat, kids." She heard the crackle of a paper bag. "It's a little cold by now, maybe, but you can't have everything. Now let me check over my very valuable little bunnies." Suddenly the beam of a flashlight sprang to life and pierced the gloom of the closet. "One, two... hey, where's—"

Lynn sprang around the door frame and tried to use the rope as a garrote. But she hadn't been able to take their captor as much by surprise as she'd wished. He had already dropped the bag of hamburgers and was backing away. She tackled him nevertheless, trying for a judo hold that would immobilize him. At the same time, Kate and Maggie leaped to their feet, cast aside their ropes and rushed to add their strength to Lynn's.

But their enemy was no easy target. Noel was wiry, agile, strong and all of his fighting skills were honed to a razor-sharp cutting edge. What's more, he was ruthless. Brutally, he clipped Lynn on the head. The blow made her see stars and for a moment she staggered back. The hesitation gave Noel a chance to whip a wicked-looking switchblade from his belt. As he waved the blade in a slow arc in front of him, its gleaming edge held all three young women at bay.

"That was stupid—very, very stupid," he hissed. "Because now that you've all had a clear look at my face, I can't give you back to your nice old gramps, can I?"

Wildly, Lynn looked around for some sort of weapon, or something to use as a shield. Her gaze fell upon a wooden kitchen chair. She grabbed it, and casting another fast look around the poorly lit room, hurled it with all her strength.

"WELL, THIS IS THE PLACE," Nick said, peering at the number on the aging brick apartment building across the street from where Jake had parked his car. Night had long since fallen. Random lights struggled out from behind the dwelling's grimy windows. A street lamp shed a sickly glow over the entry. "Do we have a plan?" Nick looked questioningly at Garrity, who sat in the backseat, frowning out at the building. "All I want to do is rush the place. But that's probably not the smartest way to go about this."

"If we're lucky," the policeman said, "there won't be anyone in there but the girls tied up or something. Then we could simply free them and wait to nab our guy."

"It's a nice thought," Jake replied, "but chances are we're not going to be that lucky. I suggest we do a little reconnoitering, find out which is 304 and how we can get to it."

"Okay." Fitch started to climb out of the passenger side. "I'll go around back and see what's in the alley. Maybe there's a fire escape."

Jake pulled the keys out of the ignition and stuck them into his suit pocket. "I'll go over and check on how hard it is to get into the lobby."

"I'm with you," Nick said.

Garrity rubbed his chin. "While you three are having your look-see, I'll keep an eye on the place."

Jake and Nick crossed the street and approached the building's run-down entry. "Locked," Jake said after he tried the door. He turned and examined a series of buzzers on a metal plate, each labeled with a dog-eared scrap of paper.

"I guess we don't want to try 304," Nick commented. "How about ringing the manager?"

"No. I don't want to have to explain anything. What's this? Science Fiction Club. They're in the basement and I think I hear noise coming from that direction. Let's try them."

He buzzed, and a moment later a stringy-haired young man in a red beret and wearing a T-shirt depicting the Loch Ness monster gulping down a mermaid opened the door. He scanned Jake's business suit and Nick in his jeans and leather jacket. "Hi, you guys new members?"

"We're thinking of joining," Jake told him solemnly.

"Well, the movie's already started. Tonight we're showing *Attack of the Crab People*."

"Exactly what I'm in the mood for," Nick growled as they followed the science-fiction aficionado through a warren of hallways toward a darkened room full of people on metal chairs. Once inside, Jake and Nick took seats in the back and then after a few minutes made a quiet exit and returned to the lobby. Silently, they climbed the stairs to the third floor and crossed toward 304.

Footsteps on the stairs behind them made them slip into a dark doorway. They waited tensely. A slim, blond young man in jeans and a sport coat, carrying a large paper bag emblazoned with the logo of a popular fast-food chain hurried down the hall, stuck a key in the lock of 304 and disappeared inside before Jake and Nick could react.

They looked at each other. "That's got to be him," Nick hissed. "If only we'd known, we could have grabbed him in the hall."

"Well, we didn't know. I'd like to break the door down," Jake said, "but I think we'd better round up Garrity and Fitch. I'll stay here. You wedge the front entrance with paper or something so you can get back in."

Nick nodded and hurried down to the lobby. Jake stood staring at 304. Every nerve in his body was as tight as piano wire. *Lynn, are you in there?* he wondered. *And, oh dear heaven, are you all right?*

He moved closer to the door, his ears strained. But he could hear nothing, just an occasional creak or rustle. What if Lynn were in there hurt, or even dead? Jake's heart squeezed and his muscles went rigid. He wondered how long it would take Nick to bring Fitch and Garrity. And what would they do when they arrived?

Maybe if all four of them broke the door down fast enough they could rush the kidnapper before he could harm any of his victims. Though Jake had seen doors kicked in on cops-and-robbers shows, he suspected it was a lot harder than it looked on television. But right now he was strung so tight that he felt as if he could break down steel with one blow.

Outside, Nick and Garrity walked around to the back of the building to get Fitch. They found him standing in the shadows, staring up at a third-floor window.

"The light just went on up there," he said when the other two men approached him.

Nick turned and studied the illuminated square. "That's got to be 304," he said. "If only there were a fire escape nearby." But the rickety metal fire escape hung from the opposite corner of the building. The only thing under the window was a pile of trash.

Garrity frowned up. "We might be able to do something with ladders. When we go in, I'd like to have everything covered."

A loud crack split through the ordinary noises of the city. Glass splintered out from the window in question and smashed to the alley below.

"My God," Fitch exclaimed, "someone on the inside just threw a chair at that window!" In fact, its wooden legs protruded through the shattered glass.

"Let's get the hell up there," Nick cried. He was already sprinting back around to the front of the building with the two other men running behind him.

In the hallway outside 304 a galvanized Jake rushed at the door that stood between him and whatever mayhem was going on behind it. He heard women's screams, cursing, furniture breaking. Using all his weight and strength, he slammed his shoulder against the wood. It splintered half off its hinges. Another well-aimed body blow, and he was past it and dashing through a narrow hall into a dimly lit kitchen.

A woman's body lay on the floor. He caught a horrifying glimpse of blond hair spattered with blood. Then the young man he'd seen carrying the bag rushed him with a knife.

Jake reacted like a madman. Had this creep killed Lynn? By God, he'd make him pay! With a skill and precision he hadn't known he possessed, Jake kicked the knife out of his assailant's fingers and slammed him back against the wall. Hands outstretched, Jake went for his throat.

But Noel was strong, and as agile as a snake. Just as Jake's hands were closing, he used his elbows to twist free. At that moment Nick, Fitch and Garrity rushed in.

The kidnapper took one look at his opposition and headed for the window. With one quick kick, he knocked the chair jammed in it all the way through, clearing the frame of most of the broken glass that remained. Then he jumped out.

The four men in the apartment rushed after him, but it was too late. Somehow he'd managed to land in the cushioning trash and bounce to his feet running.

"The guy must be half cat!" Garrity exclaimed. "That's a fall most people would break a leg on."

Jake didn't answer. White-faced, he'd already turned back to the young woman lying on the kitchen floor. "Lynn—oh, my God, Lynn!" With his heart suspended in his chest, Jake turned her over and cradled her against him. He could hear her breathing, so she wasn't dead. But the blood—"Lynn," he cried as he looked for the source of it. *"Lynn!"*

A jagged gash oozed on her hand and another on her shoulder leaked into the fabric of her blouse. But neither wound looked life-threatening. *Please God, let that be all!* He held her tight against his heart again and kissed her cheek. "Lynn," he whispered feverishly, "are you all right? Please tell me you're all right!"

It was precisely at that moment that she opened her golden eyes. Confusedly she gazed up at him. "Jake?"

"Yes, darling. Yes, it's me."

"You've got blood all over your suit."

"That doesn't matter. The only thing in the world that matters is you."

"Do you mean that?"

"I never meant anything more in my life!"

A beatific smile spread over her face. "Then you love me after all, don't you, Jake?"

CHAPTER SIXTEEN

"OF COURSE I LOVE YOU, Lynn. I think I've loved you for a long time. Much longer than I was willing to admit, even to myself."

"Then why, Jake? I know you think I did something terrible in deceiving you, and maybe I did. But even so, if you loved me, why were you so cold and distant for so long?"

Jake, who'd been standing in front of the fireplace gazing at the dancing flames, turned toward the woman imploring him from the couch. Her heart was in her eyes and she looked so damn beautiful, and so very desirable.

After they'd finished with the police and Kate and Maggie had gone back to their hotel rooms with their husbands, Jake had argued that it wasn't safe for Lynn to stay alone in her apartment and insisted that she come home with him instead. When she'd bathed and Jake had bandaged the cuts on her hand and shoulder,Lynn let him have his way. She'd wanted to be alone with him so that she could see once and for all if what he'd blurted out about his loving her was true, or only her wishful thinking.

In two strides Jake closed the distance between them and dropped down on his knees in front of the couch where she sat huddled under the blanket he'd spread over her lap. "Lynn, listen to me and try to understand. Like it or not, I'm a lawyer and I have a lawyer's plodding mentality. I want to have my feet firmly on the ground, and I want to know where I'm going. It's stupid, maybe, because just when you think you've got things arranged, life pulls the rug out from under you. I found that out in a big way when Janet died. But still—''

Lynn reached out and touched Jake's cheek, feeling the fine structure of the bone beneath. She gazed into his eyes, which looked back at her clearly and steadily. ''But you can't help it,'' she murmured. ''That's the way you're built.'' Her finger stroked downward and then gently traced the hard ridge of his jaw. ''I think that's part of what I love so much about you, Jake—the way you insist on making order out of chaos, the way I know you'll always be there for me, or whoever needs you—even when you're angry. The woman who has you will have struck pure gold—and if you'll give me another chance I want to be that woman.''

He took her hand in his and pressed his lips against the soft flesh above her knuckles. ''Oh Lynn, God help me, I'm a dull fellow. I've worn the same style of suit for the last ten years and I never ever rearrange furniture. I like my meat with potatoes, and I've been going to the same dentist since I was a teenager. And just when I thought I had the woman I loved figured out, she changed. Like quicksilver, she became someone else altogether. And I didn't like it one bit. It made me angry and frustrated. I just plain resented it.''

They continued to look at each other, the light from the fire sending warm shadows rippling over their faces. ''Where do we go from here?'' Lynn whispered.

''I don't know, but wherever it is, I want us to go there together. No, it's more than that—I *need* us to go there together.'' Jake twined his fingers more tightly with hers. ''I think we have to start fresh, Lynn. We have to get to know each other all over again, only this time it has to be—"

"I know," she quickly interrupted. "Only this time we have to tell each other the truth. No more deceptions. Not that you ever lied to me. You've always been exactly what you seemed, straight and clear through and through. I was the trickster. But Jake—" she leaned forward, taking his face between her hands and meeting his eyes with grave sincerity "—I'll never deceive you again. That I promise with all my heart. I'll tell you everything, answer all your questions—even though . . . even though . . ."

As she faltered, Jake cocked his head. "Lynn?"

Weakly, she released him and fell back against the couch with her face averted. "Oh Jake, there are things in my past that you won't like. They may even . . . It may be that after you've heard it all . . ."

"Lynn, there's nothing you can tell me that will change the fact that I love you and want you."

"I was a runaway. Before Maudie took me in, I was on the streets."

"You had a tough childhood, but you were strong enough to overcome it."

"It's more complicated. Right now you're thinking I might be Owen Byrnside's granddaughter, sort of a princess in disguise. But what if I'm not anything of the kind? What if I'm just a baby that another street person abandoned?" She looked at him searchingly.

Jake didn't flinch. "Lynn, you're beautiful and strong and brave and accomplished. I think you should be very proud of yourself. For that, you don't need to be anybody's granddaughter. You only need to be who you are right at this moment."

Lynn's mouth turned down wryly. "I doubt your sister would agree."

"Freddie isn't the one who's in love with you—I am."

"But she's your family, and they're a big part of who you are. Your family will always be important to you, Jake."

"Freddie will learn to accept you, she'll have to because I want to marry you, Lynn. I want to put my ring on your finger and tie you to me in every way I can. I don't ever want to be without you again."

Lynn felt as if her heart might burst. She flung her arms around his neck and buried her face in his shoulder. "Oh, Jake, I love you so much!"

"Do you mean that?" He enclosed her and drew her close. "Don't say it unless you mean it."

"You know I mean it."

He tipped her head back so he could study her face. Then, with a groan of satisfaction, he closed his eyes and let his mouth come down on hers. The kiss was as much a contract as a caress. It was a seal on the promises they'd just exchanged, the physical expression of the spiritual union they'd just begun to reforge.

But soon it became more than that. As he inhaled Lynn's scent, breathed in the essence of her, Jake's heart pumped with hammer blows and his body flushed and hardened.

Lynn's pulse accelerated to the rhythm of his, and every part of her began to tingle with excitement. As she felt all that her nearness did to Jake, she seemed to melt against him. Her knees went weak and a dizzying flush of liquid heat spread through her.

Jake's mouth began to move over her face. He kissed her cheeks, her throat. At the same time his hands left her back to cup and fondle her breasts.

"You're not wearing a bra," he muttered with husky surprise. His hands slipped beneath the hem of her loose sweater.

Lynn felt his fingers move up her rib cage and begin to trace delicate patterns over her hardened nipples. She inhaled sharply. Eagerly she raised her hands over her head so that he could slip the sweater off. When it was gone, Jake laid her back against the cushions of the couch and gave all his attention to her breasts. His lips went from one to the other, tugging and caressing until Lynn ached with a pain-pleasure that made her light-headed.

Her hands moved over the back of his head, winnowing through the short, crisp strands of his hair. Her thumbs massaged the smooth skin behind his ears and as her excitement mounted, she arched, thrusting her breasts more completely into his mouth. He took them ardently and against her thigh she felt his swelling manhood.

At last he moved up against her and looked into her flushed, firelit face. "I want to take off all your clothes," he said in a thickened voice.

"Here on the couch?"

He cast a glance around the shadowy room. The fire had begun to die down. Soon only a few coals would glow. "I'm the conservative type. I want a bed."

Lynn's restless fingers slipped his shirt out of his waistband and moved over the warm skin covering the base of his spine. "I'm not sure I can make it upstairs." She lifted her pelvis against his to let him know what she meant. She wanted him badly, now—this minute!

He smiled wolfishly. "I'll carry you."

"Oh, but Jake..."

Already, he was off the couch. Sweeping her naked breasts with an admiring glance, he bent, slipped his arms beneath her back and buttocks and scooped her up. Though Lynn had watched scenes like this in movies and envied the heroine lovingly pressed against the hero's broad chest, she'd never expected anything like it to happen to her.

"I'm not exactly light," she exclaimed as Jake strode toward the staircase in the hall.

"You're light as a feather." Again he flashed her a roguish grin. "Right now, to get you in my bed, I'd gladly carry you up these stairs with cement blocks dangling from your ankles." He dropped a kiss on her forehead. "Do you know how afraid I was when that creep had you in his clutches? Do you know how good it is to have you safe in my arms like this?"

She snuggled her head against his shoulder, drinking in the familiar healthy fragrance of his skin, the strength and solidity of him. Then, hungrily, she pressed her lips against the open V of his collar. As her mouth began to move over his skin, Jake took the last four steps two at a time. He strode down a hall and into a darkened room where he placed her on a wide bed.

Lynn lay on it watching, letting her eyes adjust as Jake stripped off his shirt and then his pants. Though she loved the way he looked in his clothes, she decided she liked him naked even more—the broad, hair-sprinkled chest, narrow hips and long, muscular legs with their hard thighs and well-developed calves. Her gaze moved higher. Though she didn't know that much about men, she suspected he was unusually endowed in the sexual area as well. Right now, if she hadn't been on fire for him, his arousal would have been a little frightening. As it was, she wanted him, all of him.

When Jake came down on the bed beside her, her arms went out and drew his lips once more to her breasts. As he kissed and fondled and tongued them she whispered his name over and over. It was a kind of litany against all the pain and frustration they'd been through, as well as a prayer for their future together now that they'd finally found each other, really found each other.

Jake began to move down the length of her body, softly caressing her breastbone and then her belly. He unsnapped her jeans, slid the zipper down and then began to let his mouth graze over the sensitive skin he'd bared. It was incredibly exciting and Lynn couldn't stop herself from wriggling.

Her movements were clearly inviting, and a moment later Jake slid her jeans and panties off. When they were both naked, he knelt on the bed and drew her up with him in a long, sensuous embrace. Lynn could feel his erection pressed hard against her and her own liquid feminine softness.

"Jake!" she whispered urgently when at last their lips parted.

"I know. I can't wait much longer, either."

"Why are we waiting at all?"

"Because I want to show you how much . . ."

"Jake, please!"

With their arms locked around each other they fell back down to the bed. And then Jake, his elbows supporting his weight, rolled over Lynn and parted her legs. With her knees locked around his narrow waist, she took him deep inside her.

"Oh, Jake, oh!" she cried as he filled her. This was how it was meant to be—the thought flashed across her mind— this frenzied, sacred communion between a man and a woman. Never to have such a union was to miss out on one of life's great gifts. But without love it meant nothing. She and Jake would give each other love and they wouldn't ever allow it to be lost. *Never,* she thought fiercely as her body began to crest the breaking wave of passion right along with Jake's.

Afterward they lay locked together. "Lynn, my sweet Lynn," Jake whispered. "I was afraid we'd never be together again like this."

"When I was locked in that closet I was afraid I'd never see your face again," she whispered back. She kissed the cleft of his chin and then the slightly bristly underside of his jaw. "Oh Jake, life is so precious. We can't waste a minute of it."

"We're not going to, my darling. From now on we're going to savor every last drop. Which reminds me—" He moved his head back slightly so that he could look at her questioningly. "How about a glass of champagne to celebrate this moment?"

"You have champagne?"

"There are a couple of bottles in the basement that I've kept around for a special occasion. I think this meets all the criteria."

When she nodded her agreement, he released her reluctantly and got up. His gaze still lingering on her, he pulled a terry cloth robe off a brass clothes tree, wrapped it around his lean body and then turned and left. As Lynn listened to his footsteps descending the stairs, she lay against the pillows feeling dazed but incredibly happy. A few minutes later, however, she began to look around her curiously.

This was Jake's room, the place where he slept almost every night, and she'd never seen it before. When he'd brought her back to his house and settled her in the living room, she'd admired, in a vague way, his town house's restrained elegance. But really, at that point she'd still been too emotionally overwhelmed to give interior decoration much thought.

Now she sat up against the four-poster's headboard and flicked on the candlestick lamp next to the bed. As its soft light brought the room into focus, Lynn's gaze moved from the royal-blue border of the Chinese rug, to the antique dressing table with its oval, beveled-glass mirror, to the gold-framed Oriental woodcuts that set off the gold-and-cream wallpaper.

This was not a man's bedroom. A woman had decorated it, a woman with elegant, expensive and sophisticated tastes. Suddenly Lynn felt awkward about her nakedness. She looked around for the sweater Jake had taken off her, but it was still downstairs.

Lynn was just wrapping a bath towel around her body sarong-style when Jake returned with a bottle and two wine glasses on an etched silver tray.

"Is something wrong?" he said, casting a glance over her towel-swathed torso.

"No, I was just, I—"

"You aren't cold, are you?"

"No, I'm not cold." She gestured about her. "This is a beautiful room."

"Thank you." He stood very still in the lamplight, comprehension dawning. "Janet decorated it."

"Yes, I could tell."

"I haven't changed anything. There's been no reason to."

"No, of course there hasn't."

He set the tray down on the bureau and popped the cork on the champagne, an abstracted frown knitting his dark brows. "Does it bother you that we just made love in a bedroom I shared with my wife?"

"No . . . well, maybe a little. Of course I didn't notice when you brought me in here. But now that I see it in the light, it's so clearly hers. I guess I feel a little as if I've trespassed."

"Oh, Lord, Lynn! I guess I wish you hadn't turned on the light." Frowning, Jake filled the glasses on the silver tray and then crossed to the bed and flicked off the lamp. The room was plunged into darkness, relieved only by the faint silver glow of the moon outside the window.

For several seconds, Lynn was blinded. She stood blinking, trying to adjust. She felt rather than saw Jake approach her. He paused in front of her and placed his palms heavily on her bare shoulders. "Lynn, a little while back I mentioned marriage. How do you feel about it?"

"I don't know. Jake—" Her voice caught. "Jake, I don't think I could live here."

"Then we wouldn't. I'd sell it, and we'd start fresh with a place of our own. You'd pick out your own furniture and decorate it the way you wanted."

"But what would you do with all these beautiful things?"

"I don't know. Janet's family might take some. My niece is about to get married. Maybe she'd want a few pieces. Things don't really matter." Jake's hands curled possessively, and Lynn felt the urgency he was barely restraining. "The point is that I want us both to start fresh and make a new life together, a life that's only ours. What do you say?"

"I want that too, Jake. I want it more than anything. But there's something else. What if I'm Owen Byrnside's granddaughter?"

Jake was silent for a beat. "More than likely you're not. In fact, none of you three may be his natural granddaughter. It may be that Owen's been chasing a rainbow. If that's true, it'll break his heart, but that's something I have to warn him about before he goes ahead with the tests." Jake began to draw her closer. "Anyhow," he continued huskily, "that's a bridge we can cross when we come to it. I need an answer, Lynn. Tell me if you think we have a future together.''

Lynn gazed up at Jake. Now that her vision had readjusted to the shadows, she could see that his eyes were pleading with her. The realization made tears sting the backs of her lids.

"Oh Jake, of course I want a future with you. I can't imagine the future any other way.''

"Thank God!'' Jake muttered roughly. He hauled her up against him and his mouth came down to cover hers in a fierce and demanding kiss. Lynn kissed him back with all her strength. And when at last he lifted his head, all the doubts that had sprung up between them were banished.

"Time to drink our champagne,'' he whispered and she felt his lips smiling against hers.

She drew back and retorted playfully, "That's fine, but we need a toast, don't you think?''

"Oh, most definitely.'' Jake picked up the filled glasses, handed her one and then twined his arm with hers. Both their smiles deepened, and they lifted their crystal flutes to their lips. "To us,'' Jake said, "and to Owen Byrnside's quest for a granddaughter. Without it we would never have found each other.''

Yes, oh yes, Lynn thought, sipping the dry, sparkling wine. As it trickled down her throat, joy for her and Jake flowed through her like a newly tapped spring. Yet it was tinged with sadness, too. For she couldn't help but think of the old man who was responsible for her and Jake's happiness. In just a few days he would know the truth about his search. What would happen to them all when they came together at Taleman Hall and that truth was revealed at last?

"DNA FINGERPRINTING has the ability to distinguish one person from another on the basis of their unique genetic makeups," Dr. Michaelson began several days later. Before going on with his explanation, he glanced around the large, luxuriously appointed library in Taleman Hall. The three young women in question, Kate Conti, Maggie Marlowe, and Lynn Rice, all sat listening intently.

They were certainly an attractive group of people, the doctor thought. His comprehensive gaze went from Kate, with her head of rich auburn curls and cat-green eyes to the man who stood behind her. Nick Conti was wiry, muscular, and darkly handsome except for his startling blue eyes. And the way he rested an arm along the back of his wife's wing chair with his elbow touching her curls said a lot about their relationship.

Next the doctor focused on Maggie Marlowe and her Viking-tall redheaded husband, Fitch. What a contrasting pair they made. Maggie with her wide, serene gray eyes and sweet face was like a lily. Fitch, on the other hand, looked as if he would be quite at home wearing a horned helmet and wielding a battle-ax to protect her.

And then there was Lynn Rice and her lawyer-fiancé. Good to look at and smart cookies, both of them. You could see that in the intelligence and concern they both radiated. But you could also see that they were crazy in love. It was in the way they looked at each other, the way they couldn't keep themselves from occasionally touching, brushing a finger against a wrist, allowing knees to come in contact ever so briefly. Ah, young love! In this room Dr. Michaelson felt surrounded by it.

And then there was Owen Byrnside to consider. Dr. Michaelson let his gaze rest on the old man sitting rigidly upright in his motorized wheelchair. It wasn't hard to read the fact that this was a momentous occasion for him and that despite his proud and unflinching expression, he was nervous and quite possibly frightened. What did it matter that he was richer than Croesus? He was also very human and very vulnerable.

Dr. Michaelson cleared his throat. "Humans have forty-six chromosomes, arranged in twenty-three pairs and located in the nucleus of virtually every cell in the body. DNA fingerprinting is based on the uniqueness of the molecules of deoxyribonucleic acid that contain every individual's unique genetic code. The pattern is only exactly alike between identical twins."

"All right," Kate said, breaking the uneasy silence that had fallen over the room. "I understand that everyone's genetic code is different. But how can you use that to determine who is or is not my grandfather?"

"Yes," Lynn chimed in. "It's one thing to say that I have unique DNA. It's another thing to trace the molecules in my body back to a distant relative."

Dr. Michaelson tapped his fingertips together and smiled. "My dear young lady, a grandfather isn't such a distant relative. Roughly a quarter of your genetic code comes from your grandfather."

Suddenly Maggie, who was a nurse and had a better understanding of all this, spoke up. "It's just a matter of taking blood samples and then finding which one of us carries bands in our DNA that match bands in Owen's."

"Sounds damn tricky to me," Nick muttered.

"It is tricky," the doctor agreed. "It's not a simple procedure, by any means. But it can be done. And if you all agree and Mr. Byrnside wants it, it will be done. The lab is set up on the grounds now and the technicians are waiting."

All eyes in the room went to the frail old man in the wheelchair. "Well, Owen," Jake said, "what do you say?

You know the risks. You know there's a very strong possibility that none of the girls are actually yours. Are you ready to chance finding that out?"

Owen's mottled hand clenched on the arms of his chair and his mouth went pale.

"Wait a minute," Kate exclaimed. "Maybe we've changed our minds and don't want these tests." She looked at Lynn, who nodded and then stood up.

"Owen," she said, facing the aging millionaire resolutely. "Kate and Maggie and I have been talking this whole thing over. I know how strongly you feel about leaving a living flesh-and-blood relative behind you. I respect your feelings, though I can't agree with them. But our lives are involved here, too, and our feelings have to be considered." She took a deep breath. "A lot of things have changed since we all agreed to these tests. We all like the idea of being your granddaughter, but we've also decided that we don't want to inherit your money."

Owen looked astounded. "You don't want my money? That's the queerest thing I've heard in a month of Sundays! Why in tarnation not?"

"Because," Maggie exclaimed, a mulish expression coming into her normally gentle gray eyes, "our lives are going so well without it. Can't you see? Money has a way of changing things, and we don't want our lives turned around! We like them just the way they are."

"Yes," Kate chimed in. "Nick and I are happy and so are Maggie and Fitch. And now that Jake and Lynn have announced their engagement—don't you see? Why rock the boat?"

"And your husbands agree to this?" Owen still looked flabbergasted.

"Whatever Maggie wants is fine with me," Fitch declared stoutly.

"Same here," Nick agreed.

Jake walked forward and stood next to Lynn. "This is Lynn's decision. Whatever she decides, I'll go along with."

The patter of small feet broke the gathering tension. "Oh dear, dear, dear, I'm afraid I've lost my way again," a breathless voice exclaimed. Mrs. Crumper skidded around the corner, her white curls bobbing furiously and her flowered dress dancing around her ankles. "Oh, goodness!" She pressed a soft wrinkled hand to her breast. "There you all are!" She looked around inquiringly, her gaze finally coming to rest on Owen. "Am I interrupting something?"

The old millionaire's expression went from stormy to benign. "Daisy, my dear, you're looking lovely this morning."

"Why, thank you, Owen—you are such a kind gentleman!" Mrs. Crumper's pink mouth lifted in a flirtatious smile and her hands began to flutter. "But you know, it's so lovely and quiet here in your beautiful house, and my bed is so comfortable. I'm afraid I've overslept and missed breakfast."

"Oh, no—that could never happen in a house of mine!" Owen shook his head emphatically and pressed a button that put his chair in motion. When he'd rolled it across the floor close enough, he reached out and gave Mrs. Crumper's hand a light squeeze. "You just go right back down that hall and press the pull next to the staircase. When the maid answers you tell her you want breakfast, and be sure to ask for anything at all you fancy. Anything at all, my dear and it shall be yours."

As Owen's eyes twinkled up at her, Mrs. Crumper blushed furiously. "Why thank you, kind sir. You are a prince among men, and I'll do exactly as you say." She sent a tremulous little wave around the room. "See you all later." And then, with another bright smile at her indulgent host, she pattered off.

Unobtrusively, Lynn jabbed Jake's elbow and shot him a meaningful look. His gray-green eyes glinted back at her in amused comprehension. The moment Mrs. Crumper had arrived at Taleman Hall as Lynn's guest, Owen and the old lady had taken a very obvious liking to each other. Who knew what might develop? Though Lynn had never thought of herself as a matchmaker before, she had high hopes.

As soon as Mrs. Crumper left the room, Owen's demeanor went through another abrupt weather change. "Now see here," he said, gazing at Lynn and the other two young women sternly. "A bargain's a bargain and a person has to stick by his word of honor no matter what. You three agreed to these tests of mine, and regardless of whether or not I like the results, I can't rest until they're performed. Is that right, or isn't it?" He looked challengingly from Lynn, to Kate to Maggie.

They, in turn, looked at each other. "I did promise," Kate muttered.

"And so did I," Maggie added with a sigh.

Lynn turned to Jake. "What do you think?"

"It's what *you* think that counts," he answered. "This has to be your call."

Just as Maggie had done, she sighed heavily. "If this is really what Owen wants, I guess we have to go through with it."

Owen Byrnside sat rigid as a statue. "It's what I want," he stated emphatically. "I'm no quitter. I didn't start down this road not to see it through to the bitter end. You girls go along with Dr. Michaelson and pretty soon we'll know what's what."

THE REST OF THE DAY at Taleman Hall dragged like a lead weight on a chain. It hadn't taken more than a few minutes for Kate, Maggie and Lynn to give blood samples. After that, it was just a matter of leaving the technicians to their business and waiting.

"How long do you think it will be before we hear?" Kate asked as the three young women left the newly set up lab adjacent to the greenhouses and walked across a patch of lawn. It had turned cold and blustery. Kate's red curls blew around her face in wild confusion and Lynn's short blond locks whipped back from her ears.

She drew the collar of her tweed coat up around her throat. "They're being very cagey about how long it will take them. And, of course, Owen's the one they'll bring the report to. After that, it's up to him when he wants to give us the results."

"Fitch is so impatient. Waiting around here with no end in sight is going to drive him crazy," Maggie murmured.

"Nick's the same way," Kate told her. "He doesn't like this business one bit. I guess he's afraid that if I turn out to be the heiress, Owen will take me away from him—though nothing in the world could do that!" she added fiercely.

Lynn remained thoughtfully silent. It was a little different with her and Jake, she mused. Since Jake had been working on this orphan search from the beginning, he felt some loyalty to it. But since their own commitment to each other was still so green and untried, she knew he was worried about what impact the results of the tests would have on it. So was she. Whatever way the final result went, it was really hard to gauge its effects.

Inside the house she excused herself to go to her room. After she'd stowed her coat, she headed for a back staircase that had been pointed out to her by a maid. It led to

Loretta Greene's rooms. At the top of the stairs she stood for a moment and then, taking a deep breath, tapped lightly on Loretta's door.

After a moment it opened and Owen's secretary, looking pale and tired but still immaculately dressed, peered out. She was obviously shocked to see Lynn and her hand flew to her breast.

"I'm sorry to disturb you," Lynn began a bit nervously. "But when Owen told me you were still here, I knew I had to see you and thank you for what you did for me."

"What I did for you?" Loretta looked nonplussed. Obviously she had been expecting something quite different than a thank-you.

"Yes, the plastic surgery. No matter what else happened, I'll always be grateful for that. It changed my life."

A little tremor seemed to ripple across Loretta's expression. "It…it came out very well. You're really quite lovely now."

"Thank you. But I owe the change to you, and I want to let you know that I intend to pay you back. It may take me a while, but I'll do it."

"Oh, no!" Loretta cried. Her hand tightened on the doorknob until her knuckles showed white and tears began to gather in her dark eyes. "Oh no, you don't understand. I don't want to be paid back. What I did for you may be the only generous thing I've ever done in my foolish life! And even so, my motivations were not entirely what they ought to have been, I'm afraid. No, accept the surgery as a gift and if it's made a positive change in your life, then think of me kindly now and then. Can you do that?"

"Oh yes, of course I can."

"Then that will be payment and thanks enough," Loretta said and closed the door, but not quickly enough to keep Lynn from seeing that the tears in her eyes had begun to trickle down her cheeks.

AS THE DAY WENT ON, the tension built. Fitch and Nick were both edgy. They spent much of their time in the game room, sending billiard balls shooting across the smooth green felt of Owen Byrnside's handsome antique billiard table. Jake closeted himself in the library where he pored over legal papers.

Lynn, knowing that occupying himself with office work was his way of taking his mind off what was going on in the lab, left him alone. She and Kate and Maggie spent the hours in one another's company, walking around the grounds, playing desultory games of cards and talking. Before the afternoon drew to a close they knew as much about each other as any three sisters might and they'd also developed a strong bond.

"Whatever happened to Loretta Greene?" Kate asked at one point. "Is she still here? I haven't seen her."

"Oh, she's still here," Lynn answered. "She's just staying in her rooms until we're gone, I guess."

"Will Owen keep her on as his secretary now that he knows about her relationship with Winston Deeping?" Maggie asked curiously.

"I asked him about that last night, and he said he thought he would," Lynn answered. "Even though he's angry about the whole thing, she's been with him so long he just doesn't have the heart to fire her."

"I never liked the woman, yet I feel sorry for her, too," Kate said. "Talk about falling for the wrong guy and totally messing up your life!"

"Yes!" Lynn agreed, and thought about the saddened and defeated woman she'd spoken with earlier in the day. She, Kate and Maggie were silent while they reflected on how lucky they had been in matters of the heart. But would they stay lucky after the results of the DNA fingerprinting came in?

The only two people in the house who seemed unaffected by the mounting suspense were Owen and Mrs. Crumper. The two spent the day in each other's company. Owen took the old lady through all the rooms in the house and looked vastly pleased and amused while she crowed with delight over each and offered suggestions for the ones that needed redecorating. In the afternoon, following their naps, the elderly couple played cards in the solarium and gossiped like a pair of cozy old pals.

That night, dinner in Taleman Hall's huge formal dining room was an anxious affair with the conversation so strained that even Mrs. Crumper became subdued by it. Immediately after coffee was served, Owen went to bed and the other couples soon made excuses to retire to their rooms. Alone, each pair of lovers renewed their commitment to each other by making passionate love and then lying in bed speculating for hours about the revelations the morning might bring.

Unbeknownst to all of them, Owen Byrnside had left instructions with his team of medical technicians that he be awakened as soon as the results came in—regardless of the time of night or day.

AT SEVEN THE NEXT MORNING the millionaire heard a tap on his door.

"Come in!" He was already awake, eating his breakfast on a tray and watching the sun rise over his grounds.

Dr. Michaelson opened the door and walked in. "I've got what you asked for."

The old man put down his fork, pushed his tray to one side and waited apprehensively. "And?"

"See for yourself." The doctor set a printout in front of Owen.

The old man stared at it as if it were a snake. "I haven't got my reading glasses. Without them I can't see a thing."

"I'll get them for you," the doctor said, and picked up a pair of spectacles from the bedside table.

When they were settled on his nose, Owen smoothed the printout and studied it. Slowly, the frightened expression on his lined features changed to one of pleased surprise.

"Is it what you expected?" Dr. Michaelson queried.

"No, but that doesn't mean I'm not glad it's turned out this way. If any of them had been Winston Deeping's brat I'd have wanted to shoot myself."

"No fear of that. The readings were pretty clear."

"Hmmm." Owen gave a brisk little nod and then folded the printout in thirds. "Remember our agreement to keep this information confidential."

"You needn't worry. You're to have it and no one else. Of course, if when you die one of the young women disputes your will, the information will have to be released."

"I honestly don't believe that's likely. But I also know that I have a lot of thinking to do before I make my next move," Owen allowed. He leaned back against his pillows and closed his eyes. "And I'd better start doing that thinking right now."

Two hours later, everyone involved in the Byrnside quest reassembled in the library. Looking a bit like the Cheshire cat, Owen Byrnside was waiting for them.

"Well?" Kate said, when they'd all seated themselves near him. "How long are you going to keep us in suspense?"

Owen glanced around the room, studying each young woman's anxious expression, but being careful not to let his gaze linger overlong on any one of them. "For the rest of my life, I'm afraid."

"What?" Maggie stiffened. Behind her, Fitch rolled his eyes and then folded his brawny arms over his broad chest.

Owen held up a hand. "Yesterday you all said you'd rather not know the results. You all agreed you'd like to go on being my granddaughters but you didn't want any truck with my money. Very well, I've decided to grant you your wishes."

Lynn gaped. "Are you saying that now you know which one of us is your true granddaughter but you're not going to tell us?"

"That's exactly what I'm saying." Owen gazed back at her blandly. "Any objections?"

Lynn blinked and then turned to Jake. "Can he do that?"

Jake looked nonplussed. "He can if you three agree to it."

Lynn turned to Kate and then Maggie. "What do you two say?"

"It's a little frustrating," Kate murmured. She shot a quizzical glance at Nick who merely shrugged. "But," she went on, "I don't see how we can object if we meant what we said yesterday. And I know I meant every word."

"So did I!" Maggie seconded.

Lynn turned back to Owen. "Then, if you don't intend leaving your money to any of us," she asked bluntly, "what do you intend doing with it?"

The old man chuckled. "Good question, and one I plan to answer in full right now. Lynn, a little while back you tried to convince me that it's the good deeds a man leaves behind him that really count. Well, I've been thinking on that, and I've come to the conclusion that you've got a point there. So here's what I intend to accomplish in the good-deeds department." He rubbed his hands together, obviously anticipating the shock waves he was about to set off.

The three young women looked at each other apprehensively and then focused all their attention on Owen.

"All right. First off, why should I wait until I die to see my money put to good use? As soon as possible I intend to establish three trusts, one for homeless youngsters, one for the construction and maintenance of medical clinics to be used by the poor in the Caribbean islands, and one to award grants to promising young musicians." He smiled at Maggie. "I think you can guess which of these three trusts I'd like you to administer. Feel like taking on responsibility for the clinics?"

Maggie turned to Fitch, who nodded and grinned broadly.

"Oh, yes!" she exclaimed. "I can't think of anything I'd rather do."

"Then the job is yours." Owen switched his attention to Kate. "Well, what would you say to doling out some of my ill-gotten gains to your starving musical colleagues?"

Kate jumped out of her seat and threw her arms around the old man's neck. "It's work I'd love, and I could do most of it from home," she cried. "Owen, it's a wonderful idea! And you're a wonderful, wonderful grandfather!"

Pink with pleasure, Owen peered up over Maggie's red curls and winked at Lynn. "And how about you, young lady? Do you think you could administer a grant program to provide group homes and counseling services to runaway youngsters?''

Lynn was utterly speechless. She could hardly believe that this was really happening. As tears of joy began to spill from her golden eyes, she tried to choke out her thanks, but all she could do was nod and sniff. Jake came and threw a loving arm around her shoulder.

"I hate to lose you in the office," he whispered into her ear. "But this is a job you're going to be terrific at, my darling. And to make up for what I miss at the office, I'll make sure I see plenty of you at night."

Owen, who'd finally been released by a teary-eyed Kate, beamed around the room. "Well," he said in a slightly raspy voice, "A year ago when I started my search I only hoped to wind up with one granddaughter at best. But now I have three. I think I'm a darned lucky old geezer and this story has had one heck of a happy ending!"

EPILOGUE

"OH OWEN, IT WAS BEAUTIFUL, so beautiful!" Daisy Crumper gushed. "Lynn made such a lovely bride and Jake looked so handsome in his tuxedo. And the solarium is so gorgeous with all these azaleas and spring flowers!" The voluble old lady took Owen Byrnside's hand and gave it an affectionate squeeze. "And you're every bit as handsome as the bridegroom in your tuxedo, too. You should wear it more often."

"A man in a wheelchair doesn't get too many opportunities to dress in a monkey suit," Owen responded dryly. But he looked pleased by the compliment. He squeezed Daisy's soft hand back. "You know, my dear, pink suits you. You're the one who should get gussied up more often. You're a fine figure of a woman."

Under her white curls her scalp went rosy with pleasure. She was just searching for a properly playful response when she was interrupted by Fitch Marlowe and Nick Conti. Both men came striding through the festive crowd of wedding guests.

"A beautiful ceremony and reception and a fine day all around, Owen," Fitch commented as he emerged from the throng.

"The caterers' and wedding-gown designers' unions ought to give you a matchmaker's medal," Nick added with a chuckle. "You're to be congratulated."

As he regarded the two younger men, the old man's eyes twinkled. "Oh, but a little bird told me that Marlowe here is the one to be congratulated. What's this I hear about you and Maggie being in an expectant condition?"

Fitch looked startled, then to everyone's surprise, he blushed violently. "You must have quite an aviary. Even Maggie and I can't truly believe it yet. But it does begin to look as if we might be expecting offspring about seven months from now."

"That's fine," Owen said heartily, "really fine."

"But that's not what Nick and I wanted to speak to you about," Fitch added.

"Just before we left for the ceremony, Kate and I had some news from Lynn's police-detective friend, Garrity," Nick said.

"Oh?" Owen's white brows lifted.

"He was embarrassed to have to confirm that Noel Barringer, alias Rona Chastain, alias a half dozen other people, managed to slip through their net."

"I'm not surprised," Owen commented. "I figured that if they hadn't caught him by now, he was probably safely out of the country."

"I thought the same," Fitch said. A grim smile began to play around his well-cut mouth. "But there is one amusing bit of news. You remember that the last we were able to determine, Winston Deeping had disappeared somewhere in South America."

"I remember it with crystal clarity."

"Well, apparently Deeping's contract killer is headed in the same direction. I suspect that those two are destined to meet, and when they do it's not going to be a happy occasion for Deeping."

"I suspect the same thing," Owen agreed with wry satisfaction. He shook his head. "But, to tell the truth, I don't really want to think about that now. This is too happy a day." His gaze went out over the room where the wedding guests were gathered around the champagne fountain and Lynn and Jake were feeding each other cake. Nearby, Kate and Maggie, each beautiful in their contrasting ways, stood smiling benevolently at the newly married couple. "I never thought I'd be so lucky as to see a day like this," Owen murmured. "Life is just one long surprise."

A flurry of activity distracted the three men and Daisy Crumper, after patting Owen's shoulder, hurried forward to investigate.

Kate and Maggie had taken Lynn's hands and were drawing her toward the decorative water fountain in the center of the glassed-in area. "Time for you to throw your bouquet," Kate was exclaiming.

"But I don't have anyone to throw it to," Lynn demurred. "You two are already married."

"Then you'll just have to find a creative solution," Jake said with a laugh. His eyes as they dwelled on his new bride were adoring.

But Lynn had already found a solution. As her gaze lit on Daisy Crumper, a mischievous sparkle came into her eyes and the corners of her mouth lifted. "Catch," she cried, and sent her bouquet of spring flowers spinning directly into her startled elderly friend's hands.

Back by Popular Demand

Janet Dailey

Americana

A romantic tour of America through fifty favorite Harlequin Presents®, each set in a different state researched by Janet and her husband, Bill. A journey of a lifetime in one cherished collection.

In April, don't miss the first six states followed by two new states each month!

Available wherever Harlequin books are sold.

JD-A

This April, don't miss #449, CHANCE OF A LIFETIME, Barbara Kaye's third and last book in the Harlequin Superromance miniseries

A powerful restaurant conglomerate draws the best and brightest to its executive ranks. Now almost eighty years old, Vanessa Hamilton, the founder of Hamilton House, must choose a successor. Who will it be?

Matt Logan: He's always been the company man, the quintessential team player. But tragedy in his daughter's life and a passionate love affair made him make some hard choices....

Paula Steele: Thoroughly accomplished, with a sharp mind, perfect breeding and looks to die for, Paula thrives on challenges and wants to have it all...but is this right for her?

Grady O'Connor: Working for Hamilton House was his salvation after Vietnam. The war had messed him up but good and had killed his storybook marriage. He's been given a second chance—only he doesn't know what the hell he's supposed to do with it....

Harlequin Superromance invites you to enjoy Barbara Kaye's dramatic and emotionally resonant miniseries about mature men and women making life-changing decisions.

HARLEQUIN'S "MATCH 3"
SWEEPSTAKES RULES & REGULATIONS
NO PURCHASE NECESSARY TO ENTER OR RECEIVE A PRIZE

1 Play the "Match 3" Sweepstakes Game. To enter the Sweepstakes and join the Reader Service, affix the corresponding stickers to the five rows on the Match 3 game board. This will disclose the major prize levels you are eligible for along with the number of free books and mystery gift you will receive. Entry in the Sweepstakes qualifies you for all levels of prizes. See rule #3 for total prizes to be awarded. If you do not wish to take advantage of our Reader Service, do not affix stickers to rows four and five. Return your three completed game cards in the return envelope provided. Incomplete and/or inaccurate entries are ineligible for that section or section(s) of prizes. Torstar Corp. and its affiliates are not responsible for mutilated or unreadable entries or inadvertent printing errors. Mechanically reproduced entries are null and void.

2. Whether you try our Reader Service or not, three lucky numbers will be assigned to your entry. On or about April 30, 1992, at the offices of Marden-Kane, Inc., Lake Success, NY, your Sweepstakes numbers will be compared against a list of winning numbers generated at random by the computer. However, prizes will only be awarded to individuals who have entered the Sweepstakes. In the event that all prizes are not claimed random drawing will be held from all qualified entries received from March 30, 1990 to March 31, 1992, to award all unclaimed prizes. All cash prizes (Grand to Sixth) will be mailed to the winners and are payable by check in U.S. funds. Seventh prize will be shipped to winners via third-class mail. These prizes are in addition to any free, surprise or mystery gifts that might be offered. Versions of this Sweepstakes with different prizes of approximate equal value may appear in other mailings or at retail outlets for Torstar Corp. and its affiliates.

3. PRIZES: (1) ★ Grand Prize $1,000,000 Annuity; (1) First Prize $25,000; (1) Second Prize $10,000; (5) Third Prize $5,000; (10) Fourth Prize $1,000; (100) Fifth Prize $250; (2500) Sixth Prize $10; (6000) ★ ★ Seventh Prize $12.95 ARV.

   ★ This Sweepstakes contains a Grand Prize offering of a $1,000,000 annuity. Winner will receive $33,333.33 a year for 30 years without interest totalling $1,000,000.

   ★ ★ Seventh Prize: A fully illustrated hardcover book published by Torstar Corp. Approximate Retail Value of the book is $12.95.

   Entrants may cancel the Reader Service at any time without cost or obligation to buy (see details in your center insert).

4. Extra Bonus! This presentation offers two extra bonus prizes of an expense-paid, two-week trip for two to Hawaii plus a new Buick Electra, total value $33,000. Extra Bonus Prize to be awarded in a random drawing from all qualified entries received by March 31, 1992. No purchase necessary to enter or receive a prize. To qualify, see instructions in your center insert. Versions of this Extra Bonus Sweepstakes with different prizes of approximate equal value may appear in other mailings or at retail outlets by Torstar Corp. and its affiliates. Winner will receive the bonus prize featured in this mailing or any other merchandise bonus prize offered or may elect to receive $33,000 payable by check in U.S. funds. All trips featured as an extra bonus prize are subject to availability and must be taken within one year of notification. All other published rules and regulations apply.

5. This Sweepstakes is being conducted under the supervision of Marden-Kane, Inc., an independent judging organization. By entering this Sweepstakes, each entrant accepts and agrees to be bound by these rules and the decisions of the judges, which shall be final and binding. Odds of winning in the random drawing are dependent upon the total number of entries received. Taxes, if any, are the sole responsibility of the winners. Prizes are nontransferable. All entries must be received at the address on the return envelope and must be postmarked no later than 12:00 MIDNIGHT, on March 31, 1992. The drawing for all unclaimed Sweepstakes prizes and for the Bonus Sweepstakes Prize will take place May 30, 1992, at 12:00 NOON, at the offices of Marden-Kane, Inc., Lake Success, New York.

6. This offer is open to residents of the U.S., the United Kingdom, France and Canada, 18 years or older except employees and their immediate family members of Torstar Corp., its affiliates, subsidiaries, and all other agencies, entities and persons connected with the use, marketing or conduct of this Sweepstakes. All Federal, State, Provincial and local laws apply. Void wherever prohibited or restricted by law. Any litigation within the Province of Québec respecting the conduct and awarding of a prize in this publicity contest must be submitted to the Régie des Loteries et Courses du Québec.

7 Winners will be notified by mail and may be required to execute an affidavit of eligibility and release that must be returned within 14 days after notification or an alternative winner will be selected. Canadian winners will be required to correctly answer an arithmetical skill-testing question administered by mail which must be returned within a limited time. Winners consent to the use of their names, photographs and/or likenesses for advertising and publicity in conjunction with this and similar promotions without additional compensation.

8. For a list of our major winners, send a stamped, self-addressed envelope to: WINNERS LIST c/o MARDEN-KANE, INC., P.O. BOX 701, SAYREVILLE, NJ 08871 Winners List will be fulfilled after the May 30, 1992 drawing date.

If Sweepstakes entry form is missing, please print your name and address on a 3" x5" piece of plain paper and send to:

In the U.S.
Harlequin's Match 3 Sweepstakes
3010 Walden Ave.
P.O. Box 1867, Buffalo, NY 14269-1867

In Canada
Harlequin's Match 3 Sweepstakes
P.O. Box 609
Fort Erie, Ontario L2A 5X3

Offer limited to one per household.
© 1991 Harlequin Enterprises Limited   Printed in the U.S.A.

COMING IN 1991 FROM HARLEQUIN SUPERROMANCE:

Three abandoned orphans,
one missing heiress!

Dying millionaire Owen Byrnside receives an
anonymous letter informing him that twenty-six years
ago, his son, Christopher, fathered a daughter. The
infant was abandoned at a foundling home that
subsequently burned to the ground, destroying all
records. Three young women could be Owen's long-
lost granddaughter, and Owen is determined to track
down each of them! Read their stories in

#434 HIGH STAKES (available January 1991)
#438 DARK WATERS (available February 1991)
#442 BRIGHT SECRETS (available March 1991)

Three exciting stories of intrigue and romance by
veteran Superromance author Jane Silverwood.